THE LIGHT
SOURCE

PRAISE FOR KIM MAGOWAN

"...these delicate, thoughtful stories are devoted to unpacking the intricacies of infidelity..."

Kristen Roupenian
The New York Times Book Review on Undoing

"A deeply honest, emotional powerhouse of a debut by Kim Magowan, The Light Source is told through the individual voices of boarding school friends whose lives and relationships interweave and unravel by turns. At its core, two women share a fragile, complicated love marred by denial and betrayal. It is because Magowan's people are so real, so flawed and funny and smart and hurting, that they compel us so. This novel brilliantly and movingly demonstrates the power of forgiveness and self-acceptance, and that which we so often forget: How by opening the one door we've always stubbornly refused to, we are at last rewarded with light."

Kathy Fish
author of Wild Life: Collected Works from 2003-2018

"The Light Source so exquisitely illuminates the elusive natures of both love and truth. I was riveted by Magowan's storytelling from the opening pages to the last, as each successive character both built their own narrative and also placed little charges of dynamite in the ones that had come before. An endlessly wise and devastatingly human book."

Robin Black
author of Life Drawing

"In stunning prose that renders time's passage with the fluidity of sand slipping between hourglass chambers, Magowan follows smoldering affairs over several decades, moving seamlessly between different characters' lives to explore the conflicting demands made by love in its many forms—familial, sexual, sororal. Indulging in neither cynicism nor sentimentality, Magowan explores the sacrifices, even the price, demanded by relationships confronting social sanctions and past hurts; and the ways we flourish when we are willing to grow and change, and, above all else, to take risks."

Alice Hatcher
author of The Wonder That Was Ours

"With a cast of friends who have known each other intimately since prep school days, Kim Magowan creates a smart and intricate drama about love and friendship, loyalty and betrayal, and the knife edges that separate them. Mastering a range of authentic voices (male and female) and time periods (post graduate and midlife), Magowan artfully weaves together episodes that capture in large ways and small the decisions we make that will shape our lives and hearts—and our families."

Sylvia Brownrigg
author of Pages for Her and Pages for You

"Kim Magowan writes some of the most exquisite sentences out there and her metaphors flash at you like eyes in the dark. To me she is a literary equivalent of the renowned psychotherapist Esther Perel, for all the wisdom, candor, and wit she shines on human relationships. The story of Julie and Heather is told in a composition of seven voices. As in a chiaroscuro painting, each voice is a stab of light that creates stark contrasts with the voices around it. The Light Source is a wicked smart, sexy, and devastatingly tender portrait of love in all its muddy glory."

Michelle Ross
author of There's So Much They Haven't Told You

ALSO BY KIM MAGOWAN

Undoing

THE LIGHT SOURCE

a novel by

Kim Magowan

7.13 Books
Brooklyn, NY

Printed and distributed by 7.13 Books. First paperback edition, first printing: July 2019

Cover design: Charli Barnes

ISBN-13: 978-1-7328686-6-3

Library of Congress Control Number: 2019935870

The following excerpts first appeared in these journals: "Phantom Light" *SNReview* Vol. 17 No. 1 (Spring/ Summer 2015), "Nothing in My Mouth" *Gettysburg Review* Vol. 25 No. 4 (Winter 2012), "Or Consequences" *Breakwater Review* Vol. 11 No. 4 (2014), "Like Salt" *descant* Vol. 55 (2016); winner of the Gary Wilson Short Fiction Award, "Mosaic" *Breakwater Review* Vol. 14 No. 2 (2016), "The Sticking Place" *Valparaiso Fiction Review* Vol. 4 Issue 2 (Summer 2015), "Invisible Woman" *580 Split* Issue 18 (2016)

For information about permission to reproduce selections from this book, contact the publisher at https://713books.com/

For Nora Esme Wagner
and Camille Margot Magowan Wagner,
with love

And in loving memory of my father,
Peter Alden Magowan
(1942-2019)

CONTENTS

IAN, 1994

I could always get sick. A sudden virus: it's worth considering. Bad enough getting dragooned into dinner with my friend-slash-ex-girlfriend Julie and her fiancé Porter, who is as handsome, plastic, and affectless as a Ken doll; now I must shop for the damn thing. "Please, I'm desperate," Beth said on the phone an hour ago, and when I capitulated, "Awesome! Do you have a pen?" She dictated a list of ingredients for what she calls "that Cuban meat thing." As I copied down "ground beef, 10% fat," I considered how Beth ensnared me in the first place. "Are you free for dinner on March twentieth? Julie will be there," and only after I agreed: "By the way, Porter is coming too." It's easy to picture professional Beth employing the same bait-and-switch on a hapless underling: "Want a crack at this nonfiction submission? Excellent! Reader report due Monday." Beth and I have been friends since we were kids, but still I resent being so smoothly played.

In the real world outside, dirty snow clings to curbs in lumpy piles. Inside Fairway, there are no seasons. Mangos stack in rosy-green heaps. A woman next to me pokes a melon with one talon. From under her arm peers a hideous dog. Its black eyes blink, recalling me to item #5 on my list: olives.

I remember being here last summer with Violet, an architect I briefly dated. She fed me cheese cubes from sample platters before we picked out wine and bread for a picnic in Central Park. I remember the salty bite of the cheese, the curly-topped toothpicks,

Violet's neat, black bangs. Summer, not yet disgusting. The wire grocery baskets looked like ornate scrollwork. Now they remind me less of French Quarter balconies than cages.

Shake it off.

I tick down Beth's list. I feel embarrassed ordering ground beef to her specifications. "Banal" we called Beth in high school, pronounced to rhyme with "anal": come exam time, it was always Beth's notes on Bismarck and the English civil wars that everyone borrowed. She's detailed and meticulous, and when the crap we gave her passed her tipping point, she'd remind us, "I can't afford not to be." The girl needed to earn her scholarships.

I take longer once I've completed Beth's list, first over flowers, then wine. Seasonally defiant, the flower section explodes. The guys ride me about remembering all the girls' favorite ones, but it's such an easy way of earning "You're so thoughtful!" hugs on birthdays. It reminds me of how "May I please?" functioned in grade school as a magic spell, unlocking special privileges; I could never understand why other kids didn't say it. Julie: parrot tulips. Heather: dahlias. Beth: anemones. Meriwether: sunflowers. Joy: pink peonies, balled into what Julie calls "flower fists." Ginny: doesn't like cut flowers, get her a plant. I choose purple anemones.

Then to wine. Here I go by price: thirty dollars for a cabernet. Compared to Julie, I know jack about wine. That didn't stop her, back when we were dating, from handing me the wine list. Valentine's Day, 1986: she wore makeup, I a tie, we did our best masquerade of twenty-one. I doubt we fooled the waiter, but he never asked to see my fake ID. Probably we struck him as sweet. I remember feeling both proud and flummoxed, and picking a wine as blindly as poking a spinning globe.

Not until much later, when Julie took me out to dinner for my eighteenth birthday and commandeered, unhesitatingly, the wine list—"Sancerre okay with you, Ian?"—did I realize what it meant to have me order. Another play-act, like the lipstick. There's something conventional about Julie. No doubt when she marries Porter she will take his last name. Since that scene years ago, watching Julie crisply order wine, how many times have I seen her deferentially pass the carte to her boyfriend of the moment? As if ordering herself is castrating. The night I met Porter, last December, she pulled the same stunt: "Honey, will you?" That asshole knows even less about wine than I do.

I pass the flowers again on my way to checkout, and exchange the anemones for parrot tulips. The serrated petals look like they could bite.

Beth lives at the top of a fifth-floor walk-up, and by the time I slog two packed grocery bags up the stairs I'm out of breath. On the fourth floor landing the neighbors' folding stroller and Big Wheel block the final flight. "Fuck," I say, vaulting them. I punch Beth's doorbell.

She answers immediately, and I unload into her extended arms the heavier bag.

"Thank you, Ian! You're absolutely saving my ass."

"Careful, that one's about to break."

I'm still gasping for air. We carry the bags into her kitchen, tiny even by New York standards. It could fit on a boat.

On a counter the size of an ironing board, Beth unpacks ground beef, golden raisins, light rum, a bag of tomatoes, white rice, onions, garlic, cilantro, cumin, olives, arugula, two loaves of bread, the tulips, the wine.

"What do I owe you?" She squints at the receipt.

"Well, subtract the flowers and that bottle of cab, that's my contribution."

"You are an angel. Oh, damn, black olives. I need green."

"You just said olives."

"Did I? No sweat. I can send Heather and Julie out for them."

I hear Julie's name first, because, let's face it, I am wired to. But a second later I say, "Wait. Heather's back?"

"Yeah, she got in a few hours ago. That's why I'm in such desperate need, because suddenly this dinner party has expanded to nine, and I don't have enough food. Jeez, where will I fit all this?" We contemplate her fridge, the size of the one I rented for my dorm room at Columbia to store beer.

"So Heather's here?"

"She's staying in a hotel tonight, tomorrow she gets the keys to her uncle's place in the Village. Remember that squinty uncle, you called him Igor? She checked in and then came straight to Finch. I was planning on bailing early anyway, since you and Julie and Porter were coming over, but not three hours early. And my luck, Goldstein was lurking right outside my office, breathing on everyone. But what could I do? Heather was falling asleep at my desk. So I sent her down ahead of me, told Goldstein I was sick, and left." She shakes her head. "Shit, I may have said 'cramps.' Not very professional."

Twenty-five, Beth is the youngest editor at Prescott-Finch; her assistant Nancy is thirty. Consequently Beth is obsessed with being adequately professional. It's a standard she applies to her haircuts and bagged lunches. We could tailspin for the next ten minutes, analyzing what phony illnesses sound most or least professional on some arbitrary Beth spectrum, so I divert her quickly.

"Where's Heather now?"

"Julie called when we got back. As soon as I told her Heather was here she hopped on the subway. It was lucky timing: she had no idea Julie was in town tonight. I'm not even sure she knew Julie had moved to Boston. Anyway, they're getting wine—"

The doorbell sounds like a stepped-on cat. "That's them. Will you get it, Ian?"

"Ian!" says Julie, when I open the door. "I wasn't expecting you yet."

"Yeah, Beth called in the cavalry."

I hug her, inhale the coconut smell of her hair. I haven't seen Julie for a month, since the night we went out for French-Vietnamese and she told me she was engaged. I remember the Chinese water torture of dainty course after course, trying to look cheerful, knowing Julie was observing my every twitch.

"Hey, Saltonstall," says Heather, behind her, and I let go of Julie to hug Heather. She's wearing a potato sack of a dress; underneath she's all angles. It's like embracing a cookie cutter.

"Welcome back," I say. "You look tired."

"Nine hour flight from Barcelona. I didn't sleep at all."

"Take a nap," says Beth. "People won't be coming until eight."

"If I lie down I'm never getting up," says Heather. "I'll be like the old lady in the LifeCall ad. No, what I need is something to drink."

Julie laughs. "I thought you were going to say, 'coffee.' Beth, can I open wine?"

"Sure. Pour us each a glass, will you? Wine glasses and opener under the sink."

"This is the strangest kitchen," says Julie. She pours full glasses, hands them out.

Beth drops the empty bottle into her recycling bag with a flourish. "Well, cheers, kids! Hey: this is the first time we've been together since the engagement. How about toasting Julie?"

We clink glasses. "Woohoo," says Heather, in her flattest voice.

"I can't believe you're back," Julie says, squeezing Heather's waist. "No disappearing for ten months again! That's way too long!"

"Clearly," says Heather. "You get up to all kinds of tricks when I'm not around."

Julie laughs. "You call getting engaged a 'trick'?"

Heather pretends to reflect. "Hmm. What do I call getting married at age twenty-four? I think I'll go with, 'bonkers.'"

"Man, right out of the gate," Beth says.

No one avoids conflict as assiduously as Julie Howe. At eighteen, she was an All-State lacrosse player, and Julie has a jock's meet-trouble-if-it-comes fortitude when required. But she will go a long way to circumnavigate an argument if she spots exits. After we broke up, early spring of junior year, I barely saw Julie for months. Sometimes I would catch a glimpse of her back; once I saw her literally perform an about-face. It was nearly summer vacation when I walked towards her and she didn't retreat. I remember the two of us advancing at the same measured pace, stopping outside of the Dining Hall, and saying, at the same time, "Hey." "So you're finally talking to me," I said, and Julie responded, "Well, you stopped looking like you wanted to bite me."

Ever since, I've taken that line to heart. When I'm with her and feel the least bit upset or angry, I gauge myself for "bite." It's nearly an out-of-body experience, such disciplined self-scrutiny. In the

French-Vietnamese restaurant last month, I felt like a C.I.A. agent. Heather, and this has always bugged me, has never been on the same leash.

"First of all," says Julie, "I'll be twenty-five in three weeks. Second, I know what I'm doing." She looks around, speaking to all of us. "I always wanted to be a young mother. And this isn't my first proposal. I happen to have found the right person." She turns coaxing. "Heather, you need to meet Porter, and see us together."

"I have met him," says Heather, just as evenly. "I have seen you together."

This is news; Beth and I exchange a look. Heather has been out of the country since May. Julie started dating Porter last September. I only met him myself in early December.

Julie blinks. "I mean really meet him, Heather. You'll see."

"Well, explain it to me. Because frankly I can't imagine why Porter is the right guy."

"He values me. He understands me. He takes care of me." Julie is speaking fast, tick tick tick. "I trust him."

Heather turns to me and Beth. "Guys? Do 'understanding' and 'trustworthy' sound like Porter to either of you?"

"Not getting involved," says Beth.

"You don't know him, Heather! Can't you hold off judgment and be supportive, for once?"

"You want me to be supportive or honest?"

"Supportive," Julie says, immediately.

"I just don't think Porter's all that," says Heather.

And the State All-Star is out, eyes blazing: "Damn it, Heather! What doesn't translate about, 'supportive'?"

She's grabbing her coat before we can move. "Hey Julie," I say.

"I need to book anyway. I have to pick up Porter." Her tone is modulated again, but she won't look any of us in the eye. "I'll see you all at eight." She points at Heather. "And you: I mean it, be nice."

After the door closes, Beth shakes a spatula at Heather. "Can't you be back for twenty-four hours without picking on her?"

"She's been provoking me. Ever since she got here, it's been Porter this, rehearsal dinner that. I have this wedding bullshit coming out of my ears! Let her marry him, I don't fucking care, let her turn into boring Bridal Barbie, but don't make me listen to more of it."

"You are always harsh about her boyfriends," Beth says.

"Not true."

That elicits my most sarcastic laugh, and Beth says, "See?"

Heather folds her arms. "Not true! I liked Henri."

"Only because he was French," says Beth.

"No, because he was witty and interesting. And come on, Ian, you and I have always been buddies."

"*Au contraire*, you know perfectly well you were a pain in the ass when Julie and I were together."

"That's not fair." She looks back and forth. "Do I really have to do this all by myself? You both know Porter isn't right for her. I mean, cute and all, but so fucking what? I could not believe it when she wrote she was marrying him."

"Julie wrote you? How?" I ask.

"I pick up mail at American Express offices. She always writes. I got a letter from her last week, in Tunisia. Come on Ian: don't tell me you think it's a good idea for her to marry him."

"And that's another thing," says Beth. "What's this about you meeting Porter? They only started dating in September."

"Oh, I met him years ago," Heather says dismissively. "Before junior year of high school. I was visiting Julie in Newport, and we ran into him and some friend at the Beach Club. We went on a double date."

"That's weird," says Beth.

I say, "Why haven't I heard about that?"

"Probably because it wasn't the least bit newsworthy. Look, I know exactly what kind of guy Porter is, and so do you. Good-looking and shallow and impressed with himself. You can't honestly believe Julie is making a smart choice."

There's a pause. Beth and I meet eyes again. She says, "Whatever. It's her life, Heather."

"Beth! Stop being so fucking neutral." Heather turns to me. "I know you agree. I can't always be the only one kicking up dust. He's a tool, and you know it. You're just as bummed about this as I am."

Of course I don't like Porter. While I don't entirely trust my response to him, he has never tried to win me over. He's possessive and patronizing. I can't deny that part of me welcomes the prospect of Heather as an ally. No one exerts her kind of sway over Julie. If anyone can stop Julie's forward march, it's Heather.

That said, I have a complicated friendship with Heather. Before Julie and I started dating, Heather was Julie's right-hand friend, I was the left-hand friend. We had a good cop-bad cop shtick, when it came to Julie's revolving door of boyfriends. I would settle for damning with faint praise, but Heather let loose. Chad, with his ever-present lacrosse stick, drew "He's okay" from me; "Club-wielding caveman" from Heather.

All that should have prepared me for the Mr. Hyde-Heather I experienced during my own tenure as Julie's boyfriend. Heather became the cruel goddess, the stone wall, every mythic icon to thwart lovers. She complained that I spent too much time in their room, that I prevented her from studying. Yet the needling way she dealt with me stung. After all, we were in the same circle. We'd always gotten along well. She must have slept with half my friends. And I was likewise unprepared for Julie's blithe capitulation: "Oh, that's just Heather, you know Heather." When Julie broke up with me, I half-blamed Heather. Even recognizing the irrational scapegoating at work, it was a while before I could forgive her. If, frankly, I ever did.

So I say, "He's okay."

Heather snorts. As tenderly as if she's speaking an endearment, she says, "Saltonstall, you're so entirely full of shit."

An unbidden memory surfaces: graduation night, a party at Julie's parents' house. Julie was in her bedroom with Fred Eshelman, the last of her high school boyfriends. A decent guy, I suppose. He was always masticating some cud of chaw (Heather's nickname for Fred was "Bessie") or spitting, grotesquely, into a soda can.

I'd adjusted to Julie going out with Fred, but I knew that bedroom too well. Julie had not redecorated since she left for boarding school; it was preserved in time. I can still name everything inside it: the Tinkerbell night-light, the Charlie's Angels poster on the wall, the dressing table with the checked skirt, the makeup mirror with miniature light bulbs. That room was full of memories for me, but the one I loved most belonged to Julie. When she was eleven she had sat in front of that mirror and plucked out both her eyebrows, hair by hair. I made love to Julie in that double bed with its Wizard of Oz pillowcase and tippy canopy. But it is this image of Julie at eleven, staring at the pink ridges where her eyebrows had been, that Fred Eshelman contaminated. I fled.

I sat on the beach, so drunk that the stars seemed to revolve like powdery sparkles in a snow globe. I didn't hear Heather come up behind me, didn't know she was there until I felt her fingers on my shoulders.

"Heather—what—" I said.

She kissed me. She said, "Just pretend..."

I never told anyone about that night. But here's the other thing I remember: despite the gritty sand and the way-too-much bourbon, that was the best sex I've ever had.

I shake my head like it's an Etch A Sketch, trying to physically clear the picture of Heather on all fours, her ass leeched of color by the moonlight.

"Oh, dial it down, Heather," says Beth. "You planning to go *Jane Eyre* on Julie? Madly wave your hand when the minister asks if there are any objectors? In all seriousness: what do you expect us to do?"

"Jesus, I'm tired of being the only one who ever speaks up," Heather says, glaring. "Fine, Cowardly Ian, Tinman. I'm going to my hotel to freshen up."

"You can shower here," says Beth, more gently.

"I feel like this dress is covered in fleas. I'll see you in an hour and a half, okay?"

She's rigid when I hug her. Beth kisses Heather on the cheek and says, "I really am glad you're back, Scarecrow."

"Sure, sure," Heather says, and walks to the door.

"Oh, will you get a jar of green olives?" The door closes. "Shoot, I hope she heard me."

We start cooking. Beth puts a pot of water on to boil, plugs in her rice cooker, and hands me a cutting board. I chop on the floor because there's no space in the hobbit kitchen. Beth's apartment doesn't yet reflect her fixation with professionalism. It still looks like a dorm: a futon draped with an Indian tapestry, wobbly towers of CDs, crystals that bounce pellets of color onto the walls. The grown-up exception is the dining table, inherited from her grandmother, which fills half the room.

"Those two." Beth shakes her head. "When I'm away from them I forget how sparky they are. Remember the fights they had in high school?"

I wipe the papery garlic skin from my hands. "She's not entirely wrong."

"Heather, you mean? Yeah. I need the garlic thinly slivered."

I correct and start slivering.

"It's not like Porter is a bad guy. So we don't click with him; imagine his perspective. We've known each other since we were kids. We're not the easiest crowd to please. He's always been nice enough to me."

"Really?" I say. "Not to me."

"You're trickier, the ex and all. That garlic's perfect, hand it over."

When the water comes to a boil, she drops in the tomatoes one at a time. They make a sound like stones. After a minute, she drains them. "As soon as these cool, can you peel and chop them? Do you need a bowl?"

"Sure."

I tear cilantro until Beth hands me a tomato. "These need a coarse chop."

While I'm cutting, she says, "It's always surprised me that someone as sharp as Julie is so unimaginative when it comes to boyfriends. Present company excepted, naturally."

"Thanks."

"Sure I wouldn't marry Porter, but I wouldn't date any of those dudes: Chad or Fred or Simon or Nils or Theo or that skinny French guy. Her taste has always felt opaque. Tomatoes done? You up for doing onions?"

Julie isn't close to anyone on that list except me. She has a policy against staying friends with her exes, though in the next breath she reassures me that I was "grandfathered" into a different system. Our friendship is staked on my willingness to slough off being an ex. "Just pretend," Heather whispered to me on that beach in Newport. I sometimes feel Julie and I are locked into a similar gambit: pretend I never saw you naked, never shed tears over you. That's our contract. I promised to not "let things get weird" before she first let me take off her shirt.

"Boring guy after boring guy. You are definitely the cream of that crop."

I rinse the cutting board. The water runs over my fingers. "Thanks Bethie," I say. "Even if it is a fucking low bar."

Beth sighs. I say, "What's wrong?"

"I'm just worried."

"About me?"

"Among other things. About Heather, who looks like skin and bones, right? She obviously has not been taking care of herself. About Julie. Heather won't persuade her by being so confrontational. But she's probably right. It seems speedy, this dash to the altar."

I remember showing Heather a necklace I bought for Julie. Julie and I had first kissed on my sixteenth birthday, September 15, 1985, so for our six-month anniversary, I got her an emerald on a thin gold chain. I was pretty proud of it, the first expensive present I had ever bought. Heather said somberly, "It's beautiful, Saltonstall. But don't give it to her." And when I protested: "Trust me. Don't go so over-the-top. Save it for later." St. Patrick's Day, Julie broke up with me. Afterwards, I could never figure out if Heather discouraged me because she knew what Julie intended and wanted to spare me the humiliation, or if she somehow thwarted me. Whether I believed the one narrative or the other depended on how charitably, at that moment, I felt towards Heather. The necklace sat in my drawer for years. Even when I began college I held onto it, and it seemed slimy in any case to present to some other girl. I finally gave it to my mother one Christmas.

"And sure, I worry about you. I want you to be happy."

I look at her, and Beth gasps. "Ian! Don't you know how to cut onions? You're going to cut off your damn fingers! Switch with me. You stir this beef, I'll chop."

She hands me the wooden spoon and takes my place on the floor. "This is how you hold an onion. See how my fingers curve away from the knife?"

"Got it, Julia Child." I stir for a bit, then say, "Listen, Bethie, I appreciate the concern about my fingers. And the rest of me."

"Nothing really knocks you on your ass like first love, huh? It's like some self-protection mechanism kicks in that warns you, don't go down that road again. You build scar tissue. Add these onions. They need to be translucent."

I fold them in. "I think I still love her," I say. "Isn't that pathetic?"

"You loved Julie when she was sixteen and the prettiest girl at school. You're in the habit of loving her. No, listen," she says. "Do you remember Michael? I brought him to that concert in the Park? Well, I just about went crazy over that guy."

"Crazy in love or crazy insane?"

"Both. First one, then the other. You know me, I'm not Julie or Heather. I never had a queue of guys at my door. Michael could be very sweet. He made me potatoes once when I was taking a bath. A plate of salty potatoes. Downside, he was a cheat. When I found out, I broke up with him right away. I felt good about that: at least I wasn't a doormat. For a few months, I thought I was doing well. Add those raisins soaking in rum."

I comply.

"Then I went to a party and saw him. He was with a woman, more a girl, she looked eighteen or nineteen. I had to leave because I thought I was going to vomit. So I concluded, I must be in love with him. There was no way I could feel so bad otherwise. Then I thought I was going nuts. I cried constantly. Strangers would stare at me. I had no social poise at all, or whatever you call the thing that keeps you from crying in cafes. I hid in my apartment like a mole...

"Until I met another guy. No one significant. We only went out a couple of times. But I forgot about Michael right away. It just didn't hurt anymore. I thought, where did all that misery go? Am I really so shallow? Then it hit me. You know how sunlight is eight minutes old?"

"What are you talking about?" I say.

"At the speed of light, it takes eight minutes for sunlight to travel to earth. And when you look at the stars, it's taken the light so long to travel that many of those stars aren't there anymore. Some have been gone for thousands of years. So, it had taken so long to get through my censors, my intricate system of self-denials, that by the time I admitted to myself I was still in love with Michael, it wasn't true anymore. I was looking at phantom light. I think that's your situation with Julie, precisely. Her getting married has made you finally process delayed information. You're dazzled by something that isn't there anymore."

"Interesting theory, but kind of impossible to prove," I say. "I see what I see: how can I tell if it's real illumination or phantom light? Is there any way of knowing which stars are extinct?"

"Well, that's my point. You know when you meet someone else. You will know when you realize that it doesn't hurt to look at Julie."

"That scenario sounds like the opposite of the boiling frog." When she looks blank, I say, "Haven't you heard of that experiment? Put a frog in a pot of water and incrementally raise the temperature. Supposedly if you increase it very gradually, the frog keeps adapting and never jumps out. It will literally boil to death in the pot of water. It's an analogy for the levels of pain you get used to tolerating, through immersion."

Beth smiles. "Whereas I'm telling you that you'll meet some sweet young thing, blink your eyes, and realize, hey, what nice, warm water. You only think you're suffering."

"Maybe." I don't hide my doubt, but I put an arm around her soft shoulder. "You're a good friend, Bethie."

"Ditto. Now please wash the arugula for me."

I'm cranking the salad spinner when the doorbell rings again. Beth opens it.

"I come bearing olives."

"Great," Beth says. "And wow. You sure clean up well, Heather."

She's wearing a matted white coat over all black: a sheer blouse, a bra, a short skirt, black tights, boots with heels so stacked that when Heather shimmies into the kitchen to hug me, she's my height.

"Hey, Saltonstall. Sorry for being obnoxious earlier," she says.

"Earlier today, or in life generally?" I ask.

She smirks and sniffs the pan. "What are you making? Smells funny."

Beth pokes her. "That apology didn't last very long." She strains the olives and adds them to the pan.

I take in Heather: the red lipstick, the eyeliner, the clothes. Something about the way she's dressed reminds me of those long passages in *The Iliad* about warriors garbing for battle: Hector strapping on his breast-plate, his crested helmet, to set out against Achilles and the well-greaved Achaeans.

"You look amazing, Heather. What is that coat? Abominable Snowman?"

She laughs, and Beth says, "I was thinking, polar bear. But Heather, you need to eat tonight. You're too skinny."

"First, more wine," Heather says, and I pour her a glass.

The doorbell rings again. "Shit, it's eight," Beth says, walking over to open it. I hear her greet Julie and Porter. I hear our friend Sam say, "Is Katchadourian really back?"

Heather chucks me on the chin. For a second she and I lock eyes. "Game face," she says.

HEATHER, 1994

June 27, 1994
Dear Julie,
  *It seems like I have to be five thousand miles away to talk to you, to try and
explain. I know you're wondering how I can explain...*

I arrive in Amsterdam in the middle of a heat wave. Everywhere,
I see people wearing cheap straw hats to protect themselves from the
insistent sun, I see people spending whole afternoons in museums,
huddling by air conditioning vents, looking at Van Gogh's hallu-
cinatory sunflowers. Drugs take the edge off the heat. The coffee
shops are crowded with tourists smoking hashish. The hash burns
my lungs, the sun burns my skin: to be here is to be on fire, a lit
spark, incendiary. I skulk instead of walk, I feel vaguely criminal. I
am at home here.

The first day I pace the Red Light District, looking for a hotel,
my suitcase banging my leg. At noon, sick of carrying it, I open it.
My maid of honor dress, midnight blue silk, spills onto the sidewalk.
A dress I spent four hundred and fifty dollars on, a dress I will never
wear. I stuff it into a garbage can, where it billows out, a bloated
flower.

I find a hotel at last, a youth hostel overlooking a canal. The
concierge has a Mediterranean face, brown and moist. We discuss
the rates in Italian: fifteen dollars a night, three hundred dollars if
I rent a single room for a month. Meals included. I give him three

hundred. The girl standing beside him tells me softly to have a nice stay, pushes the key across the counter. It makes a light scraping noise. I can't tell if she's his wife or his daughter.

I pass the lounge walking up to my room. A group of Australians cluster around the television set, passing a hookah like a peace pipe, watching MTV.

My room has a white ceiling, pale cracked walls. Sitting in it I feel like something waiting to hatch.

Dear Julie,

My apologies for this stationery. I had to beg the concierge for it, he charges me for each sheet. The place I'm staying is a real dump, its claim to fame is they have cable. The television is on constantly, I can't get Guns N' Roses out of my head. Guns N' Roses in Amsterdam: there's an odd logic to it.

This is the seventh time I've begun a letter to you. I don't seem capable of finishing

The first few days I barely leave my room. I lie on the bed, hands folded on my chest, like the Lady of Shalott floating down the river to Camelot. I occupy myself by counting things: the water stains on the wall, the number of times I blink, intakes of breath. I had not thought a nervous breakdown could be so peaceful, or so boring.

My brain feels stir-fried. I think in snatches, not complete sentences. Strung out. That is me, unraveling. Tangled hair. A kite string in knots.

Even going downstairs for meals demands effort. Coffee and croissants for breakfast, miniature boxes of cornflakes and Sugar Pops to appease the Americans. Soup and sandwiches for lunch. For dinner, thin slices of brown meat, defrosted vegetables: corn niblets, peas, garish diced carrots. I can't eat anything so colorful. I push them around my plate, making patterns.

Meals are noisy, sociable. It's hard to isolate myself. At first, the Americans make overtures. They sit at my table, wearing peach, yellow, lavender, Easter egg colors. They try to talk to me. I shake my head, mumble back in French. One American woman, fuzzy-haired and persistent, clicks her fingers, looking for words. "Aimez-vous

Amsterdam?" she asks. I shrug, pretending not to understand. She gives up, her group debates the merits of different breweries, they leave me alone.

Dear Julie,

Once again, I am beginning a letter to you, this impossible letter I can't seem to finish. You probably think that I don't care enough to try to explain. There goes Heather, I imagine you thinking, bouncing through Europe, not even bothering to justify herself.

That's not the case (Case: it sounds like I'm on trial—apt, don't you think?). I just don't know how to start. Saying 'I'm sorry' seems inadequate. Can you tell me, please tell me, what words to use?

Nine days after coming to Amsterdam, I make a friend. She's an Indian girl who sleeps down the hall. I first see her in the dining room. She's a tiny girl, barely five feet tall, with long hair so black it has blue in it. She holds her tray of food and looks around the room for a place to sit. Her jacket, green and gold, is embroidered with sundials. It's impossible to tell how old she is. Perhaps fifteen or sixteen. She has a child's profile, the round forehead, wide-set eyes. She walks over and sits at my table. I flinch reflexively. After nine days I have established myself as a loner; I resent this encroachment on my space. But she smiles, sweetly, and points to herself.

"Lakshmi," she says.

Lakshmi. It's the prettiest word I've heard in Amsterdam. I tell her my name: "Heather."

I watch her, trying to figure out what she's doing here. A runaway, I think. She should be carrying a pole with a polka-dotted handkerchief knotted to it over her shoulder; she looks that childlike. I bolt the rest of my dinner and stand up to bus my tray. "Bye," I tell her.

The next morning she follows me out of the hostel. I do not notice her at first. Down the street from the hostel is a row of buildings, like shabby boutiques, where prostitutes sit on stools behind plate glass windows. I identify the prostitutes by the color of the lingerie they wear: the purple prostitute, with her merry widow and garter belt and lace stockings, the silver prostitute in her shiny metallic teddy. Although it's not yet noon, the silver prostitute has pulled apart the curtains of her window, signaling that she's now open, ready to receive customers. I watch her for a minute. She scratches her leg. Two men walking down the street stop in front of her window, and she smiles at them. Even her lipstick is metallic. I turn away and see Lakshmi coming towards me. I wait for her to catch up. She doesn't increase her pace, so it takes her a minute to reach me. We smile at each other. We walk to the coffee shop on the corner.

I buy her a hot chocolate, and while she sips it I try my languages on her. She shakes her head, smiles, murmurs in Hindi. When I light a cigarette she extends her fingers. I hand it to her.

All I know about Lakshmi is what I observe. She eats by compartmentalizing her food. She picks the mushrooms out of her salad, gathers them on one side of her plate. Tomato wedges on another. A soggy handful of croutons at the top, lettuce and red cabbage at the bottom. She eats one section at a time, working around the plate counterclockwise.

She likes to sing. Since she never speaks and hardly makes a sound—even her footsteps are light, she picks up her feet like a cat, never shuffling—I was taken aback when I first heard her. Her voice is low and sweet. It reminded me of something I couldn't place. Later I remember: Julie's laugh.

I once heard a theory about how language was invented. Early man wanted to preserve tribal secrets. So they used words as veils, to keep neighboring tribes from understanding and learning their mysteries. Language was not intended to communicate, but to dissemble, to conceal.

Because Lakshmi and I do not attempt to understand each other, we never misunderstand each other. We speak no words, so we leave no words out. She can't interfere with the identity I create for her. She is a smooth stone goddess with a shattered nose and eight arms. She is a child swimming in the river Ganges, black hair floating like leaves. She is sandalwood incense and curry and myrrh. She is soft gold in my hands, to model and shape. She is whatever I want her to be.

Dear Julie,

I left the States because I wasn't brave enough to see you, but I think you've followed me here. I see you everywhere. I see you on posters and in museums, I see a woman with long red hair walking down the street and follow her thinking she might be you.

And even when I try to sleep

Amsterdam is a city of voyeurs. The prostitutes are hierarchized, three-tiered. The prettiest ones work in whorehouses. I pass one brothel on the way to my coffee shop. It's a brick building with lavender curtains, printed with small yellow flowers, sedate and prim. One morning, as I buy a *Herald Tribune* at the newsstand, a woman comes out of the house. She is wearing jeans, mirrored sunglasses, her hair is rolled in curlers like sausages, bound up with a yellow bandana. She buys Gitanes and a pack of Hollywood gum, and turns to face me. Her sunglasses reflect a double picture of myself, two pale faces, two mouths thin and straight as hyphens.

The second tier of prostitutes are the window girls. At night they turn on the light bulbs above their stools. Tourists gather around them, gesturing for them to unhook their bras, show their breasts. They are skillful at differentiating potential johns from onlookers. When they get a customer, they close the heavy, red curtains for ten or fifteen minutes. His friends wait outside, laughing. When he leaves, the prostitutes open the curtains again, reapply their makeup. You can see the sweat shine on their chests.

On the bottom tier are the heroin addicts. They hang out at the docks and canals, smoking. I don't know where they take their customers: in the shadows of the houseboats, possibly, or underneath the bridges. One morning I saw two policemen rolling one into a body bag. I couldn't see her face, but her feet were unmistakable, turquoise pumps poking from the gray plastic.

The Red Light district is crowded with doorways where men stand, promising in French, German, English, that for a few guilders you can have a conversation with a naked woman. I hear one of these solicitors exhorting a Japanese man in a light gray suit to come inside. He speaks in English, the international language of business.

"You can talk to her for a minute," he cajoles. "Very pretty girl. Very pretty tits. No touching."

I wonder what he could do with a naked woman in a minute. No time to masturbate, even. What would they talk about? The heat wave, Rembrandt, the value of the guilder? "Conversation" must be a code word, it seems too unlikely.

The Japanese man hesitates. Two cameras loop around his neck, one with a long, thick lens like a throat. His face, ringed with round glasses, seems calm and bland. This is the kind of tourist you see in Disneyland, taking pictures of his children standing next to Snow White. Focusing and re-focusing his camera while his children stand perfectly still and Snow White smiles, fixedly, her lips as red as blood. This is not a sex shop customer. But the Japanese man surprises me; he pays and walks in.

There is another place, deep in the Red Light district, that I heard the American women in their pink and yellow clothes discussing at dinner. Here, for a larger price, you pay to strip while people watch you. Apparently you strip before a one-way mirror, sealed from the onlookers. They can see you, but all you can see is your own body reflected.

On my first trip to Amsterdam, when I was nine, my mother took me to the house of Anne Frank. A line of people climbed the steep staircase to look at the rooms a dead girl lived in, the chairs she sat on, the table where she did her homework. We looked at Anne Frank through a one-way mirror of time. We peered through the window whose shutters she could never open, to look at the outside world, the pretzel vendors, the streets, the canals she could never see. The world seemed so bright and clamorous and enticing, pictured through the eyes of a prisoner.

After two weeks in Amsterdam I borrow a telephone from the concierge and track down my mother, at a hotel in Marseilles. The connection to France is crackly with static. Her boyfriend answers the phone.

"Nicolo, it's Heather. Can I please speak to my mother?"

He calls for her. I never have much to say to Nicolo. My mother picked him up last fall in Naples.

"Sweetie. Where are you?" she says. "I've been trying to reach you in New York."

"Amsterdam."

"Amsterdam? But honey, I thought you were going to spend the summer in the States. Amsterdam is so awful." She sighs. "Well, tell me, how was Julie's wedding?"

I pause, then say, "Fine. But Mom, I need you to wire me some money."

She catches the hesitation. "Did anything go wrong?"

"No, I told you, it was fine. Listen, I'd love to talk, but I have to pay for this, and I'm broke. Can you wire me some money?"

She sighs again. "You know, I went to an art supply store yesterday, and I saw a gorgeous set of paints that I was thinking about getting Julie for a wedding present. But there was a tube called flesh color. And I thought, that's really offensive, people are all different colors, brown and yellow and red, to call pinkish beige 'flesh color'—well, it seemed disingenuous at the very least."

I picture my mother, holding the phone, lapsing into some meditation on the wrongs of the world. In the last few years, she has begun to get fat. She was always beautiful, she still looks much younger than her age, but the weight drives her to extremes. She dyes her hair black, wears low-cut blouses, does everything to counteract the baffling onset of time.

"Julie doesn't paint," I say.

"Heather," she replies, her voice wintry, "I hope you aren't asking for money to buy drugs. Don't think I'm naive about Amsterdam. I know what goes on there, all those derelicts, punching needles in their arms and putting garbage up their noses—"

I stare at the wall. In a red plastic frame hangs a poster of a Van Gogh, the bowl of irises that look like curled hands. "Mom. Will you wire me the money or not?"

"It's Bastille Day," she says. "I'm looking out the window and I can see tanks coming down the street." She pauses. "I just realized, it's your birthday next week. What do you want for a present?"

"Money. About six hundred dollars. You can send me a check if it's easier." I give her the address of the hostel.

"I know you think you can take care of yourself," she says. "But I worry about you. It's a sign of strength to ask for help, Honey." She waits, but I say nothing. "I'll give your love to Nicolo."

I tell her goodbye and hang up. Then I go to my room, take two painkillers, and lie on my bed. The bed spread is white and nubbly. It feels like Braille.

When I was ten, my father, an alcoholic, prone to falling into rabbit holes of depression, lost his job and shot himself in the head. But he didn't die, at least not immediately, if you could call what was left of him alive. My mother and I found him sitting in the room we called his office, his head on the desk. The gun was still in his hand. We had been out shopping for shoes. My mother dropped the shopping bag and ran over to him while I stood in the doorway. She lifted him up and put her face against his chest, then she looked at me. "Oh God," she said, "His heart is still beating."

My mother hired a nurse, a middle-aged Canadian with red hands. For just over a year Irma spoon-fed him, washed him, gave him medication. He sat in a chair by the window, blinking. If he had a mind left, it was not a responsive one. It drove my mother crazy that there was no plug to pull. He died a month before I turned twelve, and my mother and I never forgave each other for feeling relieved.

My mother was born in Louisiana, and had met my father when she was eighteen, skiing in Switzerland. They married that summer. When he died she was thirty-three and lovely. She is credulous and sweet and vain, and more like me than I want to believe. When I was thirteen, my mother called me a slut and I told her that it took one to know one. We were standing at opposite sides of the living room yelling at each other. The furniture was covered in plastic sheets because the house was for sale. I was taller than her by then, and I remember how she looked. She was wearing a red cashmere jacket and her pretty, shocked face looked like a porcelain doll's. I imagined her falling on the floor and cracking down the middle.

After that she sent me to boarding school in the States. The first three months there I was miserable. I missed Switzerland, my friends, crepes with butter and sugar. I missed sitting in cafés drinking espresso or sweet red wine and flirting with the waiters. The school had more rules than I could keep track of, dress codes and curfews and chapel attendance, and so I even missed my mother's lazy neglect. It was hard to make friends. My clothes were wrong. I didn't have the requisite monogrammed sweaters or Lanz night gowns or James Taylor records.

And then Julie started to be friends with me, and the pieces my life had splintered into fused again. Julie, that's the terrible secret of you: you stick me together. Without you, I scatter. Without you, I disappear.

I wake up one morning with the sun on my face. I get up to close the shutters and look out the window. Across the street I see a woman holding a bouquet of purple and white dahlias. She lifts them to her face. The gesture is so pretty that I smile.

My watch stopped days ago, and I wonder absently what time it is. Early: the sun is still low in the sky, the city is not yet stifling. At some point in Amsterdam I have lost track of time, of the progression of days.

I stop at Lakshmi's room on my way out and knock on her door. She's still in bed, mummy-wrapped in sheets. "I'm going to the coffee shop," I tell her. "I am going to write a letter." I pantomime writing, make loops in the air. Lakshmi nods, as if she understands me perfectly.

The coffee shop I always go to is at the corner. Like everything in Amsterdam, its hours are random. It's supposed to open at six, but although the clock on the wall says half past seven, the waitress is only now removing chairs from the tables and sponging the counters. She hands me a menu with the kinds of hash listed in the left column, marijuana on the right. I hand it back to her and say, "Just coffee, please." She pours a cup without looking at me.

She's a beautiful young woman with a sullen, Slavic face. Over the past weeks I have invented a history for her. She's the daughter of the couple who own the coffee shop, and she's angry because she wants to be with her lover, a sidewalk artist, but her parents make her work. They disapprove of the artist, call him sacrilegious. He draws chalk Pietas who all have the broad, stony face of the waitress. It's her long-lashed blue eyes that gaze tearlessly down at the naked body of Jesus, her dead son. The waitress's parents pressure her to go out with someone more stable, perhaps the anemic man in a suit who comes here frequently and sits in the back, looking humbly at her. Lately I've been unable to stop myself from doing this, stop my mind from connecting to other people; it makes me feel raw, as if my nerves are too close to the surface of my skin.

I take stationery from my bag and smooth it out on the table, then realize that I don't know what day it is. It seems very important to write the date on this letter. If I start it correctly, maybe I'll finally be able to finish it. I try to get the waitress's attention but she is sitting at a table in the back, holding a magazine in front of her face. When I walk over and say "Excuse me," she flinches.

"Do you know what the date is?" I speak slowly, but she looks blank. "The date, what is the date?" I repeat.

"The date, I understand," she says. "July twenty."

I want to laugh: July twentieth, my twenty-fifth birthday. I can't believe I forgot my own birthday. I feel a surge that catches me off guard, a child's excitement for presents and cake. But of course there are no presents, there is no cake except for the frosted hash brownies. My feeling of happy surprise dissipates. There were so many things I was planning to do by the time I turned twenty-five: quit taking drugs, find a job I could stand, settle down. Settle down: a strange expression. It makes me picture sediment in water, falling slowly to the bottom.

I walk back to my table, date my letter, and begin to write.

Dear Julie,

You probably know that I've begun this letter fifty times. I think the reason I haven't been able to write it, the reason I start it over and over again, is that as long as I don't finish it, the letter is in my hands. But as soon as I send it, it's yours, yours to read or not read, and that scares me.

I stop and stare at the paper. I remember when Julie and I were fourteen, discussing which of Superman's powers we would most like to have. I said invulnerability. I liked the idea of deflecting bullets, of being impenetrable. Julie said heat ray vision: the ability to burn things into ashes with her eyes.

Every time I try to write, I'm blocked by the same image, same memory: that night in June when Porter and I were screwing on the floor of the pool house and Julie walked in. I remember the way she stood in the door, her hand on the wall as if she were holding herself upright, her mouth open, not saying anything, and I remember most of all the way she looked at me. Her eyes were like lasers, that sharp and precise. I remember how I pulled Porter's shirt to my chest, I remember saying "Julie" and the way that seemed to snap her out of it. She said, "Don't," that was all; not "Don't talk," just "Don't." Then she shut the door behind her, almost calmly, lightly, as if she was making a point of not slamming it. I could hear the sound of her feet on the gravel, running away. I didn't follow her. I didn't know what to say. I still don't; I keep waiting for the words to material- ize, the right ones that will make her understand, I crumple up letter after letter because the words aren't there. Since that night I haven't been the same; my bones feel loose in my skin.

I'm sure you know how hard a letter this is to write.

But it was always hard to write Julie. Even when I first knew her. The summer after freshman year of high school, I spent an after- noon sitting on the beach writing her a letter. I can't remember what it said, but it must have implied, too often, that I missed her. Or perhaps I missed her in the wrong way: too intensely. When I got her letter a few weeks later, I realized right away that the tone of mine was wrong. Hers was newsy. She had met a boy in Maine she liked but thought might be too old for her; he was in college. She asked me if I thought that mattered, if he would expect too much. She asked if I'd met any boys in California. She asked, also, if anything was wrong, if I was having a bad time; I'd sounded "weird" in my letter. It was signed, "Lotsa love." I read her letters so carefully, as if they were in code, trying to peel the skin away from their sunny banality. Not that Julie's letters were boring. They were confiding, but about things I didn't want to hear. There were no submerged meanings.

So I wrote her back in the same vein: cheerful, chatty, about boys. The first month of summer, when I wasn't playing Hearts with my mother and her boyfriend of the moment, a German named Andreas, I had spent most of my time alone. Now I started going out at night with my cousin Sean. He was a freshman at Trinity and a minor drug dealer. After dinner with my mother and Andreas, Sean and I would walk to the beach to meet our new friends, smoke pot, do lines, flirt. By August I had made out with half a dozen of the better looking boys.

I don't recall liking any of them. California boys seemed so young, fumbling and jittery. I remember writing Julie about a boy named David whose eyes were green with yellow dots, like a leaf with sunlight on it. The funny thing is I can no longer picture his eyes themselves, their shape or size. I remember my mother telling me that young ladies don't spend forty-five minutes kissing boys goodnight, and I remember reporting that goodnight kiss in a letter to Julie. But as for the texture and taste of his lips, I have no memory. It was material, to annoy my mother, to share with Julie.

Of course I played down the sexual aspect of these encounters, knowing Julie would disapprove. I remember freshman year of high school, sitting on her bed, describing making out with a junior named Owen. Julie was sitting at her desk holding Moe, her stuffed platypus. Her eyes widened. "You went to second base with him?" she asked.

I had no idea what Julie was talking about. I had a very sketchy understanding of American sports. Julie, blushing, explained the choreography. First base was kissing. Second, up the shirt. Third, down the pants. Fourth was doing it.

In fact, Owen and I had "gone" to somewhere between third and fourth base. That is, we had attempted to "do it" but Owen, in a pivotal moment, lost his nerve. After trying to force his much too soft penis inside of me, he turned his back to me, zipped his fly, and mumbled that he wouldn't tell anyone we did it if I didn't tell anyone that we hadn't. There were logical flaws with this line, but I never bothered to point them out. I didn't care if he told people. The only time the word "slut" ever hurt me was when my mother had flung it across that plastic-sheeted room. So it wasn't any loyalty to Owen that kept me from telling Julie the details. It was the fact that second base seemed shocking enough to her.

Owen's body was a source of derision; Julie's was a complicated map. She seemed to envision her body crisscrossed with dotted lines indicating places that she allowed boys to touch, places that were off limits. I looked covertly at her breasts (she was just beginning to have them) and imagined them bounded with NO TRESPASSING signs

I saw my body as skin without boundaries.

Julie knew I wasn't a virgin. In Switzerland, most of my friends lost their virginity when they were barely teenagers. We took the pill while American girls my age were still taking Flintstone Vitamins. I think in a funny way Julie was intrigued by my "experience," as if it gave me a special way of looking at the world.

But she thought sex without love was wrong. She connected sex with romance in a way I never had. She told me once how she wanted to lose her virginity, and the scenario was embellished over time. She wanted it to be in a hotel, with a soft bed and flowers. Preferably in Venice, which she thought was the most romantic city in the world. Though any hotel would do. The boy would be someone who adored her, someone she could trust, someone discreet. It would be best if he was a virgin too, not inept, but innocent and sweet. They would be each other's first lovers. And the strange thing was that her fantasy more or less came true. Or maybe not so strange: Julie usually gets what she wants.

Julie seemed to see virginity as a game that she could win or lose. Winning involved champagne, a picturesque setting, and a lover in the true sense of the word: someone who loved her. Losing was having sex in the back seat of a car or the floor of a deserted classroom, with a guy who talked about her to everyone but never talked to her again.

I had sex for the first time when I was twelve, a year to the day after my father died, with an eighteen-year-old Belgian named Jean-Charles. All I remember about him are the moles on his hands. We had sex on my bed while my mother was on a date. It took me ten minutes to remove the blood stain from the bedspread with cold water. Afterwards, we walked to a park where a movable fair, complete with a small Ferris wheel and carousel, had been imported from France. Jean-Charles bought me cotton candy in a paper cone. It was the first time I ever tasted cotton candy, and I remember liking how the fluffy pink sugar dissolved to nothing in my mouth.

I know what you're expecting. You want me to explain about Porter, what happened with him. Well, I don't know what he told you, but it wasn't a one-night stand. I wish it were. I wish I could say I was drunk, that it was a meaningless drunken encounter. Although it was meaningless. We slept together half a dozen times. It wasn't serious, it wasn't important. To tell the truth, Julie, I don't like him very much.

So why did I do it?

You must have your speculations. You know me pretty well. And I know you pretty well, too—I bet I can guess what your guesses are. How Henry James-ish our—what should I say? friendship?—has become: deciphering each other's thoughts. And we're not bad at it, either, though I bet a lot gets lost in translation. But back to guessing your guesses: Attraction. Well, slightly, sure. But you know he's not really my type: too preppie. Boredom. Wanting to shake things up. Even you know that those "reasons" are pretty thin, motive-less. Jealousy. Now you're closer, Julie, now you're getting warm. But what do you mean by jealousy? Do you think I wish it were me instead of you, me marrying Porter, me wearing the champagne or eggshell or whatever the color your off-white dress was, me with the perfect life and perfect husband and boxes of crystal I would never use?

I first met Porter the summer before junior year in high school, when I was visiting Julie in Rhode Island. He grew up in Newport too, a mile up the beach from her, but she barely knew him. Porter was five years older than us, so Julie must have been invisible to him.

Which is why both of us were surprised when Porter and his friend Tim asked us out. We were at the Newport Beach Club, ordering the fanciest drinks we could think of, because Felipe, the Puerto Rican bartender, had also known Julie all her life and would never card her: banana daiquiris, mint juleps, sea breezes, tequila sunrises. Julie was getting loaded; I remember her trying to do the samba. She was wearing a white cotton tank top and her arms were bare, her shoulders sunburned. She looked happy and pretty: not pretty in her usual All American Girl way, but seductively pretty. She tipped her head back and clicked her fingers in the air. I could see the stubble in her armpits. Her hair had all the incredible colors that sunlight brings out in red hair, violet and scarlet and gold.

She looked at me and laughed, and I felt a sharp rush of tenderness for her. I remember thinking that despite all the crap she put me through, I loved her. I love Julie, simple as that; the contortions I had to put my love through are what screwed everything up.

After Julie's impromptu samba solo, Porter and Tim walked over and bought us drinks. Tim barely spoke, but Porter was very suave, flirting with us both. I knew right away he was after Julie, and I could tell she was interested. Julie has a very specific type: clean cut, dark hair, white teeth, nice hands. When he asked if we wanted to go out with them, Julie gave me a look that I won't forget: a nervous, pleading look. I said, "Okay." So Porter asked us out for Tim and himself, and I said yes for Julie and me.

It was a car date. We drove to a cliff overlooking the beach. Porter and Julie were in the front, Tim and I in the back. I remember Porter unbuttoning Julie's shirt, I remember how she let him. He did it so slowly. She was wearing some kind of black push-up bra that I had never seen before. I didn't know what to do with my eyes; I couldn't look at them, and I couldn't take my eyes off them either. So I started kissing Tim as passionately as I could, I let him do anything to me. Skin without boundaries. He pushed my skirt up and started kissing my stomach, then he pulled my underwear down and kissed my thighs. By then I could tell that Porter and Julie had stopped being lost in each other. They were both watching me and Tim, at first surreptitiously, then overtly, watching us put on a show.

So that's what I remember: not Tim, whom I had sex with that night, in the back seat of a car, but whose face has slipped into so deep a crevice that I will never be able to fish it out: but Julie, the way she caught her lip with her teeth, and Porter, his hands lightly holding Julie's shoulders. The way they looked at me.

I left the next day. I think Julie saw Porter three or four times before she came back to school, no more. But he stuck in her mind. She wrote him a couple of letters, and I could tell she was hurt that he didn't write back. She would talk about him at odd times, long after she had started seeing other guys. So, though that night was nine years ago, I wasn't surprised when I heard she was going to marry him.

I'd been out of the country for a while, traveling. I went to Spain last May with a guy, and I woke up one morning and found him gone and my traveler's checks missing. I wired for more money and kept moving, going southeast, following the sand, until one day in March I picked up my mail in an American Express office in Tunisia, and there was a letter from Julie saying she was engaged to Porter. Ten years later and Julie's letters were still all about boys.

So I flew back to the States, spending too much on a ticket to get there quickly, talking to myself to get rid of the panicky feeling in my stomach. Beth had a dinner party in New York the night I arrived, and Julie and Porter were there, and I took one look at him and thought, it can't be this easy. He remembered me, I could tell. He was sitting across from me at dinner and all through the evening I saw his eyes sliding to my breasts. That easy: until I wasn't sure, in the end, who seduced whom. To Porter I was always the girl he watched having sex in the back of his car; to me he was the boy who had half forgotten about Julie and her push-up bra to watch me. And when Porter and I were screwing in the pool house that night, the night before he and Julie were supposed to get married, and Julie walked in and saw us, I had a heady sense of déjà vu: she, too, was watching me again.

But that's too simple, too simple to say that I slept with Porter in order for Julie to catch me. It wasn't just to hurt her; it was to connect with her too. I think Porter got that. Perhaps our motivations were the same: I slept with him because he was Julie's fiancé, he slept with me because I was her best friend. So in a funny way we might have slept together out of love after all. But it was never love for each other.

Oh, I admit there have been plenty of times when I've wanted your life. I've wanted parents who spoil me, who are nosy and overinvolved and watch my lacrosse games. You have many things I want: I would like your security, your solidity, the way you, like most well-loved people, take everyone for granted. But Porter is not one of those things, Julie. If I had him, what would I do with him?

Forgive me if I sound flippant. This letter is not intended to be an apology. Apologies are for putting a cigarette burn in a sweater I borrowed; not for sleeping with your fiancé.

I can picture your face, the way you frown when someone is telling you something you don't want to hear. That frown has stopped me so many times. But I have to tell you, don't you see?

I don't love Porter, Julie. I love you. I always have. You can take that in whatever way you want. But you know how I mean it.

I stop writing, submerged in memory. A memory treasured, hurtful, overplayed; frayed at the seams, like Julie's stuffed platypus, falling to pieces from too much handling. There was a time, fall of junior year, when Julie and I were roommates. She was kneeling in front of the mirror wrapped in a towel, blow-drying her hair, I was sitting on my bed watching her. I said something like, "Let me do that." She hesitated, then handed me the blow dryer. We caught each other's eyes in the mirror.

I remember this as being both distant and larger than life, as if on a movie screen. I see myself sitting cross-legged behind Julie, holding the blow dryer with my left hand, I see Julie's damp, red hair flying with hot wind, I see my right hand on the side of Julie's neck. After a few minutes I turned off the blow dryer and started rubbing Julie's shoulders. She closed her eyes. Her eyelids were blue, as thin as silk. Her towel was knotted in front of her, and when I loosened it, it fell to her waist. I have seen Julie naked so many times—she was my roommate for three years—but this time I could barely look at her. I moved my hands so lightly up and down her sides that I could hardly feel her pale pink and blue skin. I kissed her neck.

And I want to say this, I want to make this clear. Julie kissed me back. She was not passive; she kissed me back. She didn't pull up her towel, and she kissed me back. She cupped my cheek in her hand, and she kissed me.

There were other times, too. Julie always kept her eyes closed when I touched her. She never talked, either. If I spoke to her she wouldn't answer, as if when she shut her eyes she shut off sound. I stroked Julie's back while she lay face down on her bed, I stroked her legs, her shoulders, her ribs. I kissed her neck, her hair, her waist, the bottoms of her feet. The corner of her mouth if she was sitting up and allowed me, though she kept her face averted.

For years, however, I never touched those parts of her body which were partitioned off by the invisible dotted lines. That was the most frustrating thing about whatever was going on between us. I could handle not kissing her breasts, the breasts I saw almost daily as she dressed and undressed, I could handle not making love to her, but I hated the fact Julie could so easily elude self-awareness. Because we weren't going to second base, or third base, Julie's distinct islands in a vague sea of physical contact, my touches fell into a no man's land. They couldn't be categorized, so they didn't exist. And home plate was impossible; how could home plate even occur between women, when Julie defined "doing it" by genital penetration? There was no way for two women to do it; there was nothing, therefore, for them to do.

Julie behaved as if the Heather that she saw every day, the Heather that was her best friend, was not the same person who touched and kissed her. After that first time, she would undress in front of me as unselfconsciously as ever; she would talk about her boyfriends without a flicker of awkwardness. When I tried to get her to talk about "it," she would get angry and defensive, tell me I made her claustrophobic, and avoid me for a few days. Julie knows how I feel about her; she's no fool. But as long as we don't talk about it, it's not real. And I was such a coward, so afraid of chasing her away, that I capitulated. She was, is, my best friend. I was, am, in love with her. But I have had to separate these two things—love for a friend, love for a lover—as one is a love that Julie will accept, and one is a love that she won't.

I remember Estelle, my first "official" girlfriend, the only person

I have confided to about Julie, saying to me, "I just don't get it. I mean, she's pretty, I guess, in that wholesome I-eat-lots-of-nutrients way. But she's such a denial case, so superficial. What do you see in her?"

Can anyone explain, ever, why they love someone? I love her because she pours maple syrup on cottage cheese. I love the way she speaks French in an octave higher than her English. She loves to dance but can't keep a beat. She buys balloons so she can let them go. She's afraid of the soft, thorny part of artichokes. She likes movies where the main characters die. Sometimes when she goes to bars, she tells strangers her name is Siobhan O'Mingus and speaks in a brogue. She is like ice cream: sweet and cold. She is a favorite restaurant that no one knows about, an extra fortune in a cookie. I love her because I do. How else can I put it?

I've been trying to understand why I slept with Porter. I think it was because he was something I could share with you. I know you will have trouble believing that, I know you think that the reason I hooked up with Porter was to hurt you. That isn't true, Julie. I never wanted to hurt you, at least never consciously. But you have to remember, you hurt me too...

This is a memory I have tried to forget, and even now, with the cushioning distance of time and space, thinking of it makes me press the flats of my hands to my eyes. It was my sophomore year at Barnard, and Julie had taken the train from Princeton to visit. We were at the salad bar of the dining hall when Estelle came over. She was wearing hoop earrings wide enough to fit a hand through, which swung back and forth as she said hello. After Estelle left and we sat down, I asked Julie, "So, do you like her?"

Julie shrugged. "Do you?"

"I'm trying to figure that out." I took a bite of salad. "I'm sleeping with her."

"What?"

"You heard me."

I don't think I will forget Julie's expression. She looked at me, then looked away.

"What's the matter?" I asked.

"Listen, Heather, I don't want to get into a conversation about your sex life. Let's drop it."

"Tell me." I don't know what was making me so confrontational. "Are you jealous?"

Julie snorted, pushing her tray away. "Come off it, Heather."

"What, then?"

"All right, if you really want to know, I don't understand why you want to throw your life away. I mean, you like guys. Obviously. And you want to have children, don't you, don't you want to have a family? I'm telling you this as a friend, okay? You like being the rebel, you like shocking people, but you're not a lesbian, and I don't see what you're trying to prove."

"I can't believe you're saying this."

"I'm saying it because you're my friend, okay? Look, I get it. You go to a women's college, and they feed you all this ideology, like if you kiss a guy you're caving into patriarchy. They make you think it's anti-feminist to be normal. Stop looking at me like that, Heather. I just want you to be happy."

What got me most is that I could see Julie really meant it, really believed what she was saying. She had on that pained but composed look of someone who knows she's right and is trying to explain something self-evident to a person who inexplicably doesn't get the point. She meant it; not only did she think that being a lesbian was an aberration, not only did she see it as having nothing to do with her, she also saw it as having nothing to do with me. She saw it as another theatrical and insincere pose that she could rationalize me out of.

The fact that you've hurt me isn't an excuse. You and I are not fractions; our injuries don't cancel each other out. But I want you to understand. Porter didn't happen because I hated you, he happened because I loved you, and I was frustrated and hurt and, yes, maybe angry, maybe bitter, if I'm being absolutely honest, that you gave me no way to express that love. That is, no way except through friendship.

After that scene about Estelle, I became as fixated on those

American make out "bases" as any teenage boy, for whom sticking a finger in a vagina is valuable not so much for the sensation as for its meaning: the way it converts formless boys into men. I had never fetishized sex, but since Julie did, I believed that crossing her dotted lines would change everything. It would force her eyes open.

The first time we touched in one of her prohibited ways occurred more than four years after the initial blow dryer day. She was spending her junior year in Italy, fall semester in Florence, spring in Rome. I visited her over Christmas break. I remember standing in the Uffizi Gallery, watching Julie regard the tilted, narcotic face of Botticelli's Venus. I had just been thinking how Venus reminded me of Julie—not her features so much as her sleepy eyes and the placid way she seemed to accept, along with the silk robes they extended, the nymphs' doting gazes.

Julie said, "I know it's as boring as loving Van Gogh, but I never get sick of looking at her." Then, with a laugh: "Her boobs look like yours."

That night in some bar with jasmine cascading like Venus's hair over an awning smeared with pigeon shit, we drank two bottles of wine and shared a joint. I knew without understanding how—I imagined a divine message being whispered into my ear the way a fat angel alerted a smirking Mary that she was pregnant with baby Jesus—that I could kiss her. That she would kiss me back. And it might have been just seconds after feeling, for the first time in years, the wet interior of Julie's mouth, that I had a hand up her shirt. (Which made me think of yet another Uffizi painting, a topless noblewoman pinching her own nipple; according to the placard it indicated that she was bearing a hoped-for heir). I remember feeling not lustful as much as victorious. I win! You will not be able to deny us anymore!

I woke up in the morning so happy, which lasted the minutes Julie slept. Then she opened her eyes. For five seconds we looked at each other. She sat up in bed, in her soft, old T-shirt, and said, "Hungry? Let's get breakfast." Before I could move she was pulling on her jeans and clogs and had slipped, elusive as ever, from my grasp.

So my fantasy that this breach of Julie's dotted lines would make us, finally, an official couple amounted to nothing. Over the next four years there were similar contacts that similarly didn't matter. They tended to happen when Julie was between boyfriends and off home soil (more than once during those months two years ago when we went Eurailing, for instance: a disco on a beach in Greece, a ferry, a hotel room in Budapest with mold making Rorschach blots on the walls). Always alcohol was involved. Though I suspect that she made her decision earlier that day, and the wine or ouzo or spitty joint was a means of giving herself permission. Some tossed-off comment, like the one in the Uffizi about Venus's boobs, would alert me that this could be a night. Only once in New York, just after Julie broke up with boring banker Theo, he of the flaccid handshake, did she end up in my apartment. That night she sucked on my tits and I remember thinking maybe this would do the trick, her taking the lead.

But she was gone in the morning, and when I saw her that weekend at a bar phalanxed by our high school friends, they might as well have been body armor for the way she hid behind them.

Maybe six times since that night in Florence things have "gone further," according to her old maps, and yet not progressed at all: picture a hamster wheel. More often I kissed her neck, touched a soft cone of thigh. You'd think I would know the exact number, and the fact I don't is testament to how such events literally did not count. Nothing changed. The pattern was the same: her raised eyebrow or some modulation of tone, a dip in her voice, would spike my hopes, so distractingly that I retained less the feel of Julie's lips or nipple or thigh than my uppercase, exclamation point thought bubble, Now she will have to deal! Followed, inevitably, by the full-scale erasure of everything in the morning; her careful smile, her back-off eyes.

Often I felt crazy. Those nights were water drawings done by fingertip on warm stone, evaporating once complete.

Last summer I read my little cousin Lucie a myth about a Greek girl who, unable to settle for having her god-lover only at night, against his warnings burns his fur cape and consequently loses him. "Why are you crying?" Lucie asked me, and I couldn't say, because

I know how Psyche feels; because I want to burn that fucking cloak of fur.

I don't mean to devalue our friendship; it's the most important thing in the world to me. But sometimes I wish I could talk to my best friend about the person I love, and she won't let me. And sometimes all those feelings I swallow and have swallowed, Julie, for years, come out in perverse ways. First I hoped I would change, that I could shut off the way I felt about you. Then, for a long time, I hoped you would change. I've finally not just realized but accepted that you simply don't feel the same way about me that I do about you. I'd be lying if I said that I no longer want you to love me "that way," but I don't believe it'll ever happen.

So Julie, you have my permission to love any beautiful brown-eyed men you meet; but please, please, be my friend again. I need you, I rely on you, I want to see you on any terms. I promise, Julie: I will ingratiate myself to any boyfriend or (yikes) husband you have; I will shop for shoes with you, I will go to Lamaze classes with you, I will be your middle-aged chain-smoking fat friend whom you can feel superior to. If you hate me too much to forgive me I will get plastic surgery and change my name and acquire a Hungarian accent. I just can't face you disappearing from my life.

A feather-light touch on my arm makes me stop writing and look up. Lakshmi is looking at me with her dark eyes. I smile hello and move my chair to make room. She arranges herself at the table. She is wearing a thin, red cotton dress, and her hair is pulled into a fish-bone braid down her back. Lakshmi holds two fingers to her lips, and I nod and grab a package of smokes out of my bag. I strike a match, light a cigarette, and pass it to her. One thing I have learned about Lakshmi is that she's afraid of fire. She takes the cigarette, closes her eyes, and exhales a ribbon of smoke. The expression on her face is one of such pure pleasure I laugh.

I return to my letter.

Did you see that it's my birthday today? My mother once said to me that the only way to give a gift is to lose all interest in it once you give it. So I'm going to try to do that. Just as this letter, once I send it, is yours to read or not read as you wish, my love for you once I've given it is yours to accept or reject. And if you do accept it, it's yours to accept in whatever way you want. It belongs to you.

*I'll be back in the States in September, or when I run out of money, which-
ever comes first. I'd like to see you then, and talk.*

My pen slips from my fingers and rolls across the table. I sit very
still. My body feels like it has turned to water. If I move, I might just
flow away.

Lakshmi taps my wrist, very lightly, and I raise my eyes and look
at her. The expression of her face, intent and kind, reminds me of
how my cousin Lucie once plunged herself into my lap when I was
crying, and with round, six-year-old fists batted the tears on my face,
willing me to smile. I hold Lakshmi's gaze, and for a dizzy moment
I can no longer differentiate whether I am the eyes looking or the
object seen.

The waitress comes over and asks Lakshmi, in Dutch, what she
wants. She points to my coffee. Even the waitress cannot resist her
smile. She pours Lakshmi a cup of coffee and gives her a space cake
free of charge. I watch Lakshmi lick the silky icing. Then I finish
writing.

Or not talk. Maybe we can just forget words for a while.
I love you. Heather

BETH, 1994

What I mean to say is, "Can I help you?" Julie's on a step-stool, stretching to reach the cabinet over the fridge. But what comes out is, "Help." Like I'm the one in need.

Her shirt rides up to expose a wedge of back. She's gotten so damn thin: her vertebrae remind me of knots on a rope.

"Can I help?" I try again. Julie hands me a bottle of bourbon, then scotch.

"Thanks Beth," she says, then louder, for everyone to hear, "Libations!" Descending the stool, she bumps into me. Her fingers dig into, then release my shoulders. "Whoops!" She gives me her brightest smile, the one Heather calls "photo-op." I haven't seen it since the night before she was supposed to get married.

That was June. It's the beginning of September now, and we've gotten together at Julie's house in Newport for Labor Day weekend. By "we," I mean mostly a crowd of us who went to prep school together: Ian Saltonstall, Ginny Kanute, Meriwether Burns, Sam Pitzer, Lawrence Stone, Joy Wiley. There's also Becky Ferris, Julie's roommate from Princeton, a tall, intense woman I've met a couple of times, once in Boston at the Head of the Charles and once at Julie's wedding. She sits on the porch by herself, playing Leonard Cohen songs on her guitar.

This weekend was Ian's idea, though I made most of the phone calls. We had a beer two weeks ago and he said, "I'm worried about Julie."

"She seems okay," I told him. "I talked to her last week. She's taking a ballroom class." I snapped my fingers, cha cha cha, but he didn't smile.

"I got a letter from her yesterday, and all she talked about was her vegetable garden. She's doing that Julie thing, donning her mask."

That's Ian, always the first to send flowers to hospitals. Julie went out with him for six months junior year. He can push her further than I can. I used to tell her, "You should marry him," and she would laugh and say, "I know, I know, that's exactly why I won't."

"Off" is how Ian described her that night we had drinks, making me picture a light switch. I was a little drunk: I'd worked through lunch that day, so my stomach was empty. In the bar I had to restrain myself from scarfing the bowl of peanuts. Now, thinking about Julie stumbling off that step-stool, I imagine it in another sense. Off-balance. I feel as if I'm on the deck of a boat: tilted. Through the kitchen window I see Julie's garden, the tomato plants tied to bamboo stakes.

Ginny has been sitting on the porch swing, smoking a cigarette. Now she puts on her sweater. "I'm going for a walk on the beach. Beth, come with?"

"Sure."

"Be back for lunch," Julie tells us. "It's saffron rice, and gazpacho—"

Ginny says, "We'll be back."

We walk a quarter of a mile down the beach and sit on a large piece of driftwood. I take off my flip-flops to feel the sugary sand on my feet. Near the water, a little way from us, Sam, Lawrence, and Meriwether are throwing a frisbee.

Ginny lights another cigarette and we watch them for a while. Then she says, "So, have you heard from Heather?"

I hug my knees. "I got a postcard from Amsterdam in July, a picture of someone smoking a roach. Nothing written on it except a heart. I figured it was from her."

Ginny smiles. "Yeah, sounds like," she says. "Well, she's back."

"Really?"

"I got a call from her Tuesday."

Tuesday. Was I working late? "What did she have to say?"

"You know Heather. She's been traveling all summer, Holland, Italy, Greece. She sounded pretty burnt."

Tuesday unrolls back: no, I was home, making lentils. Opening the window to release furls of steam. The phone never rang. It's an old, dull hurt that only being with these friends produces. I remember sitting on my bed in high school, staring out the window, then swiveling to the door when Heather opened it. "Hey Beth. Why weren't you at the dance? Why are you sitting in the dark, you goon?" Completely forgetting she'd promised we'd walk over together.

"I told her we were all coming here this weekend," Ginny says.

"You did? Why?"

"She wanted to know how Julie was doing. She feels really bad." Ginny buries her cigarette butt in the sand. "Well, what should I have said? I'm not shunning her. This is between her and Julie."

"I know, but—"

Ginny motions with her head. Sam, Lawrence, and Meriwether are walking over. "Later."

We all head back to the house. Joy has set the table and is arranging daisies in a vase. Ian is making his special dressing: Dijon, olive oil, lemon juice, chives, kosher salt.

"Where's the drug paraphernalia?" Lawrence asks Julie, and she points to the coffee table, where a hookah is lying in several pieces.

"I took it apart to clean the pipe. You'll have to put it back together."

Lawrence and Sam start reassembling it.

"Is this real brass?" Sam asks.

"Yeah, I got it in Nepal, summer after eleventh grade. Beth, you remember, don't you?"

"Sure," I say. "How could I not? You hid it in my laundry bag all senior year."

Julie comes out of the kitchen with a platter of bread, laughing. "Well, we knew if there was a room inspection, they'd never look through your stuff. It was the safest place to keep it."

"Thanks! Your hookah in my laundry bag, Heather's Smirnoff's in my underwear drawer. I'm lucky I didn't get expelled."

Ian puts his arm around Julie. "We all are." He shoots me a

completely legible look: don't mention Heather.

We sit down to lunch, but now that getting kicked out has been brought up, everyone wants to talk about their close shaves.

"Do you remember how we'd keep gin in the Vidal Sassoon bottle, and every time we drank it, it tasted like shampoo?" Joy asks Meriwether. They roomed together junior and senior year.

"Or smoking a joint in the shower stall before chapel, and then singing the hymns so loudly Mr. Boardman kept giving us weird looks?" adds Meriwether.

"I don't get you all," Becky Ferris says. "If you hated that school so much, why do you go on about it all the time?"

There's a pause. I say, "Well, it's a shared experience. Like war. You hate it but you never forget it. All the rules—table wipes if you walk across the precious grass, dishwashing if you skip chapel—we were in it together."

"You talk about high school like it was a mystical experience. High school was something I just had to get through."

Sam says, "We learned a lot there, though. I don't mean academics, those Catullus poems we memorized, *Vivamus mea Lesbia, atque amemus*, or how to write a three-part thesis sentence, all that crap. We learned to do anything you could for a friend, hiding them when they were drunk, writing their papers when they were hungover. Anything."

The thing I learned in boarding school was how to be aesthetically unhappy. We weren't depressed; we were melancholy, we were angst-ridden, we carried the weight of the world, we read *Letters to a Young Poet* and thought Rilke was talking to us. That narcissism now seems bizarre. It's been years since I thought my problems were relevant or interesting to anyone besides myself.

"Not to interrupt this trip down the lane," Julie says, "But I forgot to tell you guys, I'm going into town tonight to have dinner with Catherine. We made plans weeks ago and I can't bail. So you're on your own tonight, but the fridge is full, and I'll give you numbers for take-out pizza and Thai."

"Who's Catherine?" asks Joy.

"Porter's sister."

"His sister? Seriously? You still see her?" Ginny says.

"Well, I'm not thrilled about dinner, believe me. But I can't blow her off. After I called off the wedding, she came over, so upset, and said that she hoped she and I could still be friends. So what could I do?"

"Say, 'No,'" says Ian.

Julie turns to him. "Catherine's sweet. It's hard to be rude to her. Porter's girlfriend before me was a real wreck, a speed freak. His family was so happy he was going out with someone normal. Catherine especially."

Ian snorts. "Julie, you have no obligation to be nice to Porter's sister. He's an asshole. Why dredge up crappy memories?"

"Oh, Ian, you never liked him," Julie says.

Last night, after everyone went to bed, I came downstairs to get a glass of water, and I saw Julie and Ian on the living room couch. They were very close together, talking. It occurs to me that they might have slept together last night. Over the years I've seen Ian with other girlfriends—I remember a twitchy woman he dated at Columbia—but part of him never got over Julie. I try to catch his eye, but he's looking at her. It's like when Julie was on that stepstool: I'm watching everyone through the wrong end of a telescope.

"Who wants to get stoned?" Lawrence says.

Ian helps Julie clear the table. Lawrence, Sam, Becky, Ginny, and I crowd around the coffee table and take turns with the hookah. I take two good hits and stop when the smoke burns my chest. I walk out on the porch to see the ocean. The water looks flat as a gravestone. I watch it for a minute. Then I see Joy and Meriwether sitting on the swing, looking at photographs.

"Whose pictures?" I ask them.

"Oh, hi, Beth," Joy says. "Jeez, you sounded like Julie."

"They're of Julie's wedding," Meriwether tells me. "Or whatever. Aborted wedding. I know it's in bad taste to bring them here, but the photos are really cute."

"Let me see." I squeeze between them.

Joy passes me a picture of the rehearsal dinner. All the bridesmaids group around Julie. It was one of those huge weddings: six bridesmaids, six ushers. The theme was blue, and the bridesmaid dresses were in six different shades, lightest to darkest. The ushers had blue bow ties and cummerbunds and were to wear forget-me-nots in their button holes. We were supposed to walk down the aisle with the ushers in matched pairs. I was the first bridesmaid, sky blue.

"Look at this one," Meriwether says, and hands me a photo of Heather, holding a glass of champagne and laughing.

"Wow," I say. I stare at her, wearing a gold dress that looks like a slip, her dark blond hair in a french braid, her eyes red points from the flash.

"That was some night," Meriwether says. "Julie in hysterics, and Heather just vanishing. I looked for her everywhere, I thought she might have drowned herself. I finally found her sitting on the beach, eating a snow cone. Where the hell did she get a snow cone at two in the morning? She said, 'Oh, here come the furies.'"

"I slept through it all," Joy says. "The next morning I heard Julie fighting with her mom. Her mother kept saying, 'You can't just call it off,' and Julie told her, 'Watch me.' Then Mrs. Howe ran into the hall, and said to me, 'The wedding's off.' And the first thing I thought was, Shit, I just spent two hundred dollars on these shoes."

"Did you hear what happened with Becky?" Meriwether says. "She didn't know. She was dressed in her gown wondering where the rest of us were when Julie came into the church and made that announcement."

We fall silent, thinking about Julie's announcement. The wedding was supposed to start at three o'clock, and at exactly three, Julie marched down the aisle and stood at the altar. She was wearing jeans and an Indian shirt. Meriwether, Joy, Ginny, Julie's cousin Serena, and I waited outside the church. We could hear Julie say, in a loud, clear voice, "Can I have your attention, please?" Everyone—there must have been three hundred people there—got quiet. Then Julie said, "The wedding is canceled. Last night I found my groom having sex with my maid of honor. So you can all go home now."

"Can you imagine, all those faces?" I say. "I'm almost sorry I didn't go inside."

"God, I'm not," Meriwether says. "Do you know Porter's

parents were in the church? I guess Porter was hoping Julie would change her mind. They were just sitting there, waiting to see their son get married."

"Ouch," Joy says. "That was mean of Julie, not to warn them."

"They're Porter's parents," says Meriwether. "It's not Julie's responsibility to tell them, 'Your son's a dick, I'm not going to marry him.'"

"Still, they must have felt so ashamed," Joy says. Soft-hearted Joy: in high school we used to give her crap for seeing every side of a situation.

"Heather's lucky her mother wasn't there," Meriwether says.

Sam comes out on the porch. "What are you three doing? Conspiring?"

I look up and he smiles at me. When I was sixteen, Sam gave me my first kiss. We were running across the grass to our dorms, late for curfew, and I tripped and fell. Sam pulled me up, and, almost as an afterthought, kissed me on the lips. That was nine years ago. I don't know if Sam even remembers. But when I think of sex, I think not of the handful of guys I've slept with, but of that kiss: the pressure of Sam's hand on the back of my neck.

Joy and Meriwether follow Sam back into the house. I stay on the swing, looking at the picture of Heather Katchadourian in my hand.

I am amazed by how present Heather is in her absence. I feel her all over this house. I remember Heather sitting on this swing, letting her varicolored hair dry in the sun. I remember her in the kitchen, eating cocktail onions straight from the jar.

When I first met Heather, she was fourteen, and the most exotic person I'd ever encountered. She spoke French, Italian, and English. She smoked cloves. She wore lipstick and spicy perfume. Even then, Heather was sexy. The guys didn't know what to make of her. Heather scared them. She was the only girl in my freshman dorm on the pill. At first, the girls were wary of Heather, too. Most of us still had stuffed animals and posters of horses. We didn't know what to think of Heather and her lacy underwear.

Then Julie adopted her, promoting Heather to Brahman status. They became best friends, despite the fact they were so different.

Heather had lovers, Julie had boyfriends. Heather was the authority on sex. When Julie finally decided to lose her virginity to Ian—an orchestrated event that involved sneaking off campus to a bed and breakfast—Heather took Julie to Boston to get fitted for a diaphragm.

I sometimes think that Julie and Heather asked me to room with them senior year because they needed someone to mediate their fights. They fought constantly. Julie would become exasperated with Heather's flakiness, her theatrics. It was at these times, when they were pissed at each other, that I was closest to them. Julie and I would ride our bikes into the hills. Heather would climb into my bed and, while we ate entire tubes of processed cookie dough, tell me things. During one of their fights Heather told me about her father.

But in the end they always made up. Heather and Julie did their yearbook pages together. I did mine with Ginny Kanute.

So I'm used to being a pinch hitter, Julie's friend when Heather is out of favor, and I am used to regarding their fights with skepticism. Even that awful night in June, when Julie caught Heather with Porter, I found Julie's assertions hard to credit. She came to my room just after midnight, crying. "Beth, you're the only person I can talk to," she said, while I searched my makeup bag for a Valium. "I never want to see Heather again." How long will that last? I wondered.

I got very little sleep that night. Julie stayed in my room for hours, while Ian, Ginny, Meriwether and I huddled around her. At one point, Porter tried to come in, to explain, he said, but Ian made him go away. "Julie doesn't want to see you," he said. (Her exact words were, "Tell him to fuck off!").

Then, at about four in the morning, after Meriwether and Ginny left and Ian and Julie had gone for a walk on the beach, I heard my door shut. I opened my eyes and looked up at Heather.

"Hey Beth," she said. "Did Julie talk to you?"

"Yes."

She sat down on my bed. "What's happening with the wedding? Is she still going to marry him?"

"No."

"Wow," Heather said. "I guess if I were her, I wouldn't marry him either."

We sat in silence.

"Will Julie talk to me?" Heather said, finally.

"I think you better wait for her to calm down."

"What do you mean, wait?" Heather said. "Wait for ten years?"

"God, I don't know, Heather," I said. "I mean, you slept with the guy she was going to marry tomorrow."

"So you hate me too." Heather closed her eyes. "Can I have a Kleenex?" I handed her the box, and she blew her nose. "Well, I guess I better bail before morning."

"Where are you going?" I asked. She looked so desolate. But then she stood up, shook her head, and pulled herself together.

"Oh, where I always run from the law. Europe. I have a ticket to Amsterdam in July, but I'll try and fly tomorrow instead." She bent down and kissed my forehead. "Bye, Beth. Don't think too many bad thoughts about me."

I haven't seen Heather since.

The afternoon unrolls languorously. Lawrence naps on the living room couch. Sam and Ginny play backgammon on the porch. Julie begins a new project: spooning a tureen of her homemade blackberry jam into small jars with cork tops. I know each of us will get one when we leave. I try to talk to Julie, but she is stubbornly jovial: chipper, my mother would call her. Once Ian walks into the kitchen, toting a grocery bag of beer, and Julie presses her palm to his cheek. This is the first gesture of real tenderness she's made all weekend.

If I were with my friends in New York, we would always have a fallback topic: our jobs. But here work is something to forget, mostly because it sucks. Sam works for his father, who owns a chain of antique stores in New Hampshire and Vermont. Ian has deferred law school for the second year in a row. Ginny takes illustration and graphic design classes at Parsons, and works part-time in the Metropolitan Museum bookstore. Lawrence teaches an SAT prep course. Joy and Meriwether waitress in Boston in the fall, then after Christmas fly to Sun Valley to ski. I'm the only one who has anything resembling a career.

Translated from Latin, the motto of my high school was, "To serve is to rule." A generation ago, you could predict the pedigree of a Massachusetts Senator: Harvard Law School, Harvard College, the Hasty Pudding Club, Phillips Academy at Andover, a chain whose links extended as far back in time as the Mayflower. No one warned us that we would have to compete for what we thought would be handed to us. I remember Joy describing her interview at Random House. "All the editor asked was if I knew Excel," she said.

I find Meriwether and Joy in one of the bedrooms, talking about orgasms.

"I never had one until I was twenty-two," Meriwether says. "One day Roger—did you guys ever meet Roger?"

"The one with the funny ears?" says Joy.

"Does he have funny ears? I was going out with him senior year, then for a bit after graduation. So one day he decided, We're going to make Meriwether have an orgasm. We spent the whole day in bed, trying this, trying that. I felt like he should sell tickets at the door."

I smile, remembering something. "You know, Heather has never had an orgasm," I tell them, "Despite all her lovers—she's lost count of how many. One guy told her an orgasm was like a sneeze. So after every time they had sex, Heather would say, 'Ahchoo.'"

Meriwether laughs.

Joy says, "Countless lovers and she never had an orgasm? I wonder why she likes sex so much."

"I wonder if she does," Meriwether says.

At half past six, Julie gets ready to leave. "I should be back by nine at the latest," she tells us. "Take-out menus are in the drawer under the kitchen phone, Ben and Jerry's is in the freezer."

"Tell Catherine you've become a lesbian," Ian says. "Spill red wine on her. Chew with your mouth open."

"Oh, Ian, grow up," Julie says, smiling.

After she leaves, Sam takes command. "Who wants a refresher?"

We group around the hookah and everyone takes a hit. Lawrence turns on the TV. A Charlie Brown special is playing, and we watch for a while.

"One time I got really high and watched Saturday cartoons with my little brother," Lawrence says. "And I developed this theory: Scooby Doo and Shaggy are stoned."

"Come off it," Sam says.

"No, seriously, listen to the evidence," Lawrence says. "Think about what Shaggy looks like: that goatee, those pants he wears. And think about that car they drive: the Mystery Van. Shaggy and Scooby Doo always have the munchies. They're always paranoid. And here's the *coup de grace*: they'll do anything for Scooby Snacks."

"That reminds me," Ginny says. "Me and Rachel—she was my roommate in college, you guys remember her—we'd always have these great thoughts when we were stoned. We could never remember them when we sobered up. So one time, we were really high, Rachel got all excited and said, 'Okay, I'm going to write this one down.' So she put this folded-up piece of paper with her amazing thought in a drawer. We looked at it the next morning. And you know what it said? 'There's a bad smell in this room.'"

"Fine, ridicule me," Lawrence says. We all laugh.

"Okay, troops, what should we do?" Ian says. "How about poker?"

"Not poker," Meriwether says. "I can never remember what counts more, a full house or a flush. How about charades?"

"No," I say. "Not without—" I stop, and Ginny looks at me and nods.

"Then how about Truth or Consequences?" Meriwether says.

"God no," Lawrence says.

"Come on, it'll be like the olden days."

"How do you play?" asks Becky Ferris.

Meriwether explains. "We used to play in high school. Everyone sits in a circle and takes turns being the questioner. You ask someone, Truth or Consequences? If they say 'Truth,' you ask them a question, and they must answer honestly. And if they say, 'Consequences,' you tell them something, maybe something about themselves, that they don't necessarily want to hear."

"It's a fucking evil game," Lawrence says.

"You're outvoted," Sam tells him.

Becky turns off the TV and puts Dylan's *Blood on the Tracks* on the CD player. Ian goes into the kitchen to order pizza and brings back two six-packs of Sam Adams. We all take a beer and arrange ourselves into a circle.

"Becky, if you get how to play, you go first," Meriwether tells her.

"All right," Becky says. She thinks for a bit. "Joy, Truth or Consequences?"

"Truth."

"What's the story with your hair? Do you dye it?"

Meriwether laughs.

"I get highlights in the winter," Joy says.

"Winter starting in June," Meriwether says, then smiles at Joy. "Kidding."

Sam goes next. "Lawrence, Truth or Consequences?"

Lawrence looks mournful. "Truth, I guess."

"Senior year, when you told everyone that you screwed Missy Enright. Was that true?"

"No," Lawrence says. "God, I hate this game."

Everyone laughs.

"Okay, my turn," Joy says. "Ian, Truth or Consequences?"

"Truth."

"Tell us about the most romantic time you ever had."

"Look at him, he's blushing!" Meriwether says.

"Shut up, it's nothing racy," Ian tells her. "It was this night with Julie. We were at this Bed-and-Breakfast in Concord. It was the first time—well, you get the point."

"Dude, I thought this wasn't going to be racy," Sam says.

"I haven't gotten to it yet. So, we were both really nervous. And we started talking about all the words there are in the English language to express affection. Love, care about, et cetera. And Julie started saying, 'Do you like me? Do you cherish me? Do you desire me? Do you adore me?' I kept saying, 'Yes, yes, yes.' And I saw my life in front of me like a road, and I knew exactly what I wanted to do with it: keep telling Julie how I loved her."

"That's so sweet." Joy beams at him.

Ginny is next. "Ian, Truth or Consequences?"

"Why's everyone picking on me? Consequences."

"When are you going to learn that you're not going to end up with Julie? If she wanted to be with you, she would. You can't spend the rest of your life trying to revert to sixteen. Julie will keep letting you down."

Lawrence says, "Maybe we should play something nicer. Like guerrilla warfare."

Ian says, "That's okay. I'm cool," and we keep playing.

I steel myself when Meriwether asks me, Truth or Consequences. But I say "Truth," and her question is harmless: she asks if I ever fooled around with Todd Miller, this creepy, little guy who used to follow me around in high school. I say, "No."

We're on the third round when someone knocks on the door.

"Pizza," Ian says. He opens it and stands there.

It takes me a second to recognize Heather. She's cut off all her hair. It's a pixie, like Mia Farrow's in *Rosemary's Baby*.

"Can I come in?" Heather says. Ian doesn't say anything, so she walks into the house. She has a tense smile on her face. "Hey, everyone."

"Heather!" we say, like an idiot chorus.

"What happened to your hair?" Joy asks.

"I got sick of Italian men hassling me. It's a pain to be blond in Italy."

"Tell me about it," says Joy.

"Well, how are you guys?" Heather says. "Don't everyone jump up and down in delight at once."

"We're glad to see you, Heather," Meriwether says. "You just surprised us." She gets up and kisses Heather on the cheek.

Ginny gets up too, hugs her. "Welcome back," Ginny says. I look at her, trying to figure out if she knew Heather was going to show up. But her face is, typically, inscrutable.

I collect myself and stand up, kiss Heather's cheek.

"Hey, Pop-Eyes," she says, hugging me. "You need to work on that poker face."

"Nice entrance," I tell her.

She smirks.

"You look gorgeous, Gorgeous," Sam says behind me, and Heather reaches for him.

While Sam, Joy, Lawrence, and Ian hug her, I study Heather. She's wearing a sleeveless dress, slate gray, and her skin looks paler than ever, almost colorless. Her haircut makes her features too large for her face: enormous gray eyes, hooked nose, wide mouth. Becky says "Hi" to Heather, tersely, and turns away.

"So where's Julie?" Heather says.

"Oh, Julie's out..." says Joy, and falters.

"In town," Ginny says.

"How was Europe?" Meriwether asks.

"Disturbing." Heather rubs the back of her neck. She has shadows under her eyes that seem more than tiredness; she looks frayed. "There's this district in Amsterdam where the prostitutes wear lingerie and sit behind plate glass windows. When they get a customer, they close the curtains. One time I was sitting in a cafe across the street from one of those rooms. I was only there for an hour, but I saw the curtains open and shut three times."

"I hear there's a real AIDS problem in Amsterdam," Sam says.

"That's because half the prostitutes are heroin addicts," says Heather. "So what have you all been up to? I see Julie's hookah." Last spring, we smoked hash that Heather brought to Newport. I can picture the bars of hash: brown, thin, like slivers of chocolate.

"We've been playing Truth or Consequences," Meriwether says. "Want to play?"

"Oh, that game." Heather smiles. "What the hell. Can I have a beer?"

Ian hands her one, and we all sit down again. We settle back into the game, because it's easier than talking about what everyone is thinking: what is Heather doing in Newport, after the wedding that never happened?

It's Meriwether's turn again. "Heather, Truth or Consequences?"

"Truth."

"How many guys have you slept with in this room?"

"Down to the dirt, huh?" Heather says, calmly. "Well, there was Sam..."

I remember that night: senior year, Julie was away for the weekend. I was rattling the locked door of our room. Heather opened it, wearing her coral bathrobe. "Hey, Beth, can you crash somewhere else tonight?" she said. I glimpsed Sam behind her, lying in Heather's bed. That was when I still had a crush on him, and seeing Heather's quilt pulled over him made my stomach fall. I spent the night in Ginny's room.

"And Lawrence. But you know about that. We actually went out for a week."

"Two weeks, babe," he says, and we laugh.

Heather pauses, takes a sip of beer. "And Ian, Graduation night," she says. He looks at the floor and won't meet her eyes.

To fill the silence, Lawrence says, "Sam, Truth or Consequences?" and we keep playing.

But I stop paying attention to the game. This is the first I've heard about Ian, but it makes sense. He avoids touching Heather, as if he wants to keep a cushion of air between them. I wonder how that feels, having someone you slept with be ashamed to admit it.

Still: why didn't either of them tell me? My close friends, supposedly.

Sometimes when I'm stoned, I am subject to strange visitations, intuitions, as if I've answered "Consequences" to a voice in my head, and it tells me something I would rather not know. Last year, I was involved with a man I really liked. We were high, and Michael was comparing our relationship to his theory on how to grow healthy marijuana plants: not to nourish them, not to coax them into life with expensive artificial sunlight and bat guano fertilizers. Instead, he said, they should be left alone; this forces them to grow healthy and strong. And I realized that Michael wasn't directing me towards independence and self-sufficiency for my own sake, but rejecting all responsibility as a caregiver.

I have been friends with the people in this room for half my life, and I have seen them through periods of suffering. I was with Meriwether when her mother died. Ginny stayed in my apartment for a month when her boyfriend kicked her out of their Park Slope brownstone. And yet, and yet. We hurt each other so carelessly, pretending that we do so in each other's best interest. The wounds we inflict are, by and large, not deep or obvious ones, not knives aimed at hearts, but many small splinters that embed themselves under our skin, that no tweezers can extract, that our skin grows over and encloses, until they are almost, but not quite, invisible.

A key rattles in the door, and Julie walks in.

We all turn. Julie is wearing a caramel suede jacket; she looks very pretty. She has a smile poised on her face, a hostess smile, which freezes and dies when she sees Heather.

"Guess who came to dinner?" Lawrence says. But no one laughs. I am afraid that Julie will walk back out the door.

"Hi, Julie," Heather says, softly.

"Heather," Julie says. "What are you doing here?"

"I wanted to see you."

Julie takes off her jacket, starts to hang it up, then hugs it to her chest. "When did you get here?"

"Twenty minutes ago."

"Well, this is a surprise."

"I know." Heather flushes. "I should have called first, but—"

"But?"

"But I thought this would be better," Heather says. "Julie—"

Julie shakes her head. Slower than usual, her face recomposes. This is what Ian calls Julie's "Jane Jetson" mode. Her expression slides into place like a steel grate descending over a storefront.

"Everyone's looking at me like I'm going to spontaneously combust," she says. "I'm just surprised, okay, people?"

"Do you want a beer?" asks Ian. I feel bad for him; there are such limits to what he can offer Julie.

"Sure." Ian hands her one, and she takes a long sip. "Well. Heather. *Quelle surprise.*"

"Did you get my letter?" Heather asks her.

"Yes."

"Did you—"

"Not now," Julie says. "Let me just chill for a minute, okay?"

Heather falls silent. Julie sits by Ian on the floor, and says "What a weird night."

"How was dinner?" Becky asks, touching Julie's arm.

"Weird. I ordered something disgusting."

"What?" asks Ian.

"Borscht. I thought it was going to be something else. I confused it with Vichyssoise."

"Borscht, yuck. I hate beets," Meriwether says.

"Pizza's coming, if you want something else to eat," Ian says.

"Good, I'm starving."

"God, where is that pizza?" says Sam. "We ordered it ages ago."

"Were there any calls for me?" Julie asks.

"No," Ian says.

There's another pause. I'm afraid someone will start talking about the weather.

"So what have you all been doing?" Julie says. "Getting more stoned?"

"Playing Truth or Consequences," says Joy.

"What's stopping you? Let's play."

"Are you sure?" says Ian. "Maybe we should—"

"Ian, stop treating me like I'm glass," Julie says. "Whose turn is it?"

"Mine," Ian says, after a second.

It's like we have been holding our breath. We all exhale at once. Ian says, "Meriwether, Truth or Consequences?"

"Truth," Meriwether says.

"What's your favorite sexual fantasy?"

"I guess the one where I'm at this party. I'm making out with this guy. I can't really picture his face, but he's good-looking. Kind of foppish. Anyway, he starts taking off my clothes. We're on this stage, and everyone is looking at us. Watching, commenting." She laughs. "I suppose I'm an exhibitionist at heart." She looks at Julie. "Your turn."

"Okay," Julie says. She takes another sip of beer, then puts the bottle on the floor. "Heather, Truth or Consequences?"

Without hesitation, Heather says, "Consequences."

"When you slept with Porter, I wasn't surprised. I always knew you would fuck up something I loved."

Heather and Julie stare at each other, not saying anything. I don't know how to read the way they look at each other. There's so much hurt in it. I am afraid Heather will cry.

Instead, she leans over, puts her hand on Julie's cheek, and kisses her on the mouth. The way they look at each other reminds me of a Giotto fresco I saw in Italy of Judas kissing Jesus. Jesus and Judas stare at each other, transfixed, as if they're the only two people in the world. Then Heather gets up and walks out of the house, closing the door behind her.

No one says anything for a minute.

Lawrence laughs, humorlessly. "One thing you have to say for Heather: she never fails to surprise you."

Sam says, "God, she's gone completely around the bend."

"Shut up, Sam," Ginny says.

Julie stares at the door.

I walk out onto the porch. My hands are shaking. I'm trying to make myself think, but a wind blows through my head. It's like my old dream of taking a chemistry exam. I know exactly what page of my book has the answer; I can visualize the way the columns of text look, where the pictures are laid out. But I can't answer the question.

From the porch, I see Heather walking towards the ocean. She's five foot nine, but looks so small and fragile.

An old memory surfaces. Sophomore year in high school, in Heather's and Julie's double, I asked them how to kiss. I remember that room so well: the beeswax candles that smelled like honey, the Klimt poster on the light blue wall. "It's easy," Heather said. "Like this," and she kissed Julie on the lips. Julie pushed her away, laughing. Kidding around. One of those memories that the mind weeds as superfluous.

Images click through my head like slides: the fights they used to have. How Heather would complain about Ian: "He's always here. And he's such a puppy. Don't you get bored?" Heather's lovers she never fell in love with. The way they kept each other's pictures in their wallets. How they kicked everyone's asses when we played charades. There never was a charades team like those two. I remember one time, Julie was guessing and Heather was performing, and she bulged her eyes and pursed her lips in a prissy way and blinked, and Julie shouted, "Arthur Hoffman! Arthur! *Camelot!*" Arthur Hoffman was this guy in our class who blinked in a distinctive way. So it took them all of five seconds to guess *Camelot*: that made the rest of us clap and cheer. Vulcan mind meld, Lawrence called it: the way those two simply got each other. All the times I envied their friendship, tried to figure out why they were close—Julie so collected, Heather so emotional—and I never could. Click, click, click: a montage of images that I never really saw.

I lived with Julie and Heather for a year, and I have known them for eleven. Yet what strikes me now is not what I understand about them, my two best friends, but how much I missed.

The back door of the house opens. I watch Julie walk out and cross the beach. Heather turns and looks at her. I can't see the expressions on their faces, but I can tell they are not fighting. Julie touches Heather's hair. I imagine she's talking about it—*It's so short, why did you cut it?*—but they are too far away for me to hear. From the porch they look like lovers.

I look at them and look at them until I don't know what I'm looking at anymore.

PORTER, 1996

For the past two years, I've rarely looked back, rarely allowed myself to even think about Julie Howe. If I open that box, who knows what harpies and monsters will burst out? Once it was clear to me that there was no fixing that situation, it was simply easier, in the interest of survival, frankly, to run 3,000 miles away and put all that mess behind me. I wasn't in any kind of shape to be involved with women after Julie and I so explosively split up, but that didn't stop me, a week and a half after our canceled wedding, from fucking a tall, rangy girl with beach-browned legs that I met in a Tiki bar just hours after my plane landed in L.A. And frankly there was something cleansing about that fuck. It exfoliated some dead layer of me, skin that Julie's whorled fingertips had touched.

But three things have conspired to make me, unwilling as I am, revisit 1994 and everything leading up to it.

For one, I'm briefly here again, on East Coast soil, or rather pavement, the concrete plains of New York. For two, Nadia, who was supposed to accompany me to Thanksgiving at my sister Catherine's, to meet my new nephew and to placate (me) and to charm the pants off (her) my parents, sister, and hefty, monosyllabic brother-in-law, has bailed at the last minute. "You need to figure things out, Porter," were her parting words. By her calculus we should be engaged by now, or at least engaged to be engaged, whatever that means; she's made it clearer and clearer that the clock is ticking. Nadia and I started off almost a year ago, holiday season '95, as companionable eggnog/rum punch swillers and fuck buddies. That migrated through a series of shifts and skips to exclusive dating (my friends liked her, hers liked me, she's good in bed, and, until lately, fun and uncomplicated, the kind of girl I can read the Sunday paper with and then accompany on winding hikes overlooking the ocean). I don't know what started all this, some friends whispering in her ear, some alarm clock detonating in her head: but suddenly, come August, the pressure to make a formal commitment was on. She's lost all patience with what she calls my "post-traumatic stress excuses." Her mode lately has been a disorienting combination of carrot-and-stick. Sex has always been great, but lately Nadia has pulled out all the stops. I never know when I come over what sort of corsets, edible massage oils, mood music, and high-tech manacles I'm walking into. But these choreographed rolls in the hay are offset by black silences, and, earlier this week, a "Screw it, I'm not going to New York under these circumstances," which I have no problem admitting feels like a low blow: Nadia knows perfectly well that I only agreed to go East for Thanksgiving because I had her as my warm, flexible shield.

And finally, there's a third thing that has made me, despite all resolutions of forward march, think hard about Julie: but for now that can wait.

Where exactly is the beginning here? It can't be picked up like the tail of a snake. No doubt there's a context to all this, like my parents, with their ongoing but difficult marriage. The body part I most associate with my mother is her square jaw, which I picture set at a canted angle, either tilted downward, her eyes staring at some low place on the wall, perhaps some electrical socket, or rigidly upward, so her line of sight beams straight over my father's balding head.

Then there's my own dating history. For two years in high school I went out with a drama queen named Tina, and our relationship seemed mature, not just its duration but also its enterprises: the lines of blow we'd do, the constant sex, the mutual cuckoldry. In high school this felt very adult, though of course when actual adults have such stormy, drug-addled, treacherous relationships, we characterize them as adolescent. That girl was forever slinging the horns on me, and I'd hurl them right back on her like a hot potato. We were always having retaliatory cheats and fiery splits and weepy reconciliations. Tina was my original dysfunctional relationship, and now that I pull her out of Pandora's box, pretty Tina with her hair bleached orange from Sun-In bastings and her soft thighs and banal, scheming mind, I recognize she wasn't the most auspicious start to leading a life of responsible, empathetic conduct toward one's partner.

Of course the obvious place to start is when I first saw Julie Howe. The trouble is I've known her pretty much all her life. She grew up a mile down the beach from my family in Newport, Rhode Island. But Julie is five years younger than me, so I paid no attention to her. I have one clear picture of Julie building a sand castle with her younger brother Andrew, carefully packing wet sand in a bucket to make turrets, which she then ornamented with shells. In fact I may have even helped her decorate: I seem to remember being thirteen or so, giving her a handful of small shells I'd scooped from the shallow water, and her looking at me with shy, assessing eyes. I recall some bikini she was wearing, printed with watermelons, the top function-less on that eight-year-old body. And I can picture her at the tennis club too, maybe eleven, swinging a croquet mallet, or stretched on a shiny raft in the swimming pool, toes dangling in the water. The point is I always knew Julie, registered her as a pretty, red-headed girl with a good-looking father and a nice backhand and big, blue eyes, but she was barely on my radar, especially after I went away to college.

The first time I saw Julie in any real sense was the end of July, 1985. It was the summer before my senior year at Duke, one I remember as both raucous and annoying: a Congressional intern-ship fell through at the last minute, after I'd already committed to renting a house in Georgetown with a bunch of college friends. So except for a shit job waiting tables two nights a week, I did practi-cally nothing. I'd watch my buddies go off to work in their ties and jackets in that ghastly summer weather, then loll around, drink beer starting at noon, and take walks down streets so sweltering I could see the heat waves shimmer and bend the air. On these excursions

I toted a stained copy of *The Sound and the Fury* I had bought at a used bookstore, and which I held cover side outward, in hopes some pretty stranger would comment on my great taste. But of course all the smart girls were busy slogging away at their internships.

Given that I had no real job, I couldn't fend off my mother's demand that I visit home for at least one week that summer, so in late July, D.C. a sweaty cesspool, I dragged my friend Tim Wainwright to Newport for the weekend. Tim was a Sigma Chi with me at Duke, not much of a talker, but fun to smoke dope with and a kick-ass pool player. We were at the Newport Beach Club Saturday afternoon, getting drunk on Jack and Cokes, when Tim said, suddenly, "Who's the girl dancing by the window?"

I looked over. In that club populated by limp seniors, drinking their beachcombers, playing backgammon, two teenage girls were shuffling their feet and twisting their sunburnt arms in an impromptu samba. The scene reminded me of a *Sesame Street* song: "One of These Things Doesn't Belong Here." The girl facing me wore a tank top and a prairie skirt. Arms lifted over her head, she spun in a loose circle. "You mean the redhead? Her name is Julie Howe."

"No, the blonde."

I looked again. "I've never seen her before." She was tall, thin, flat-chested. Her dark blond hair fell just past her shoulders.

"You know the other girl, though?"

"Barely."

"Well? Let's go talk to them."

"Tim, she's like sixteen."

"So?"

Feeling like I had to be a good host made me agree. After all, I'd dragged Tim here for the weekend; I'd forced him to make conversation about post-graduation plans with my father, who grilled Tim about his job at an advertising firm in a pointed way meant to drive home the wastefulness of my own summer (the internship falling through had been no fault of mine, but my father blamed me for not "hustling"). All this indirect aggression wasn't pleasant for Tim, and I'd promised him beaches and their accessories, girls in bikinis. So, although I wasn't psyched about chatting up teenagers, I felt Tim required some marginal effort on his behalf.

Lord, the guy needed it. He was never a wordsmith, but Heather seemed to sink Tim into solid inarticulacy, like he'd forgotten English altogether. The way he stared and mumbled seemed to amuse Heather. Her lips curled into a kind of cat smile. Frankly, Julie, who I now know to be a generally adroit conversationalist, wasn't a hell of a lot smoother. So Heather and I took up all the slack.

My first impression of Heather Katchadourian I recall well. I understood why Tim found her so hot, but "not my type" was almost my first thought. She told us, with a crooked smirk, that she was nineteen. At this, Julie smiled, touched Heather's elbow, and shook her head.

"Bullshit," I said.

Julie said, "Heather, Porter knows me."

"Ah well," Heather said, and smiled at me shamelessly. "Then I'm also not an agent for the Mossad, or a Hollywood starlet, or a tennis professional."

"Tennis pro, doofus," said Julie.

Revised introduction: Heather was Julie's roommate at boarding school, she was sixteen "as of Tuesday." She had grown up in Geneva; she had a European way of saying "the States." Her American mother still lived in Switzerland. She had not so much an accent as hyper-precise enunciation. Like Tim, she was visiting for the weekend.

We kept drinking. Felipe was the bartender, and he must have known that the girls were underage. But that club had its own rules and he kept the cocktails coming. I remember they were drinking all these frothy concoctions with so many wedges inside—pineapples and orange slices and cucumbers, melon balls and strawberries—that Heather said, "It's like eating lunch on a toothpick." At some point the girls excused themselves to pee, and Tim lit into me in almost military fashion. We rehashed our earlier conversation.

"Dude, they're sixteen."

"So? Ask them out."

"If you think the blonde is so hot, ask her out yourself. I'm not Cyrano Fucking de Bergerac."

"What's the matter with you, Porter? Don't you think the other one is pretty?"

"Maybe when she grows up."

"Oh, stop being a pussy."

So when they came back, freshly spiffed up in that girl way—both were wearing lip gloss and had brushed their hair—I asked them out for both of us. I addressed Julie, but she wouldn't meet my eyes, just smiled and studied her sandaled feet. But clearly they'd had their own debrief, because Heather looked at Julie, then turned to me and nodded.

It was a car date. That wasn't our original intention. When we were driving to pick them up, Tim and I discussed movies we might go to, and Tim was perfectly amenable to that plan; probably he thought a movie would afford him enough popcorn-scented darkness to make whatever moves he had in mind. Heather was after all barely sixteen, we were twenty-one, and I don't think, for all his "So what?" bluster, Tim envisioned more than kissing. After we picked up the girls and he hopped into the backseat, all four of us talked about what was playing in the theater downtown. But first, we'd drive up to a nice lookout spot to see the ocean. We'd stashed a bottle of Jim Beam in the glove compartment, and passed it around.

It's funny, because I was the one who kept drilling into Tim that they were only sixteen, jailbait. But I was also struggling with having known Julie for all her life, thus with the image of a little girl in a watermelon bathing suit carefully brushing sand off the bottom edges of her castle turrets like loose crumbs off a plated cake: that is, Julie rendered about as sexual as a wax baby doll. So I think it was a defiant overreaction to my own picture of Julie-as-eight-year-old that induced me, after she took a slug of whiskey and wiped her mouth, like a kid, with the back of her hand, to make the choices I made; my attempt to defy my vaguely child molester sensitivities that put our date on the course it took. A course that has determined much since.

Julie was wearing a blue shirt with red piping that was just too juvenile to take, and I think it was more about getting rid of that little-girl blouse than real desire that made me, apropos of nothing, say, "You have beautiful breasts."

She looked at me, startled, and I knew Julie, with her prep-school manners, was grasping for the correct response.

"I've watched you on the beach." I believed it when I said it: I pictured her wearing a bikini, rubbing lotion on her arms and belly in a dreamy way. "I wanted to undress you."

It was all very bizarre. I hadn't even kissed her yet, and here I was unbuttoning the tiny pearl catches on her blouse, small as baby teeth. There's only one other time in my life when the initial make out has moved in this out-of-joint, skipping steps fashion, and the connection is most likely relevant, but more on that later.

I remember Julie's cheeks reddening, and her hands coming up, like she was going to stop me, but then, instead, her finger-tips pressing the backs of my wrists: not helping, not deterring, just resting there. Like my piano teacher when I was a kid, her fingers making sure my wrists were positioned correctly.

Underneath the shirt she was wearing a black push-up bra, which seemed sophisticated for Julie, out of context with that little girl blouse, her bare, sunburnt legs. She was looking at me like she expected me to kiss her, and I could sense Tim and Heather in the backseat watching us. Still I didn't. The bra was one of those front-clasp easy-access ones. With her fingers still on my wrists, I unclasped it, and before she could move, exposed her tits.

"Porter—" she said, but I just repeated like a spell, "Beautiful." I felt relieved by the size of her breasts. It was the first time Julie's prettiness seemed at all erotic to me. Julie took a deep breath, and who knows where things would have gone from here: but suddenly there was an explosion in the back seat.

It was like we were in one of those restaurants with tables pushed too closely together, where you can hear everyone's conversation, and the way to block it out is to talk to your own dinner mate as loudly as possible. I'd felt, ever since I started unbuttoning Julie's blouse, Tim and Heather's attention. And it was as if the only way they could pull away from us was to fold together. Because suddenly they were kissing, loud, wet smacks like movie stars.

Heather's arms looped around Tim's neck; I remember the sharp points of her elbows. Then she tugged his shirt loose from his belt, and he peeled off her shirt, and the camisole under it, and I remember seeing a flash of Heather's breasts, much smaller than Julie's. It's hard to pin down the performative nature of all this, which is clearer in retrospect than it was that July evening in 1985. The way their bodies, growing slicker over the next hour, would stick and unstick in little popping noises, like someone scaling a wall in rubber suction cups, is a sound I will never forget; nor Heather's breasts, so white that they made her pale shoulders look brown; nor how Tim hiked her skirt to her waist; nor the exposed triangle of her underwear and then, when Tim dragged down her panties (a word Julie hates), the thatch of pubic hair; nor Tim pushing apart her thighs and dipping his head between them; nor Heather arching her back and the slow, languorous rotation of her hips; nor the way she twisted her face, not away from us, as you might expect, but towards us. Even at the time I remember thinking she looked like a professional model, bending towards the light source.

At first Julie and I tried to ignore them, using the same strategy of diverting focus to each other. I finally started kissing her. I closed my eyes and tried to block out from the back seat the moans and random phrases ("Wait, you're on my hair"). I can't say at what moment we stopped pretending to tune them out. I remember Julie shifting in her seat and gazing at them. I moved behind her to the passenger side of the car. Her blouse was open, her bra was open. She looked like an unwrapped box.

A strange, surreal night. We watched them without speaking, barely moving. My own attention shifted between watching Julie watch them and watching their bodies stick and come apart. Heather was facing us by then, in her reclined model pose; Tim's head bobbed between her legs. Every so often Heather's gray eyes would open for a second, just a beat, as if to confirm that we were still watching her, and then close again. The first time this happened I dropped my right hand from Julie's breast to dip it under the elastic waistband of her skirt—she was still wearing that prairie skirt from the afternoon—press the sweaty plane of her belly, and then plunge inside her panties. She was as wet as any woman I've been with before or since.

"Wait, I have something in my purse," Heather murmured, and to the soundtrack of tearing foil I fingered Julie. Her underwear was comfortably elastic, so there was no real reason to do it, except to make Julie feel more naked, more exposed: but I wanted her to feel those things, I wanted her to feel undone by me. So I yanked her panties down to her knees and, while I held a breast with one hand, my other hand entirely palmed her. Julie's eyes never closed. By the time Tim was actually fucking Heather I'd hiked Julie's skirt to feel her bare ass against my thighs, and I had two fingers hooked inside her.

I drove the girls back to Julie's after that. Tim and Heather leaned against the car, kissing. I walked Julie up to her front door, and we stood facing each other.

"Can I see you again?" I asked.

Softly: "Okay."

"Monday?"

"What time?"

"Eleven in the morning?"

She nodded. She unlocked the door, spun around. "Sweet dreams," she whispered, then disappeared. After a minute Heather followed her, turning at the door to give the formal, closed-fingered wave of a royal.

I said before that in the past two years I've done my damnedest to box up Julie, to relegate her into the murky past while I push forward; but there are things one can't control, and among them are the images that kick up when one is in the throes of something, some warm body or even one's own hand. In these moments, the images of Julie Howe that emerge despite my repressive efforts are not of her eight years later, the Julie that I had sex with at least fifty times and very nearly married, but Julie from that night in 1985 and the five days that followed; Julie biting her lip with half my hand inside her; and, of course, of Heather. These are the flesh and bones and blood of my erotic life.

At noon the next day I dropped Tim off at the train station.

"You should call Heather," I said.

"What's the point?" Tim shrugged. "Besides, I doubt she expects me to."

I'd chosen Monday for my date with Julie for two reasons: Tim and Heather would be gone, and my parents would be out of the house.

When I picked up Julie (I was early, but she was sitting on her front steps, waiting for me), she looked even younger. She was wearing a polo shirt, Bermuda shorts, her hair was pulled back in a ponytail.

"Good morning."

Her formality made me smile. "Good morning."

She climbed into my car, looked at me with uncertain eyes. "So what are we going to do?"

"What do you think?"

She blushed. Julie has a redhead's skin: it betrays her constantly. "Listen, Porter, I should explain something—"

I put up a quick hand. "No need."

"No, really." She looked away, biting her lip. "I'm not like Heather. Saturday night—I don't know what you're expecting. I like you. But I can't—"

"You're a virgin."

The blush deepened. "Yes."

"No sex until you're married?"

"Well, hardly! But not until I love someone."

"Julie, that's fine. I get it. I don't want to make love to you."

"You don't?"

"Well, sure, but it's irrelevant. I won't."

"What, then?"

"I want to make you come."

I've had sex with four dozen women in my now thirty-two years, but with the exception of my high school girlfriend Tina, who was a first for me in so many ways (not just my first lover, but in the months preceding, those months of protracted foreplay that were both tortured and ecstatic, the first body I meticulously explored; and later, my first love, first betrayal, first heartbreak), there are no women's bodies I've committed to memory in the intimate detail that I absorbed Julie's. Just as it is sixteen-year-old Julie rather than her twenty-five-year-old incarnation who makes unsolicited appearances in my fantasies, it's sixteen-year-old Julie whose body I can summon up, effortlessly, even now, simply by closing my eyes. Eight months later in a figure drawing class I took spring semester at Duke, the model called in sick. During the ensuing hour-long free draw I penciled in, nearly without thinking, Julie sitting naked before me. But this almost automatic drawing quickly became so pornographic (Julie sitting in my arm chair, her legs spread open; the whorls of pubic hair; her bottom lip caught in her teeth; her eyes staring in that beseeching way), that I had to tear it loose from my pad and quickly stuff it in my backpack when I heard Callahan approach my drawing table.

Over those next five days, as soon as my parents left the house, I hustled Julie into my room and in quick rotation had her naked and recumbent. The first time I brought her there, that Monday, I made her take off her shirt and stand in front of me while I pulled down her shorts and then her (unbelievable!) Hello Kitty panties: I sat in my armchair, cupping her ass, my face buried in her crotch. I made her leave on her bra that time: "No, I've already seen your breasts," I told her, when she started to hitch it off. That made her blush too, and I realized that exposing her involved choosing which parts to keep concealed.

I liked to embarrass her, I liked to watch her cheeks fill with blood. The image I'd had of her in the front seat of the car, as an opened gift box, kept returning to me. Before long I had her sitting in my armchair, spreading her legs, and it was more to make her blush yet more deeply and squirm and protest than because I really wanted to document all this that I pulled out my camera to take pictures of her, though God knows in the years to follow I was happy to have those photos. "Open your legs wider. No, wider," I said, pointing my camera.

Our routine over that week was the same. For an hour, or two, or three, I'd play with her in my room, making her come and come again until she could hardly stand to be touched. Then I'd take her to some restaurant on the beach where we would eat fried clams and sliders. Sometimes I wouldn't let her put her panties back on. We'd sit on the same side of a weathered wooden bench, I'd hitch one of her legs over mine, and while she tried to eat her lunch I'd finger her. I must have kept three pairs of Julie's underwear as souvenirs (not the Hello Kitty ones, though; they freaked me out too much).

I always had her home in time for dinner. I'd drop her off at the corner and she'd hurry to her house without looking back. We decided that first Monday that, given our age difference, it would be best if our parents, who had a nodding acquaintance, belonged to the same beach and tennis club, had no clue that we were "seeing" each other. That verb was Julie's, and I might have bucked against it if "seeing" didn't seem such an accurate encapsulation of how I was absorbing every molecule of her. "Feeling" was the only lexical improvement.

But this looking and touching was all one-sided. I took off my shirt to feel her skin on mine, but I never took off my pants. I honored that no sex stipulation, and it seemed that undressing would lead to ungovernable temptation. I never forgot the term I'd used with Tim: jailbait. Keeping my pants on seemed to technically follow the letter of the law.

We'd talk too. She surprised me once by pointing to my battered copy of *The Sound and the Fury*—for some reason I'd brought it to Rhode Island—and saying, "Oh, I loved the Quentin section!" (This is a girl who'd only recently finished her sophomore year in high school; I was too abashed to admit I had yet to make it past the Benjy slog).

More often we talked about sex. I extracted from Julie the highlights of her until-now tame history. She'd spent her two years in high school paired with some boy or other. More than a couple of these boyfriends had been granted the privilege of touching Julie's breasts, even sucking on the nipples that, at this moment of confession, were still swollen from recent attentions. Only one, however, had been allowed to "third base," and it sounded more like he'd gotten some prize on a scavenger hunt than particularly stimulating for Julie. This guy, Chad, had been her boyfriend for a good portion of her sophomore year, and shortly before he graduated (he was going, of all places, to Duke), she'd allowed him access to that lovely red delta I now had three fingers inside. He'd never kissed her there, though: he probably had no idea how. Chad: the name was absurd. I made a mental note to look out for him at Duke. He sparked a strange flare of jealousy.

But mostly, this freckled body was hitherto unexplored territory. I had the conquistador's gratification of planting my flag: of making her shake and clutch my head by the ears. "Why me?" I asked her, after she trotted out this PG sexual timeline.

She responded with a shrug. "I've always had a crush on you."

But I knew why: because I was five years older, and some part of Julie liked being abject, submissive, literally under my rotating thumb. I had the impression that Julie was very popular in school, especially with boys. One afternoon when she had her house to herself I spent an hour or two in her bedroom, and the walls were covered with photos of her friends. I had mixed feelings about popular girls; Tina had been on both homecoming and prom court, and her popularity kept her insulated from the consequences of outrageous, slutty behavior. I suspected that Julie's poise, her prettiness, her intelligence, kept her in the driver's seat in most of her high school relationships. Whereas with me, she'd been quite literally in the passenger seat. Part of Julie, I sensed, craved submission. Even when she was saying, "No, please don't," when I pulled out my camera, she still let me spread her legs.

And we talked about Heather. Unlike Julie's, Heather's sex life (as I'd witnessed first-hand) was mature. She'd been fucking guys since before she'd started high school, a fact that weirdly enough shocked me more than Julie: "She's Swiss, you know." They'd been best friends since the beginning of their freshman year. They'd even dated several of the same boys: "Well, not 'dated,' exactly," Julie amended. "Heather doesn't 'date,' she fools around." I wondered aloud whether these shared boys caused any tension, but Julie shook her head emphatically. It was never concurrent, it was always with the other's permission. Neither of them would go near a boy the other liked. Besides, it was interesting to know—Julie's grin was sly—information that only Heather could procure. Joe Malladay, for example, had a penis that curved to the left.

"So where does she hook up with all these boys? Your room?"

Oh, there were a thousand places you could do it. My virgin girl was a regular *Michelin Guide* of places to have sex on campus, though her information was all secondhand. Empty classrooms, especially in the west wing of the Schoolhouse, where the floors were carpeted, the rooms heated, and the doors rarely locked. The boathouse. The ninety acres of woods, when it was warm. The playing fields were risky, too exposed, but exciting to try in a gambling mood, particularly, for ironic purposes, the goalie box. Their shared double, but only when Julie wasn't there. In a pinch they had a code, Heather's comb outside the door, but that had only happened once. Heather was very considerate.

"Have you ever seen her have sex?"

"Of course not! I mean, not before Saturday."

I wondered, not for the first time, whether any of this unpredictable week would have occurred—whether, for instance, Julie would be at this moment naked, sprawled in my armchair—had it not been for Heather's performance in my car. I had an image of Julie as a hot, bare light bulb, recently turned on.

"Does anything about her shock you?" I asked.

"No. Well—" she hesitated. "She once let Mitchell Connelly do it in her butt."

That, of course, was irresistible: Julie's scandalized face. So on Thursday, our last full day, I made her crouch on my bed with her white, womanly rear in the air. I couldn't find Vaseline in any of our medicine cabinets, so I rubbed Julie's lavender anus with sunscreen to lubricate it, then inserted two fingers. This was the only sex act Julie put up real resistance to; she had her face buried in her crossed arms. More than the sensation itself, the grip of her sphincter and that weird, subsequent hollowness, Julie's shame was such a turn-on that for the first time I felt truly tempted to unzip my pants and enter her. Anal sex seemed in keeping somehow with the backwards way our courtship had gone: the way, for instance, I'd sucked on her nipples before kissing her for the first time. I liked the idea of leaving her still a virgin by her definition but molested in all essential ways. And I suspected she'd let me: for all her talk about wanting to love the first guy she had sex with, she had proven a consenting party. But "jailbait," I reminded myself, and so I settled instead for spreading her legs further apart and taking yet another picture of Julie, this of her on all fours, ass and crotch in the air. Of the dozen pictures commemorating that week, this one was the most indecent.

The next day I left. I seized the opportunity of Mrs. Howe's tennis lesson at the club to briefly visit Julie's house and strip her one last time, lay her out on that little-girl's bed with its filmy canopy while the photos of her friends looked on. Afterwards she tried to get up, but I said, "No, I want to remember you like this." She seemed like one of those thin-skinned stone fruits, a plum, that has been so well-handled by grocery shoppers it's almost squishy: I saw my fingerprints all over her. I gave her one last absorbing look—her pubic hair so slick it was more purple than red—and was out the door.

Three weeks later, when I'd returned to Duke, a letter from Julie was waiting for me. I didn't answer it. Away from Julie's pliant body, reality set in. With her, I forgot she was barely sixteen. Naked, she had a womanly look (C-cup breasts, curvy hips, a shapely ass) that disappeared when she put on her tennis club clothes. But a thousand miles from her, confronting the return address of her boarding school, I freaked. I had paranoid fantasies of Dr. Howe hunting me down. I kept my photos of her in my sock drawer, and though I would often look at them—they became my substitute for all other porn—I didn't show them to my fraternity brothers. A few weeks later, another letter came from Julie, this one shorter. I read and re-read it, touched the neat cursive with my fingertip as if the paper were Julie's warm skin, but once again, I didn't write her back.

Funny: the Julie I knew more recently, the Julie of three years ago, would have waited for a response before sending a second letter. She'd never have tolerated a single rebuff.

My senior year unspooled. My family went to Vail that Christmas to ski, so I never went home for the holidays. But I had strange reminders of Julie. Her ex-boyfriend Chad rushed my fraternity, and I did nothing to obstruct him, or, once he was a pledge, to haze him, though I never liked the guy. And more than once, I'd hear this dude rhapsodize about Julie Howe, his high school honey, in ways that made me wonder if she'd ever, as claimed, formally broken up with the douchebag. Once when a bunch of us were in the common room playing pool, he passed around a picture of her. In her hairband she looked like Alice in Wonderland. Tim was chalking his cue, and when he saw the picture he caught my eye and grinned. Later I took him up to my room and showed him my stack of Julie photos. He thumbed through them, shaking his head. "Whoa, man," he said. Which was something, coming from the guy who had fucked a teenager in the back seat of a car.

By Thanksgiving I'd started dating a girl at another college. Candy was a junior at Davidson, from Charleston, a real Southern belle with blond hair and perfectly applied makeup. Of all my girl-friends before and since, she most reminds me of the 1993 version of Julie. Candy was wife material: pretty, slim, sweet, the kind of polite and put-together girlfriend parents love. (She did in fact marry young. I hear she has three children now, the oldest in second grade). So Candy, and school, and my House kept me occupied, and I was sufficiently into her that when I was screwing her my mind felt peacefully blank. But when I was alone, it wasn't Candy's body that floated before me. Despite (or because of) my image of Julie as a well-fondled plum, she'd left her own imprints on me.

The first weekend of April my house had our spring formal. Many brothers who had long-distance relationships, like myself, had their girlfriends stay the weekend. Candy drove up Friday afternoon. I was in the common room, waiting for her to get ready so we could go out for dinner (that girl took her time getting dressed), when Tim, standing next to me, grabbed my elbow and nodded towards the door. Chad had just entered, his arm around Julie.

She wouldn't meet my eye. Before I could approach, Candy was in the door frame, swinging her car key, saying in her twangy way, "Porter, I'm starved!" The next afternoon I loitered around Chad's hall, but I never saw Julie. So I didn't get a chance to talk to her until Saturday night at the formal, when I followed her outside the dance hall.

She was sitting on a bench, smoking a cigarette, and when she saw me, she frowned. She answered my questions tersely. She was here to visit Chad and her friend Angie (another freshman, they'd been on the lacrosse team together), and also to check out Duke.

"You're applying?"

"Maybe. I need a safety school," she said, and looked at me with molten eyes.

"Julie, why are you so pissed?"

She turned away.

"Hey. What'd I do? I was always respectful of you."

"No. That would have meant answering my letters."

There was nothing I could say to that. So instead I said something that, while tenuously connected—some lame way of shoring up my claim of respecting her—had no bearing on my failure to write her back. "You're a virgin."

"Not anymore."

Again, a surprising flare of jealousy. "Really?"

"I was seeing someone all year." (That familiar verb bugged me). "We broke up three weeks ago. That's why it seemed okay to visit Chad."

"So what does that mean? You're fucking Chad?"

Silence, again. I grabbed her cigarette-free hand.

"Julie. Don't have sex with him, okay?"

She snorted.

"Please?"

She looked at me, finally. "Only if you don't with what's-her-name: Hershey's Kiss."

"Deal."

She studied me, then gave a short nod.

"Okay then." I hoisted up the slippery fabric of her dress, put a hand on her knee and tried to slide it up her leg. But even if she hadn't stopped me, removing my wrist with two firm hands, the thick nylons she was wearing were prohibitive.

My whole fraternity was in the dance hall behind me; my date was looking for me and the drink I'd promised to fetch. Yet all I wanted to do was yank those nylons to her ankles and finally screw

Julie. For all the anger in her eyes, I knew that if I could just get her stockings off she'd be as wet as ever.

I can't speak for Julie, but I broke our promise: Candy would have found it so out of character as to provoke suspicion if I hadn't, once we were in bed, promptly entered her. This was the first time I lied to Julie, and set a significant precedent. When I saw her the next morning in the dining room, spooning scrambled eggs on her plate, we exchanged a brief, conspiratorial glance that suggested she'd stayed true to our breached bargain. The way she looked at me, like we were in something together, made me feel in trouble: committing myself in ways I was reluctant to honor to someone whose innocence filled me with equal portions of desire and shame.

After I graduated from Duke I went to L.A., first to law school and then to work in a firm (Kresge, Hatch, and Petersen) with a lobby as yellow and dry as a desert. My avoidance of Julie wasn't deliberate, unsettling as that last encounter had been. My parents were building their retirement house in Maine, and though they still lived in Newport, Bar Harbor was where we congregated. That is, when I made it to the East Coast at all. I'd never had an easy relationship with my father, and my mother, much as I loved her, depressed me: her disappointment with her life was so palpable. Now work was an acceptable excuse for spending holidays in California.

The one time I thought I saw Julie in those intervening seven years was not in Newport at all, but in New York, at MoMA. I walked into a room and saw a redheaded girl looking at a Rothko. Before I could absolutely confirm it was her, I walked right back out of the room and then the museum altogether. I can't explain this flight: it felt like instinct.

So I was twenty-nine, and Julie twenty-four, and it was the end of summer in 1993, when I saw her again at a barbecue at the Newport Beach Club.

Her hair was longer, reaching halfway down her back, her face a little thinner. From the animated way she was talking to the guy in front of her, I suspected that she had seen me first. Surely no conversation about sailing required such unwavering eye contact? When I approached to say hello, she discernibly swallowed. But then she kissed my cheek, and asked me about my mother in a way that indicated she knew my mother was recovering from surgery while remaining inscrutable to the beefy, eager guy next to her.

I remember feeling a bunch of things when Julie said, "And how is your mom?": admiration for her social poise; irritation at the way this big, blond moose of a guy hovered, clearly believing I was some interloper; awareness that she had changed considerably in the seven-plus years since I had seen her at Duke. My immediate impression of Julie was polish: she reminded me of a lacquered doll. It sounds silly to be making so much of a five-word question, but that impression later received no significant jolts. It was essentially accurate. Julie at sixteen had been unreserved in a way that this beautiful woman with her mermaid hair and sharp jaw was not. I felt all these things immediately, and I decided to wait Moose out.

He looked first puzzled, then pissed; I don't think the guy ever figured out Julie's prior interest had been about me in the background, rather than his bulky charm. But he finally gave way.

"We should get together," I said to Julie, when Moose lumbered off.

She raised an eyebrow. "The gentlemanly thing to do," she said—and the fact that she was smiling didn't hide that she meant it—"Would be to ask for my number."

So Julie delivered new cues. Initially, I'd been picturing a drink, yet when I called her up that evening, I asked her to dinner on Saturday. Somehow I knew that I needed to take her to a restaurant with pale tablecloths and ambient lighting, though when I pulled out her chair and sat facing her, I couldn't help but think of those benches at waterfront restaurants, the wood weathered to silver, that I'd taken her to long ago: her leg hitched over mine, my hand wandering up her thigh. Somehow I knew that conversation over dinner should be friendly-respectful rather than intimate. I knew to kiss her goodbye, on the lips, but not push for anything further, and to call her the next day to make another date.

I had run across Julie at an in-between stage: that quickly became apparent. She'd worked at Sotheby's for a year after graduating from Princeton, earning slave wages while dressed to the nines. After twelve months of trotting around in fancy heels and making barely enough to cover her share of an apartment with two roommates, she bailed. She went Eurailing with Heather (her eyes flicked up when she said Heather's name). In Provence she met a French guy, fell in love, and stayed, but after nearly a year of living with him in Luberon, she decided she didn't want to be a Madame, raising kids in an eighteenth-century farmhouse surrounded by fields of lavender. "Too hard to be an expat," she told me. "I want to be closer to my parents when I have kids." So she left France, and the guy—"It wouldn't have been fair to stay, knowing what Henri wanted"—and came home to re-set. She had applications on her desk for museum school, for business school, for Columbia's Teachers College. Sometimes she doubted her decision to come home. She was not without residual longing for those blue French fields.

I was at an in-between stage too. My mother's health problems coincided with a knotty, lucrative case that was in the early stages of pre-trial motions. So I had asked to be temporarily transferred to the Boston office to work on the trial prep team. Through early spring, I would be close to home. In March I would turn thirty. My own sense of the future had its shadows.

So much of life is determined by chance and timing (my choice of college influenced, for instance, by the tour guide we had at Duke, a gorgeous sorority girl with hypnotically bouncy tits whom I never saw again). In 1993, timing was propelling me towards Julie. A certain weariness with L.A. and the women there and my refrigerator of yogurt cups and sliced turkey; anxiety about my mother's newly diagnosed breast cancer.

Yet here's the thing: I don't believe I would have fallen in love with Julie, never mind proposed to her, had we not had that passionate fling eight years prior, and had that fling not been kept alive in those intervening years, preserved in an amber of masturbatory fantasies and documentary evidence. The Julie photos were one of the few things I'd brought to Boston. I don't think I would have had the patience to go through that song-and-dance, five weeks of

Saturday dates, kissing her goodnight at her parents' door, the kisses getting longer and steamier but, still, kisses only, were it not for eight years of wanting her.

Then again: who knows if Julie would have felt a need to be a chaste Rules Girl, if she weren't over-compensating for her craven sixteen-year-old self? Yes, there were obstructions: Julie was living with her parents while she figured out her next steps. But still, I was only an hour and a half away in Boston, pining in my sublet. There was no reason it should have taken her six weeks to visit for the weekend, other than to perform a ritualized inaccessibility.

By the end of five weeks (every Saturday, I drove to Newport to take her to one of its nice restaurants), my frustration was open. She laughed as I kissed her neck at her front door, and whispered, "Porter! My parents are home."

"This is ridiculous. I feel like I'm in high school."

Julie's expression was victorious. It occurred to me that I had been guided to this point.

"Come stay with me next weekend," I said, and she bit her lip— it was the first time I had seen her do this in years—and, after a long pause, nodded.

So, finally, after six weeks, plus or minus eight years, I had unchaperoned, legal-age Julie in my Boston sublet, wearing a black sweater dress that was both conservative (high neck, the hem below the knees) and clingy-alluring. We made dinner together. (I have learned, over the years, the seduction utility of knowing how to roast chicken: it's impressive without making one seem effete). She snapped green beans to toss with sliced almonds; I made salad. Occasionally her hip or elbow would brush against me. We drank most of a bottle of wine before sitting down to dinner.

"Before this proceeds—" she said later, pulling back. We'd finished eating, though she took her sweet time lingering over a bowl of maple-walnut ice cream. We were standing in the door frame between the hall and bedroom. I was kissing her when she withdrew.

"What?"

The look on her face was distinctive: I can perfectly picture it today. Tense, embarrassed, but resolved. "Do you still have those pictures?"

"What pictures?"

She made a face. "You know. Those photos you took."

Six weeks of seeing her once or twice a week, and this was the first direct reference she'd made to that July. Every so often it implicitly emerged, like when she mentioned Heather's name, and we exchanged a fleeting glance. But there was a tacit taboo over that week. I knew better than to refer to it. The one time I'd asked her, kiddingly, if she were in touch with Chad, she shot me such a freezing look that I shut up.

God knows why I didn't lie about the pictures: it's like Julie was Wonder Woman and had me in the Lasso of Truth. And something about the way her cheeks were pink, the way she looked suddenly familiar—rosy, beseeching. "Yeah, I still have them."

"Here?"

I nodded.

"Give them to me." Not a request.

I leaned against the door frame, studying her.

"Before we proceed."

We stood two feet apart. Julie made an impatient noise. "Honestly, Porter!" she said. "Would you rather have those disgusting old pictures, or me?"

"Seriously?"

She nodded. So I went into the bedroom, opened the top drawer of the bureau, and got them out. She stood in the door, arms folded. If she hadn't been watching, I would have looked through them one last time—not that I hadn't done so, plenty, in those recent weeks, returning to the apartment late Saturday night from Newport. I had even considered putting them in the glove compartment, so right after being dismissed by smiling Julie, her breath slightly rapid from goodnight kisses, I could scrutinize her nipples, her slick pubic hair. So I could privately correct some upended power imbalance. But, tempting as it was, keeping them in the glove compartment wasn't worth the risk. Now all I could do, with her eyes piercing my back, was quickly slide the top photo to the bottom. Then I handed them to her. Without looking at them, she put them in her purse, which I only now noticed was on her shoulder. So this had been a setup.

Part of me wondered how far that setup extended: if she had dated me only to get her hands on those pictures, if she would now, like some noir heroine, prod me with her pointed toe and walk out the door.

Instead, Julie relaxed. "Now was that so hard?"

I'd been watching my words so diligently over the last few weeks that when I said, "Yes," it surprised us both.

She laughed. It was a complicated laugh: sharp, warm, amorous. "I'll make it up to you." Then her arms were around my neck, and I scooped her up and carried her, like a bride, into the bedroom.

And did she make it up to me? Yes and no. I finally (six weeks plus eight years) fucked her that night (well, Julie would call it, "made love," and that's more accurate). It was... good. Her body, when I pulled off the sexy black dress, the sheer stockings, and the bra and panties, lacy, matching, carefully selected, was both very familiar (as I said, this was a body I'd committed to memory) and strange somehow. She'd lost a little teenage roundness; her pubic hair was thicker and perhaps a duller red; more freckles dusted the plane of her chest; her thighs were both slimmer and softer (Julie was no longer doing her three varsity sports). She tasted the same.

It was a double-exposure experience, because I knew her body well enough to trust my sense of accuracy (breasts maybe a touch lower now, et cetera) and to question it. I wondered if my memory burnished her somehow.

And her behavior in bed, without question, was different. When I started licking her, she was quick to pull me away. That first night I thought it was eagerness, wanting me inside her, and God knows I wanted that too, so I didn't process it. But this persisted. She liked oral sex, don't get me wrong, but she didn't want to come. When she was sixteen I'd go down on her for, literally, hours: she'd come and then as soon as she wasn't too tender to touch I'd make her come again, until just breathing on her would make her shiver and moan— that was my cue to take her for a slider.

Though we were now technically lovers, I'd had more dominion over her body back then.

For instance, whenever she went to the bathroom to pee, or even to brush her teeth, she'd lock the door. After sex, she'd put on panties, socks, a long nightgown. She said she got cold, but I felt there was more to it, that she didn't like being naked around me: she didn't like anything that reminded her of the way I used to spread her apart, open her up.

Open: that was the difference. She wasn't open to me as she had been in the past: not her body, nor, in some respects, her mind. She frowned when I asked her about former lovers. She wouldn't even tell me a number. "Come on, Porter! I'm not asking you!" That was true, so I desisted; I didn't want to lie, and I knew the face she'd make if I gave her an honest answer. But still, how could I avoid comparing this Julie, discreet, guarded, to the one who had shown me, fingers guiding mine, exactly where and how different boys had touched her?

It bugged me most when I met her friend Ian Saltonstall, a spaniel hanger-on so transparently devoted to Julie that I cross-examined her after we had dinner with him. Only under duress, and with real irritation, did Julie finally admit that Ian had not only been a high school boyfriend of hers ("Join the fucking crowd!" I said), but the most significant one, the one she'd first screwed. I remember feeling cold and angry, thinking of being on that bench with Julie back at Duke. "It's ridiculous to be jealous," she said, annoyed by my annoyance.

My friend Paul has a theory about sex: it's so subjective, so prone to distortion, that the only way to evaluate whether sex is "good" or not is through quantifiables. He has three: 1) Is the woman willing? Which translates for him to, does she assent at least two times out of three? 2) Is the quantity satisfactory? (He emphasizes that no arbitrary number can be assigned to this, as everyone's libido is different, so satisfaction is the only thing that counts: but his own number for a gratifying monogamous relationship, and personally I agree, is twice a week at least). 3) Does the woman ever initiate?

According to Paul's rubric, my sex life with Julie was good. She rarely said no. We had sex most nights we saw each other when we were still living apart, two or three times a week when she moved in with me at the end of February. And she did initiate, though rarely, and in subtle ways: I knew Julie wanted me to fuck her if she was listening to Nina Simone, or if she wore to bed a certain black camisole.

So why, then, do I put ersatz quotes around that initial assessment; why characterize sex with her as "good" rather than straight-forwardly good?

I guess the only answer here is that I missed the way, as a girl, she had let me take her over: subdue her, dominate her. Once she had burst into tears after I spent an hour fingering her: I missed that unrestrained passion.

None of this stopped me from loving her, or from wanting her. But I have always valued great sex—possibly I overvalue it. No question my high school relationship with Tina would have more quickly stuttered to a halt were it not for the way her body captivated me, and I wouldn't consider, now, marrying Nadia, were it not for the way she rubs scented oil over herself while I watch, or her deft touch with a blow job. Great sex isn't everything, I know, but it's hard to imagine making a commitment without it.

All this is to say, much as I loved Julie, attracted as I was to her, much as my friends admired her and my parents approved and the rest, I never would have proposed had I not believed I could revitalize that sixteen-year-old girl who had held my fantasy life in such thrall for so many years.

And I have a feeling the reverse is also true. Julie was only twenty-four when we started dating, but I was the third man to propose to her. The French guy had geographical liabilities, at least for such a homebody as Julie, but her boyfriend the year she worked at Sotheby's had been seriously eligible: rich, handsome, et cetera. So why me? This was the same thing I'd wondered back in the day: why is it me with two fingers inside her? This girl/woman everyone seems to want? And my intuition is that, again, it's because of that week in 1985: that Julie would never have agreed to marry me, if I hadn't eight years prior spread her legs and taken pictures of her.

Oh, I have no doubt that she genuinely wanted to destroy those pictures (and no doubt she did). But I believe that she decided to marry me both to own me and to tame me, in the same way that I proposed to her partly so I could finally come inside her round ass. To some degree, all lovers are time machine conjurers, seeking to recover and to repair the past.

In my mental timeline, scored to eight years of beating off to Julie, things had moved damn slowly; those five weeks of Saturday dates in particular crawled. To everyone around us, things moved fast. Circumstances pushed our courtship forward. I was working long days on trial prep, and the three-hour round trip drive to Newport was bad use of my time. But Julie wouldn't even consider moving in with me unless we were engaged. She had sensible reasons for taking this Victorian position: the year in Luberon, she claimed, had convinced her never again to move in with someone whimsically. I wanted to return to L.A.—the proximity reminding me of the inadvisability of being within 1,000 miles of my father—and Julie was intractably opposed to L.A., if smilingly so: she claimed to hate freeways, surfing, frozen yogurt. Nor did she think much of long-distance relationships. Then there were the different ways Julie's life might fork, and none of those routes (Columbia, Wharton, NYU) led her from the East Coast.

"Of course, if we were married... that would be different," she said.

Plus, I never lost my impression that Julie was out of my league. But because of our history, because I had eight years ago, for once in her life, wielded some contingent mastery over her, she was accessible. She chose me, even though her choice didn't make much sense.

And my intuition that I didn't deserve Julie was corroborated by pretty much everyone: by her snobby friends, with their tiresome in-jokes; by my parents and my sister Catherine, who were pleased to the point of dumbfounded elation that we were dating; even by

Phil Petersen, a name partner at my firm, who took us out to dinner one night and was bowled over by my hot and intelligent girlfriend ("And you went to Princeton?" he said, then gave me a look of approbation that I had never before received from this dude, never in five years of billing an average of 2,200 annual hours and being consistently ranked above class, never). She was, everyone around us signaled, the total package, a bewildering prize.

Also influential was my mother's health. She loved Julie. Julie was the one sitting with her at the Harvard hospital for Mom's chemo drip, those days when my father and my sister and I were working and couldn't be there. Julie would make chicken soup and deliver it to their house in Newport (my parents were staying far from icy Maine while my mother recovered). Julie would read Mom *New Yorker* articles while she rested in bed. In this sense, Julie's protracted stay in her parents' house really paid off, and no fucking wonder my family thought she was God's gift, with her homemade muffins and her broth from scratch.

Stage three breast cancer is no joke. I began to wonder whether my mother would be around to see me get married. I realized that her being there mattered to me.

And there was one more thing.

People were always asking us how we met, that generic conversation-opener to couples. And there was this halting, awkward issue with answering. Julie would say, "Oh, goodness, I've known Porter all my life," but it wasn't the kind of reply that held up well to follow-up questions ("So when did you realize...?"). Only Julie's social polish would navigate us through those hazardous waters. One night in January I brought it up with her. We were cuddling in bed, and I asked why all this cloak-and-dagger secrecy about how we got together? After all, it wasn't like she was still sixteen, and I was dropping her at the corner and hunching in my car to avoid being seen. This was as explicit as I'd ever been about July 1985, and it took Julie a minute to answer me. She sat up in bed and stared out the window.

"You know, you really hurt my feelings," she said, finally.

"What do you mean? Now?"

"No, silly! Back then. When you blew me off. There was this girl in high school, Annie Carpenter. Everyone called Annie 'Kleenex' because all the boys used her. When you didn't answer my letters, I felt like her. Like a disposable fling."

Something clicked for me, that second. Of course it wasn't surprising information, or even the first time I heard it (there was that night at Duke). But it occurred to me that everything might be different now, had only I been less freaked then. Maybe the issues I had with our sex life, the way Julie was prudish, reserved, would disappear if she felt truly safe. My distance then had produced her distance now. So I apologized, and kissed her, and kept kissing her, and for once she didn't put on that damn nightgown afterward. She fell asleep with her arm over my chest. While she slept I made certain decisions.

I proposed on Valentine's Day, with my grandmother's ring. We were drunk when we got home: we'd had champagne, a bottle of wine, and then ruby port (porter, she called it) with dessert. She was giggly and amorous. But when I said, "Hey, can we try something new?" she was slow on the uptake and then aghast. It was covered over smoothly, with giggles and kisses, but she wouldn't let me so much as put my fingers in her ass. Lying beside her that night, I experienced the first chill feeling that it was always going to be like this: I would never again get her to do exactly what I wanted ("No, spread them wider;" "Lift your ass higher"; "Cup your breasts and smile at me"). I felt, and this is a very strange thing to feel the night you get engaged, but perhaps more common than I suppose, something close to despair.

At that moment if I could have reversed time and traded Julie-now for the Julie pictures, I would have seriously considered doing so.

Into this situation, at the tail end of March 1994, careened Heather Katchadourian.

I should clarify that all this emphasis on my sexual disappointment with Julie doesn't mean I was unhappy. On the contrary, despite the stresses of my mother's illness, this was the happiest time of my life. Our wedding plans were on a fast track. I hadn't given up hope that I could construct a safe enough space for Julie that she would lose her inhibitions: my perfect bride would become, in all senses, my perfect bride.

The whole time we'd been dating Heather was out of the country. Though I'd seen plenty of Julie's high school friends—frankly more than I cared to, especially mopey, cow-eyed Ian—I hadn't seen Heather since that night in 1985. We went to a dinner party in New York one Friday at Julie's friend Beth's, and Heather sauntered in. God, I still remember what Heather was wearing: a short black skirt, suede I think; a black blouse, long-sleeved, chiffon maybe, sheer enough to show her black bra; black tights, black high-heeled boots. Some kind of hairy, white coat that looked like the skin of a Yeti.

Nearly nine years before, I understood why Tim Wainwright was attracted to Heather, but I hadn't felt it myself. I did now. She reminded me of a girl I'd dated in L.A., a real train wreck, but a maniac in bed; Danielle would actually scream, loudly enough to hurt my ears. From the moment Heather said, "Hello, Porter," I felt time reverse. I was in the front seat of that car again, and she was opening her wide-set eyes to watch me watch her.

She was magnetic: I don't know how else to put it. I felt like Tim, all those years ago, unable to string together a sentence.

She was sitting at the head of the table, the prodigal girl, the surprise guest of honor, and all through dinner I kept trying not to stare at her face, or worse, her sheer blouse. Beth Carlson kept shouting, "Give that girl more wine!" The men fawned. Even generally composed Julie was almost giddy about having her best friend back. "I'm so happy you're here!" she said, reaching for Heather's hand. So I blended in, just another riveted person listening to her travel stories. Though something about the way she would grin when she caught my eye made me think that she knew perfectly well I had an erection all through dinner.

"Porter, do you mind if I stay out with everyone tonight?" Julie called across the table. "You have that early meeting. And I can sleep here."

For a second I was sorry—I'd been hoping to relieve myself of some brutal sexual energy by screwing Julie when we got to our hotel.

Then Heather said, "Great. Porter and I can share a cab."

"Oh! Won't you stay with us?" Julie drooped.

"Yes, come on, Heather! We haven't seen you in a million years. You and Julie can sleep here, you can rock-paper-scissors for the couch," Beth coaxed, but Heather was already standing.

"I'd love to, but I'm so jet-lagged I'm falling over. I'll call you both tomorrow. Porter, just give me a sec, and then we can catch a cab. Your hotel is Midtown too, right?"

Half in a daze I kissed Julie and said goodbye to that obnoxious prep school crowd. Ian was so pleased I was leaving, he was practically wagging his tail. In a minute Heather emerged, wearing the Yeti coat. She hugged and kissed everyone; it took an eternity. Finally we were on the sidewalk, Heather as tall as me in her boots. She waved a hairy, white arm to hail a cab.

I didn't trust my instincts. Heather is Swiss, for one: who knew what passed for signals with her? So it wasn't until we were in the cab, and Heather leaned forward and told the driver, "Torch Club, please," gave him a Chelsea address, and then asked, "You don't mind if we take a detour, do you, Porter?" that I began to get the drift.

By then she had shrugged off the Yeti coat. She turned to me, half-smiled.

It was close to midnight, but it was New York, and there was enough light whizzing by in slanting bars that I could see some things. For one, Heather's legs were now bare; she wasn't wearing the black tights. For two, she was no longer wearing her bra. The blouse was as sheer as ever, and my eyes dropped straight to her nipples. They were sticking out like beads.

And now I was in the back seat.

Her smile widened. With an audible moan, I scooted over. My hand roamed up her bare leg. First she clamped her legs to trap my hand; then with a dark laugh she opened them. She wasn't wearing underwear. It was impossible not to think, as I hitched her leg over mine, of being at those waterfront restaurants with teenage Julie.

Impossible to stop my other hand from squeezing Heather's barely covered breast.

"Easy, Tiger," she said, and nodded towards the cab driver. Her own hand drifted, lightly as a cloth napkin, onto my crotch.

"Let's go to my hotel."

"Nope, I feel like dancing. Keeps me awake."

Outside the Torch Club I tossed money at the cab driver— God knows what I paid him. There was a line waiting to get in, but Heather took my hand, nodded to the bouncer, and he waved us through. It was packed. She pulled me to the middle of the dance floor. I tried to embrace her but she stepped two feet back, lifted her arms, and danced in front of me. I shuffled and stared. Her breasts were bigger than I remembered them being when she was sixteen, though still small. I couldn't take my eyes off her nipples. I closed the distance, pulled her against me, kissed her. Under the skirt my hands clutched her bare ass.

"I want to fuck you."

She shook her head. "I told you, I feel like dancing. Whoa, you're hard, aren't you?"

I pulled her off the dance floor, down some stairs, down a corridor to the restrooms. Both doors were locked. I moaned again. She laughed, and I turned her so her back was to me. Fingers locked, I pressed both hands against her: scratchy and wet-slick. Again, impossible to not think of Julie leaning against me in the front seat of that car, while I explored her.

Finally, a moan from Heather. "Well? Do you have anything?" she asked me.

"No, damn it. Don't you?"

"No, stupid. I just rolled off a plane."

"I thought you were the girl who was always prepared."

She laughed. "Try the bathrooms; they sometimes have machines."

She disappeared into one. I banged on the door of another until a man finally emerged, swearing at me. There was indeed a condom machine, but it was empty. Back in the hall, Heather nodded. "Yeah, the ladies' was empty too. High demand, I suppose."

"Aren't you on the pill?"

"So? Haven't you heard of safe sex, buddy?"

I was feeling her ass again. Smaller than Julie's, less soft, higher up. Heather must have been six feet tall in her boots. She was perfectly situated against my body.

"I was tested last spring. I haven't been with anyone but Julie since the summer."

"Lucky you." Her voice was dry. "Unfortunately I can't say the same. Come on." She led me back to the dance floor.

For the next hour she drove me bats. We danced. She moved away from me, smiling, sliding her hands down her sides. I reeled her in. People were all around us. I pulled her back down the stairs, dragged her into a bathroom, and licked her while she sat on the sink with her legs spread. Someone started banging the door, ironically the guy I had harassed earlier. His look, when we left, was malevolent.

"That was... frustrating," said Heather, with a sigh. More dancing.

"What about finding a twenty-four-hour store? City that never sleeps, right?"

"New York doesn't, but I need to. I'm still on Barcelona time. I'm not responsible for my actions. No wielding heavy machinery, et cetera."

"So let me act."

"Any chance Julie is going to head back to your hotel instead of staying at Beth's?"

"I don't think so." But the thought deflated me. For a second, I couldn't breathe.

"Listen, I think we better call it a night." She leaned against me, sighed on my neck.

"Ugh."

"I know. But there will be other... opportunities."

"Tomorrow?"

"I told Julie I'd have breakfast with her, I bet we'll spend the day together." Her palm rested on my crotch. I was starting to wonder at how many hours before a constant erection required medical attention. "Rain check?"

When I finally collapsed on my hotel bed, the woman starring in my fantasies was Heather.

Trying, is how I would describe the next couple of months. Exciting, certainly: but not peaceful, or especially happy. I flew back to Boston after my meeting the next morning, and it took three days for Julie to rejoin me. She returned with shopping bags and stories about Heather, whom she had been with nearly non-stop.

I didn't see Heather again for three weeks, when she came to Newport for Julie's twenty-fifth birthday party, and honestly I thought the first night, watching Heather in her low-cut dress carouse with their prep-school friends and flirt with some Australian guy who had gone to college with Julie, that I would go completely around the bend. The next morning, everyone hungover, Heather volunteered to shop with me for pickled green beans, celery, and hair-of-the-dog Bloody Mary mix (Julie's parents were still knee-deep in vodka). She laughed her dark, hoarse laugh when I drove us first to that lookout spot on the cliff. And though it was broad daylight and I was in my thirties now and too old for these shenanigans, it did seem fitting that the first time I fucked Heather Katchadourian was there, in the back seat of a car (the condom had been in my wallet for weeks).

That was essentially how I "saw" Heather: over a stolen hour when she came up to Boston or when we met her in Newport. Julie, who didn't have a job, saw much more of her: she would go at least twice a month to New York to spend days with Heather, sometimes also Beth.

It was maddening. The three of us lying on a beach together: Heather in a tiny bikini would apply sunscreen, almost in slow motion, to her chest. "I hate tan lines! I wish I could take off my top," she'd say, and I would glare while Heather grinned and Julie said, "You have to readjust to Puritanical Rhode Island." It amazed me that Julie was so obtuse—that she never seemed to catch on to her best friend's efforts to drive her fiancé nuts.

I'd spend hours lying on my stomach in the sand, waiting for the fifteen minutes when Julie would walk back to the house to get a new novel, so I could be alone with Heather, covering her with a towel, and shoving three fingers inside her.

Twice I flew to New York for meetings and stayed overnight, and these were my only untracked hours with Heather. She was... adventurous. In those two nights, we did some things I'd always wanted to do. She was also selfish. She sat on my face with her legs acrobatically spread, grabbing fistfuls of my hair, but when I later tried to get her to reciprocate, she shook her head. "I just went down on you."

"You wanted to, and who am I to deny a man what he wants?" Her sly grin. "A blow job, that's Julie's department." My face made her pause. "Or... not?"

This was our second night in New York, and spontaneously, I unloaded everything. I told her about the way Julie was: the night-gown, the primness, the reserve.

"I guess I'm not surprised."

"But it's not how she used to be," I said, and then I told her about 1985. In detail, because she wanted them: for once Heather, who often seemed tuned-out around me, almost bored, was fasci-nated. Strangely, it reminded me of how I used to talk to Julie for hours about sex: how she liked to be touched, what she wanted me to do, what other (lesser) boys had done. I told Heather about the photos, the waterfront restaurants, the way Julie would pull away because she got too sensitive to touch: all of it.

"Do you still have the pictures?"

"No, she made me give them to her."

"Well, it sounds to me like the version of Julie you miss is a blow-up doll. Someone who does whatever you want and never says no."

"That isn't it..."

"Really? Because other than the modesty stuff, which I concede is a drag, I don't really get what you're missing." She shrugged. "I guess that's just not what turns me on, Porter: I don't want a lover who will do whatever I ask," she paused, "them to do. I want someone who pushes back. But it's interesting..."

"What is?"

"Well, it explains some stuff I always wondered about. I knew Julie had seen you a couple of times that week, but she never told me details. She's so damn cagey! I figured it was her same old *inamorata* routine. But now I get it. She came back to school junior year...how can I explain it? Ready, all of a sudden. You know Ian Saltonstall? He was always waiting in the wings, but Julie was too busy toying with the seniors. Then suddenly she wanted a real boyfriend. I think you primed her." She laughed. "Interesting. Okay, as a reward for that illuminating narrative, what do you want to do? No blow jobs, I reiterate, but I'm open to suggestions..."

I had plenty of them.

Bipolar, Heather seemed to me. Sometimes, like that night, she was game, even effusive. She answered all my questions, reminding me, again, of voluble, teenage Julie. "The oldest guy? Well, he said he was fifty-six, but I bet he was lying. His skin had no elasticity at all, it was like the skin on a raw chicken, you know, how it just pulls away from the meat? How many? Oh, lord, I don't know Porter. More than you have." I raised my eyebrows, but she nodded confidently. "No, believe me; more than you. Married guys? A few, sure..."

Other times, she was curt. The morning after that second New York night, for instance, she woke up grouchy and somber. Zipping her boots (those same high-heeled ones: I could never see them without thinking of dancing in that club), she asked, "So is this your MO, Porter? Do you cheat on all your women?"

Still riding on the confessional prior night, I didn't process her tone. So I told her about Tina, "Which I feel absolutely no regret about! That slut cheated on me just as much," and others: Candy, and a girl in L.A. whom I had been fairly serious about, but couldn't stop myself from cuckolding with Danielle the psycho screamer.

"Do you plan on sleeping around after you marry Julie? Are you going to be some kind of Jack Kennedy?"

"Does that make you Marilyn?"

"Only if Marilyn were a duplicitous bitch. Hey, let go."

Belatedly, I caught her mood. "I don't know, Heather." I thought of a conversation with Julie several nights previous about the wording of our vows, whether we should say "forsaking all others" or "and be faithful to each other." "I'll do my best to be faithful to Julie. That is, unless you happen to cross my path." I grabbed her again. She gave me a crooked paper cut of a smile.

"You know, in Geneva this is normal. No one really expects their spouse to be constant. But here—" she paused. "Julie will absolutely assume fidelity."

"What she doesn't know..."

A snort. "Right, JFK."

"So tell me then. Why are you here?"

Fidgeting again with her boots, Heather averted her gaze. "Meaning what?"

"Julie told me you kept your hands off each other's guys. Or, rather," I spider-climbed my fingers up her warm thigh, "You fooled around with plenty of her guys, but only after she was through with them. With her permission. You'd report back things."

Her eyes met mine then, smoky gray. "When did Julie tell you that? Recently?"

"God, no! When she used to be forthcoming. Back in the day. She talked about you a lot..."

"Huh," she said, finally. I couldn't read her expression.

"So what changed for you?"

Her eyes jerked up again. "Porter," and her voice was light, but warning nonetheless. "Anyone ever tell you not to look a gift horse in the mouth?" She stood up, glanced at herself in the floor-length mirror. "Some gift horse!" With a bleak laugh, she scraped her hair into a ponytail. "More like a Trojan horse. Though oddly enough, I think that's where the expression comes from. Wasn't the Trojan horse first presented as a peace offering? But then the expression makes no sense, because of course you'd want to look at some trap, some hidden weapon, in the mouth, so you could identify it..." She turned to me, brooding, and slipped on her jacket. "On that note: guard your battlements, Porter," and she was out the door before I could kiss her goodbye.

Mercurial Heather. Sometimes she acted like she couldn't stand me.

I left several messages for her without getting a response. The next time I saw her, a Saturday in early June in Newport, she brought a guy, some cute, dumb shmuck who'd just graduated from Middlebury. It was like Julie's twenty-fifth birthday party all over again, except then I'd had the sense that Heather's performative flirting and cut-to-here dress were for my benefit: every so often she caught me watching her and smirked. This time, she wouldn't meet my eyes. I couldn't shake the notion that this goofy hacky sack dude was operating as some kind of shield, though I wasn't sure whom Heather aimed to protect. The one time I caught her alone (in the corridor, waiting to use the bathroom), she muttered, "Cut it out, Porter. This can only end badly."

And then it was my wedding.

Heather came up early Friday morning to help Julie with the eight hundred things she needed to do (pick up her dress and veil, get manicures and pedicures, and so forth). I was hanging out with law school friends and doing my own chores, so we didn't cross paths until that night, at the rehearsal dinner.

Heather sat next to me at the front table. She appeared to be in a great mood: buoyant, sparkly, making everyone laugh. Julie's younger brother Andrew, twenty-two then, almost hyper-ventilated. (He'd had a crush on Heather, apparently, since he was twelve: this was something of a family joke). She barely drank, and when she got up to give a toast, she seemed quite sober.

"I'm saving the juicy stories for tomorrow," Heather said. In her gold dress, she looked like a trophy. I remember the way her voice, bell-like, carried (their senior year she'd starred in every play). "For now, all I want to say," and she stopped, and turned to both of us. "Porter, you've got a real prize there. Treat her well." I nodded, aware of everyone's eyes. "And Jules—" she paused. "I wish you every happiness. And I love you so very much! But you know that already." Her smile blazed; Julie wiped her eyes. "To the bride and groom!"

I remember that night through a champagne haze: the asparagus soup, the rare steak, the crème brulee, the endless toasts. My friend Jonah's toast remains the most dazzling feat of speech-making I've witnessed. Ian gave a tortured, spastic encomium. Julie smiled and smiled. She wore a bright green dress, her eyes reflected the candle flame: not a bit the nervous bride.

I didn't feel nervous either. I turned down a joint that Jonah and Paul and Andrew were passing around, wanting to keep my head clear, and it wasn't so I could be on guard, or resist temptation, but simply so I'd retain the night: I felt like what Jonah kept calling me: a flucky (fucking lucky) guy.

And then.

It must have been close to midnight. I stood on the porch with my friend Paul, now so stoned he had to clutch the rail, when I saw Heather walking on the beach. Her gold dress caught the moonlight; she dangled her heels from her fingers. Something about the hunch of her shoulders made me look around for Julie, or Beth, or any of that high school crowd. None were on the porch.

"Hang on Paul," I said to him. "I think my friend might need some help."

Despite being barefoot, Heather moved quickly. I had to jog to catch her. I put my hand on her shoulder.

"What's up? Are you feeling okay?"

I was expecting her to be drunk, but that wasn't it exactly. Her eyes looked like holes.

"No," she said, and there was something in the way she said it—a kind of despair that I'd never heard from Heather before. It reminded me of my sister Catherine's voice when she called to tell me about Mom's cancer. No tears but worse than tears, like when it's too cold for snow.

"What's wrong?"

"Everything," and then her hands were clutching my sleeves. Her long, white face and twisted mouth reminded me of the Munch painting. "I'm so fucking sad," she said.

For the first time, it occurred to me that Heather was in love with me. That might sound really dense, but you have to know Heather. The brittle expression she often wore, the way she seemed sometimes to dislike me: I had thought I was only an intrigue to her.

"I'm sorry," I said.

At that moment I felt shame, guilt. And the only appropriate (the word that comes to mind is "gallant") thing to do seemed to be to take her hand and lead her off the beach to the Howes' pool house.

The next few minutes unrolled in sharp lucidity: the door of the pool house was unlocked; we looked around to see if anyone was close by (no one was). I wanted to talk to Heather, to comfort her, to exert damage control. She was clearly unraveling. But once inside, the best way of dealing with her seemed to be to pull her dress over her head so that, for a few seconds, her hopeless, white face was hidden in stretchy gold. She seemed bewildered: I thought she was drunker than I had realized. And then she was kissing me back, and unspooling my belt. We were on the floor, Heather on top of me, my pants were at my ankles, the heels of her hands pressed my shoulders. My eyes were closed because her face was so alien and disconcerting.

So I heard rather than saw the door open. We'd forgotten to lock it.

I opened my eyes and saw Julie standing in the door. Her eyes were wide, her mouth open. For a second it was like there were two "Scream" paintings, Julie and Heather, mirrors. Then Julie's mouth clamped shut.

"Julie—" Heather said.

"Don't," said Julie.

What they say about car crashes, how everything slows down and ruptures into freeze-frames: the door opening, Julie's mouth opening, Julie's mouth closing, the door closing. Like a palindrome composed of images.

Then Julie was gone, and I was rolling Heather off me, almost throwing her, and pulling up my pants.

"Oh my God," I said, and Heather's face was another mirror, shocked and blank, staring at me but not seeing me: staring through me. She was still on the floor when I left.

That was the last time I saw Heather.

And really, for all intents and purposes, the last time I saw Julie. I finally tracked her down in the middle of the night to Beth's hotel room, but she wouldn't speak to me, and that sanctimonious moron

Ian wouldn't open the door more than a crack. "Go away, Porter. Julie doesn't want to see you," he said; there was no missing the smugness in his voice. I waited on the beach outside for another hour, but when she finally came out, she was with Ian, his arm around her, and they never saw me. I watched them walk down the beach, Julie's head leaning on his shoulder, one darker mass in the dark.

And I saw her, some fifty feet away, the next afternoon. I was hiding in the nave of the church when she marched to the pulpit and announced in a ringing voice that the wedding was canceled. This is all stuff I've done my damnedest to forget. I remember Jonah holding my elbow. He was keeping me company as we lurked in the dark. I'd told him about the shit storm, of course, but neither of us knew how it would conclude. There was that off-chance that Julie would succumb to momentum, and I would see her on her father's arm, in her white dress—well, of course now it seems beyond delusional. But her silence was so thick and impenetrable, who the hell knew? Even Jonah said "Maybe..." I clutched onto that possibility, sustained by her radio silence (she never called, she never did formally break up with me, our relationship was like Schrodinger's theoretical cat in the box, alive until pronounced dead). So I hadn't warned my parents. They were in the front row, looking up at Julie in her blue jeans.

She never turned her head. I have no idea if she saw me.

By the time I got back to our apartment in Boston, her stuff was gone: the drawers empty, the medicine shelves clear. She took the Band-Aids, the tampons, the Advil. Nothing, no trace, no note. The one time I phoned the house ("Never call here again, Porter!" her father said before hanging up) convinced me never to call again.

Would a braver man have insisted on a face-to-face? Pushed past Ian's obstructive body into Beth's room, or knocked him down on the beach? At the very least, loitered around Julie's haunts (the falafel place, or that cafe with the green lamps where she spent afternoons reading)? Probably.

But her face, that decisive clamp of her mouth, that "Don't": they felt to me like steel grates. I fully acknowledge my wimpiness here, but I trust my instincts, and here's what they told me: there was nothing I could do or say to get Julie back, and any attempt was a waste of energy and hope. So the most boneless gestures (picking up the phone, getting out the two words "May I" before James Howe's bludgeoning voice cut in) must suffice.

My family was disgusted. Catherine even more so than my mother, who, leaking tears and more tears, still tried to do the Mom thing and deflect blame elsewhere: on Julie's hard resolve ("She should at least talk to you!" she kept saying), and of course on Heather. Still, disgust wasn't an atmosphere conducive to recuperating, nor was the Boston office (Phil Petersen had been a wedding guest, had heard every blazing syllable of Julie's "May I have your attention please?").

I fled Dodge. Within ten days I was back in L.A. I let that silence, so thick, so dense, wrap me up. I welcomed the way it cut out everything, all static, all obligations, like the thickest plate of bulletproof glass.

Home, I focused on action: work, exercise, party, surf, fuck (the Tiki girl, Liz from my Ashtanga class, Danielle the screamer, Yvette, Rebecca, that angry dancer, Gina or Nina, my assistant Jamie who finally requested a transfer, it got so awkward, and, eventually, Nadia, who felt like a refuge, before she began making her own trouble). I avoided reflection.

You see why it's been better, even necessary, not to dwell. Think of what happens to the figures in myth who look backwards: they turn to salt, the Underworld reaches out to claim them.

It's the day before Thanksgiving, 1996, two years and five months after that nightmare June (and "nightmare" is no figure of speech, for that's how that time reappears to me now: in my dreams, Heather's twisty Munch face, Julie's mouth clamping, the closing door, her ringing voice: "May I have your attention please?"). Wearing my too-thin black coat, I walk into Williams-Sonoma, looking for the jars of pumpkin-pecan filling that my sister Catherine requires for her two pies.

Catherine and I have never gotten along, except for those

months when I was dating Julie, whom Catherine, like everyone else, really liked. Julie induced her to revise an entrenched opinion of me (slimeball, to keep far away from her pretty friends). Of course when Julie and I split up, that opinion only solidified. Even when I was at my very lowest, Catherine was too pissed to sympathize, and I left the East Coast in a mutual spirit of Fuck You. Over the past two and a half years we've tried to patch things up, evidenced by the cherry-wood high chair I bought for her baby shower, a beauty, and not cheap. But Catherine is the biggest reason why Nadia's defection is a pain in the ass. Nadia is cute, chatty, eager to please, and I'd hoped Catherine would warm up to her, and through her, perhaps to me.

But of course Nadia has deserted me, so here I am, trying to appease my cranky, judgmental, sleep-deprived sister, who is all too happy to take out her own frustrations (four-month-old baby, tedious husband) on me, by shoving through the crowd at Williams-Sonoma for pumpkin-pecan filling. I escalate to the second floor, turn a corner.

Directly in front of me is Heather Katchadourian.

It's funny: my body recognizes her before I do. My jaw tenses, my arms clench, there's a nanosecond of wondering why I suddenly feel like throwing up before I process the woman in the trench coat contemplating a shelf of roasting pans. It's a crazy, fight-or-flight response, so intense that I take a step backwards towards the escalator.

Before I can move, Heather sees me.

And it's mirrors again; horror and shock on her face that must reflect mine. And, mirrors, how we both stifle those expressions, straighten and smooth our respective faces. She doesn't try to fake a smile.

"Porter," she says.

"Heather."

She looks the same, yet not the same. Her hair is shorter, shoulder-length now, as it was when I first met her. She's still thin, but no longer gaunt (an unbidden image of the ridge of her hipbone floats in my mind). She looks—healthy is the word that comes to mind.

I half-raise my arm, but she doesn't raise hers so it falls, lamely, to my side. "How are you?"

"Fine," she says. "You?"

"Decent."

It calms me that she seems just as freaked out and discomposed as I do. Her face is almost white.

"Do you live here?" I ask.

"No, just here for the holiday."

"Yeah, me too."

We both leave out the obvious follow-up information: where we do, in fact, live.

Indeed, every potential line of inquiry seems to slam straight into a wall, and I stand there baffled by what the fuck to say while Heather, like a reflection, tilts her head.

But it's the "Don't think about elephants" quandary. Against my will, I say, "So are you in touch..." She's already shaking her head before I can finish the question, but I keep going, I can't stop, it's like the compulsory completion of a fall. "With Julie?"

She stops shaking her head and stares at me. Her face chills and settles like it's been set in a mold.

After a long pause, she says, "I won't..." She pauses again. "Talk about her."

And that's all the answer I need: I understand, instantly, that Julie cut Heather off just as surgically as she severed me, enforced the same impenetrable plate-glass silence. Heather can't even say her name.

In the early months, I'd hear crumbs about Julie: my sister was unable to stop harassing her, and I gather they had dinner at least once. But since then, it's been all quiet on the Western Front, and I have to assume that Julie's hardness eventually overcame her politeness, and she cut off Catherine just as ruthlessly as she did me.

Still, though I was the one who lost a fiancée here, Heather and Julie were best friends for more than ten years before our wedding. Knowing that Julie is that unforgiving makes me sad for Heather.

"I'm sorry," I say. That phrase is forced to cover a lot of bases. I'm still speech-stymied. Even without rage it's hard to talk to Heather coherently.

She nods. Her face seems to relax.

I see Heather more accurately, without this filter of horror.

"You look good."

Her mouth twists.

And then there's a kind of squeak, almost a mew, and Heather hurries to a large stroller parked several feet away by a stand of cookbooks. She leans down and picks up a baby. "Sh, sh," she says.

My mouth must drop open like a character in a cartoon or farce, because when she turns back to me, she actually laughs.

"Yours?" I say.

"Yep."

"Nice outfit." It's pajamas, I think, printed with gingerbread cookies, though it's hard to tell the difference between sleepwear and day clothes. Over that, a parka and a pom-pom hat.

Heather laughs. "Just trying to keep her warm, Mr. Fashion Police."

The baby wrestles off the hat with one fist, exposing a round head and fuzzy, orange hair.

"She's a girl? She's beautiful," I say, leaning in. The baby's blue eyes stare.

Heather nods.

"Doesn't look much like you, does she?"

"No, she doesn't."

"My nephew doesn't look like my sister either. Isn't the theory that they look like their dads so the fathers won't kill them?"

Heather laughs again. I've never seen her like this: she's almost lighthearted. "Yeah, I've heard that."

"How old is she? My nephew's four months. I'm in New York to meet him, actually."

"Just over seven months. She's on the small side."

"What's her name?"

"Mamie. Short for Margaret." She hesitates, then says, "And that's Genevieve. Viva, we call her."

That's when I see the other baby, still sleeping in the stroller.

"Christ, Heather. You have twins?"

"Crazy, huh?"

"How's it going?"

"Oh, wild. Exhausting. But—" and her smile is wide, not forced at all. "Wonderful, I have to say. I love it."

I shake my head. "Wow." It's like the prior "I'm sorry," doing extra legwork, but Heather understands all I mean and nods.

"Strange, isn't it?"

"You seem happy," I say.

"I am."

There's a long minute where we smile at each other. Heather cuddles the baby.

"Do you want to get coffee?" I say, finally.

She shakes her head. "No thanks." And though she makes no effort to come up with an excuse, or even to gesture toward one—indicate the stroller, or the crowded store—her smile is friendly.

"Well, then can you help me find this damn thing I need to get? Pumpkin-pecan filling. For—"

She's already pointing. "Over there. See the display?"

"Thanks." I stand there for another minute, taking in Heather, the stroller, her smile. "Well, it's good seeing you."

She nods. I'm half turned away when she says, "Oh, Porter..." She indicates the shelf in front of her. "Which roasting pan, do you think? Blue or red?"

I look at the stacks of Le Creuset pots. "I like the red."

"Thank you," she says, and my last image of Heather is of her laughing, and reaching pointedly for the blue one.

It's hard for me to comprehend at first, as I walk back up Broadway with my jars of pie filling, why I feel so cheerful, so hopeful—certainly not the emotions I anticipated should I ever cross paths with the girl who ruined my life. But then I understand it. Because even under those awkward circumstances, there was no questioning the truth of Heather's assertion that she was happy. In fact, she almost seemed reluctant to admit it.

Back in the day I often saw her prance around, but this Heather (relaxed, content) is a visible, unfakeable change. And it's happened in spite of the fact that her best friend hates her and cut her loose. Or why not, even—and here my hopes inflate even more—why not because Julie exiled her? Maybe she dragged and anchored Heather. For so many years Heather had been the unruly sidekick to Julie's polished queen. Maybe Heather could only become truly stable herself when Julie, by firing her, vacated that space.

And what does all this suggest for me? Well, if Heather can find peace and a spouse and babies, then so the fuck can I.

I told myself more than once over the past two years that splitting with Julie might in fact be a blessing in disguise—salvation from a life of missionary sex with my sweet, remote wife. I told myself this, but it always tasted of sour grapes.

Now for the first time I think it might after all be true: that it's a good thing, and not a tragic wrong turn, that I lost Julie. I have options for happiness myself, if I am willing to reach for them (sexy, affectionate Nadia; or, hell, someone better, someone I haven't been ready to meet, who is waiting for me to let go of regret and self-disgust and find her).

My mood holds all the way to Catherine's. I practically bounce up the three flights to her brownstone flat. I'm so visibly cheerful that she turns from the stove to give me a rare smile when I approach the tiny galley kitchen and put the bag on the counter.

"Thanks, Porter. That's really helpful."

It's not until I've poured us each glasses of wine and am sitting at the barstool chopping walnuts for tomorrow's stuffing that I say, "You'll never guess who I ran into at the store."

She's stirring a pot, her back to me. Without turning, she says, "Who?"

"Heather Katchadourian." There's a long pause. Despite the fact that Catherine cut me no slack over the Heather debacle—unlike my mother, she didn't thrust all the blame onto Heather—Catherine's dislike for Heather is at least as intense as my mother's.

"How is she?" she says at last.

"Really good, actually. You'll never believe this," I address Catherine's rigid shoulders, "But she has twin babies! Not much older than Alexander, actually. Two girls." Another long pause. "Well, don't you think that's surprising?" I say, at last. "I never pictured Heather getting married. Especially not at, what is she, twenty-seven?"

Slowly, Catherine turns. The wooden spoon is in her hand; she's shaking her head. I watch the expressions crossing her face. They move so quickly that only in retrospect do I realize she exhibited no surprise, none at all, when I mentioned those baby girls. It's a strange initial expression, stiff, concerned, expectant, but it alters now to amusement, then to a familiar malice—I've seen my sister look at me with exactly those glittering, incredulous eyes since she was five and I was seven—and, finally, to pity.

"Dear God Porter," Catherine says, shaking her head, shaking the wooden spoon like a metronome. "Were you always such a total fool?"

PAM, 2012

At the night class I'm taking, we're doing a Word paper. Pick a word you see as problematic. First look it up in the OED; find its etymology, the root, the first known usage in print. Stuyvesant doesn't specify that the word be controversial, but when we go around the room telling him our words, the pattern emerges quickly: "Bitch," "Faggot," "Black." The way Stuyvesant nods makes me understand, prompt or no, these are the kinds of words worth writing six to eight pages about. When I tell him my word, he gives me a look before writing it down. Later, when I get up to leave, he waves me over to his desk. I stand there, watching him put his pens, one by one, back into his manpurse.

"Why 'like'?" he says, once the pens are secured. "I'm not sure I understand your word, Pam. In what sense are you using it?"

"Well, multiple senses. I was listening to these two teenagers I live with talking the other day, and it's the same as when I was in high school: they constantly use 'like,' it's like the salt they sprinkle on conversation. I wrote this one down." I read from my Moleskine book: "'Then Eileen was like, 'Viva, that makes no sense…'"

Stuyvesant is smiling; I see a wet curl of lip under his beard. "Pam, did you hear yourself use 'like'? It must be infectious. 'It's like the salt,' you said."

"But that was the proper use of 'like,'" I tell him. "Simile form: the word is like salt, the moon is like a balloon."

"True," he says, and the smile unbends like a twisty tie, as we both process which one of us is the English professor.

I say, "Which I also want to explore in my paper, how similes are different from metaphors. More tentative. And then I want to look at like's function as this all-purpose verb, something that substitutes for 'said' or 'exclaimed.' 'She's like': it grates on my ears but also intrigues me. Why do they prefer 'like' to 'said'? I remember doing the same damn thing when I was a kid."

"These teenagers you were transcribing: are they your sisters?"

"No, my girlfriend's daughters."

"Ah." We both study his purse, the color of licked toffee. "Well, it seems like you have a handle on this paper, though you will need to articulate, of course, your issue with the word 'like,' that is, what you see as problematic about it."

What is problematic about the word 'like'? Let me count the ways.

The next night I sit with Viva at the kitchen table. She's studying for a history test. I have divided a sheet of paper into three columns. I have "Vernacular," "Simile," and "Verb" at the top, and underneath in red pen I've started writing down "problems." Under Vernacular, "Makes you sound ditzy"; under Simile, "hedging, concedes at the outset that the comparison is not exact." Under Verb, I've simply written "Heather." When she sidles over I cross my arms over the paper.

She notices—Heather always notices—but she addresses the table at large. "Either of you worker bees need some hot chocolate to help with your studies? I have tiny marshmallows."

"I can't memorize any more damn battles," says Viva, despairingly.

"Want me to test you?"

Viva pauses—her first instinct is to say no; she can do everything for herself these days—but then her shoulders relax, and she says, "Thanks, Mom."

"Pam? Will it bug you if I test her here?" Heather asks. "What are you working on?"

When I remind her about the Word paper, she grimaces. "This is really an English class? In my day, people wrote papers about, you know, books. And poems."

"I need the writing credit for nursing school," I say—I've told her this before. "And we do read stuff. Lewis Carroll this week."

"Which sounds very appropriate for college."

Only Heather can jangle my nerves to this extent. "We didn't all go to fancy Seven Sisters colleges."

She rolls her eyes. "Pam: your college was plenty fancy before you dropped out to, what the fuck, grow pumpkins."

I told her about dropping out of UVM, in the early, confessional days of falling in love. It was heartbreak, plain and simple. I'd fallen for and slept a few times with and then been cruelly rejected by Dolores Sanchez, and now everything was hell—soccer in particular torture. I'd gone to UVM on partial scholarship to play. Before I had sex with Dolores, soccer encapsulated everything beautiful about college: the salty smell of the locker room, the sopping tiled floors of the community shower, my surreptitious peeks at Dolores's brown nipples. But after she dumped me, I went into a full-on tailspin, was a no-show for classes. The nicer professors gave me UWs for 'Unauthorized Withdrawal,' the harsher ones F's. It wasn't easy, nine years later with that kind of paintball transcript, to even get into state college.

And Heather knows all this: she knows I didn't drop out to be some hippie farm girl, she knows my heart was as ruptured as if I'd had a literal coronary... My eyes communicate my let-down, the let-down Heather submerges me in again and again.

She sighs and says, "That professor just seems like a tool."

I fold my paper, with dignity I think, and withdraw to our bedroom. Under the "Simile" column, under Examples, I write, "Tool." I study Heather's name, under Verb.

There was a time, of course, when "like" had a different effect on me. I could feel blood heat my cheeks the first time Heather said it. We weren't in bed though we'd done it already, "made love" were the private words in my head. A couple of days after that first time, she picked me up early at work. We were sharing a cone of Black Raspberry. September, a year and a half ago. I remember watching the tip of Heather's tongue scoop a dollop of lavender ice cream. To think that same pointed and flexible tongue had been, two nights before, between my legs...

"What is Black Raspberry, anyway?" she said. "We're in New Hampshire, for Christ's sake. Why not call it Blackberry?" I laughed, and she bent forward and kissed, with cold lips, my ear. "Hey you: I like you."

And that had graduated, of course—"I really like you," "I like you very much"—until it stopped. Or stalled. I liked "like" until it started meaning, instead of affection, enthusiasm—Hey, you're lovely!—not-love.

When I first said "I love you" to Heather, and that was well over a year ago, before Christmas, several months after that ice cream date—she said, "Thank you." The second time she kissed me. Funny how speedily the giddy-fluttery-scared-as-shit feeling of saying those words twisted into misery. For a while, when compelled to respond ("Don't you have anything to say?" I asked her once: that is pretty damn compulsory!), she would say, carefully, "I really like you." Now she says nothing, because she's sharp enough to know that nothing is better: that to have "really like" become something that hurts one's feelings rather than boosts them up is not endurable.

"Lesbians are such processors!" she said yesterday, when I tried to explain this to her.

"But you love artichokes. You love Puttanesca sauce. You use that word, I've heard you."

"That only means I'm more emotionally promiscuous when it comes to food." When I didn't laugh, she said, "Come on, Pammy: that was a joke."

"Knee-slapper."

"Look." There was a pause, and as the minute unrolled I felt something close to terror: I'm too pushy, I'm demanding things she can't give, she's going to break up with me. "You know me, Pam," Heather said, finally. "I'm shuttered. I'm a closed door. There's hardly anyone I love. I suppose my mother, though she drives me batshit. Viva and Mamie, of course: I love my girls. Maybe the issue is that my daughters demand so much of my heart that there is not a lot to spare? You know how much I like you. Why is that not enough?"

"Because I love you."

"So you say." My face must have transmitted all kinds of protest, because she held up a disclaiming hand. "And I believe you mean it. But really: what is love? It's not like we weigh it on a scale, or measure it in, whatever, milliliters. Maybe I'm just really particular. Maybe what I mean when I say 'like' perfectly balances with your 'love.' People use words differently."

I shook my head. "No, Heather. You and I both know that our feelings for each other aren't balanced. If they were sitting on opposite sides of a seesaw, my love would have its ass on the ground, and yours would be high up in the air, waving its feet."

She laughed. "I like that one! See, you should take poetry, instead of this phony English class with that jackass. You are good with figures of speech."

"How is writing a poem going to help me be a nurse?"

"How is writing a paper on some stupid word?"

I didn't bother answering, and after a minute Heather clasped my hand. "Pammy, I'm sorry I'm so shriveled and circumspect. I do think part of it is I deplete all my resources on those two creatures." She bobbed her head in the direction of Mamie's and Viva's room. "I love them to death, you know, but the problem is there's not much left over." She sighed. "Should I be lying about this? Would that work better?"

"Probably."

Her eyes averted. "Maybe motherhood has also used up my ability to deceive. Santa, Tooth Fairy, 'Sure I like your obnoxious friend who kicks the back of my seat every car pool.' I think all I can be with you is honest."

Now I sit on our bed, on the nubby crimson spread, and think about whether I can stand Heather's honesty.

I have options. There's that bartender Dara, for instance, at Pirate's, with the trumpet-vine tattoo climbing her arm; I can tell she thinks I'm sexy. My age, too, more or less. That's another thing that drives me crazy about Heather, the way she holds youth against me, sometimes even lumping me with her twins: we're young and dumb and full of energy. We're puppies with giant, dirty paws. Heather makes herself sound brittle and geriatric at forty-two. I have options. There are nights when I'm tempted to take them. When Heather seems like an almost empty toothpaste tube, it's barely worth the effort to squeeze it for the last smear of paste...

Toothpaste tube, I write under the Simile column, and after a minute, under Verb, *aimer bien*. Because suddenly I remember something Heather-of-the-many-languages, Heather who grew up in Geneva and who sometimes sleep-talks in Italian, told me last week about French. *Aimer* means "to love"; *aimer bien*, which literally translates "to love well," means "to like," because, as Heather explained it, love exists without measure. If you can put any kind of boundary on it, even if the boundary is capacious, you limit by quantifying love. She was explaining to me why she objects to qualifiers in writing, why she thought even the big ones such as "very" or "extremely" diminished rather than emphasized their adjectives. "It's counter-intuitive, I know," she said. "But I'll give you an example in French..."

Tears spring in my eyes, and I think, Later I will remember this as the moment when I gave up.

MAMIE, 2012

This place is crazy. To the eye, other things about it are more impressive: the chapel that looks like someone shrunk a Gothic cathedral to scale, graystone and witch-hat spires; the brick school building with trim so white it dazzles, and I have to fish my sunglasses out of my backpack. But somehow what gets me most is the grass: fat, manicured blades like the lawn at Grandpa James's house in Newport. But there, the grass scrapes the soles of my feet if I walk barefoot. Here, it's as soft as hair. I stretch my legs on it and lean back. Through my half-closed eyes, the flowering apple trees blur into snow.

Viva plops down beside me and tosses a sticker in my lap. "I feel like I'm sitting on a golf course," she says.

"The grass is insane, isn't it?" I say. "Mom told me that they'd get demerits if they cut across the Circle—table-wiping duties or something—but it was fine to sit inside it. It was all about protecting the grass. So she'd walk to the middle, sit down for a minute, then get up and cross."

"Mom and her loopholes." Viva stretches. Our legs are a double set of parallel lines. Viva's are beaten up from hurdles and soccer. Below her cut-offs, I can see bruises, blue and mauve, a shaving cut. Even hacked up, her legs are beautiful: sunlight bounces off them like they're sheets of metal.

"What's this?" I pick up the navy-bordered sticker.

"Nametag. I made you one inside. There's also donuts and shit.

Coffee, too." She waves the paper cup in her hand. "Would've got you one but I couldn't carry anything else."

I peel the waxy paper off the back of the sticker and examine it before pressing it onto my T-shirt. Mamie Katchadourian, it says on top, in Viva's block print, and below, in parentheses, Heather Katchadourian, '87. "We have to wear these?"

She shrugs. "Everyone inside has them on. How else are these geezers going to identify each other? Must be embarrassing, to not recognize someone who used to be your girlfriend or roommate."

"Do you think—" I say.

"What?"

"Do you think we should list Julie too?"

"Are you kidding? And blow her *Real Housewives of Greenwich* cover? Nope."

"But it's not like all their friends from here don't know about us. And don't you think her feelings might get hurt?"

Viva shakes her head. "Trust me. Julie does not want us in her face."

"Have you seen her?"

"Nope. She isn't in the Schoolhouse. When I was filling out the nametags I saw she hadn't picked up her reunion packet. Maybe—" Viva pulls up a handful of the perfect grass, and lets it fall. "Maybe she isn't coming."

"Mom said she was."

"And how would she know? It's not like they talk, ever."

"I don't know. Satellite supervision? Tracking system? Mom always seems to know when Julie's around. I bet people warn her."

"Yeah." Viva sips her coffee. "Well, I for one would like to avoid being the juicy headline story of the fogey convention, so let's keep in the background, okay? Honestly I debated whether to write Mom's name on the card, or to make a nametag at all. But then it seemed annoying to have to keep introducing ourselves. Ugh. I feel like we're Brangelina's kids."

"At least it's pretty here." It's our mode: Viva bristles, I placate. It's like having a pedigree cat for a twin sister, or a cactus.

"It's a fucking country club." She squeezes my arm. "I can't believe you considered going here."

"Well," I say. "I didn't, did I?"

"Thank God! Me alone with Mom! We would have killed each other."

"Not alone. There's Pam too."

"And Pam would have buried us and put flowers on our graves." She frowns. "Why isn't she here? I thought she wanted to come."

"You think? She doesn't know these people."

"Obviously she did! Hinting and hinting. Why didn't Mom let her? The whole thing feels shady."

"Maybe Mom thought she had enough on her plate already, old friends she hasn't seen in forever, and Julie too."

Viva snorts, pulls up another scoop of grass. "Maybe Mom didn't want a chaperone."

"What about us?"

"We're not chaperones, we're walking iPhone pictures. If Tommy weren't going to be here for that crew race, I'd think we were nuts for coming. When is it anyway?"

"Three," I say. Tommy's my boyfriend, but you'd think from the way Viva talks that he's hers. Frankly they do have more in common. They both like getting stoned. Viva drinks tequila with him from his hammered aluminum flask; tequila makes my head spin. They like the same music, bands I've never heard of. I like old stuff: Lou Reed and Dylan and the Stones. Classic Dork, Viva calls me, and one time when she did it in front of Tommy, he laughed and ruffled my hair. I wonder, for the hundredth time, why I'm the one dating Tommy instead of Viva.

"Where is Mom anyway?" Viva asks. "I didn't see her in the Schoolhouse either."

"She was headed that way. She wanted to look up her name in the Schoolroom. The room where all the students' names are engraved on the walls? Each class has its own panels. Didn't you see it? It's the giant room, where they have morning roll-call."

"No, but 'Schoolhouse' makes me think of a log building, not that billion-dollar thing." She jerks her head at it. "It sounds so quaint. False advertising."

"It's a gorgeous room, actually." That's the place I remember best from the tour. The honey-gold desks, that mellow color of wood that looks like the skin of a perfectly roasted chicken, and the bright windows with beveled glass, and all the students' heads, pointing towards the Senior Prefect, actually listening to the announcements. Morning Assembly at our school is a madhouse, Mr. Levins on stage a red-faced, gesticulating puppet.

"Let's head over. You can get coffee, and we can see if Julie's shown up." And from the casual way she proposes it, I know that Viva, like me, wants Julie to be there, even if she'll never admit it.

After the bright sunlight, walking into the Schoolhouse is like entering a cave. I'm blind before I remember to take off my sunglasses. Viva loses hers every other week, but I keep track of mine. I even wrap them in a chamois cloth to keep the lenses from getting scratched. Most make me look like a fly. Viva can wear $5 sunglasses from the revolving racks at Walgreens and look like Sophia Loren. Mom's the same. She walks around in a ribbed tank top and jeans smeared with paint and looks like a fashion model. I don't have their effortless glamour.

Behind me, Viva steers, her hands on my shoulders. "Coffee over there. Look, even the coffee's fancy. They have half-and-half in those silver pitchers."

"Are you hungry?" I ask, grabbing a glazed donut and a napkin.

"Not for that shit." Viva doesn't like anything sweet. She lives off kumquats, cornichons, grainy mustard, sauerkraut, and kimchi. I tell her that's why she's so tart, pickling herself.

I pour myself coffee and scan for Mom and for Julie. It's crowded. I can see what Viva means by fancy: the coffee table has a linen tablecloth over it, and the donuts and scones are served on three-tiered cupcake plates that belong in an Art Nouveau illustration of a Parisian patisserie. My napkin is embossed with the school crest. The people are fancy, too, decked out; they're dressed casually, but the clothes are expensive. Linen and cashmere, ferny tweeds, pearl buttons on sherbet-colored cardigans. Fingers sparkle.

Looking around, the range of ages hits me. Damp, red babies dangle in Bjorns. There are men and women so old their backs are curved like spoons. I scan nametags, and actually see one Class of '37, worn by a man whose bald head is covered with liver-spots the size of olives. Then there are people not much older than Viva and me, Class of '07, back for their fifth. They shriek when they see each other and fold into bear hugs.

I see a navy-trimmed '87 sticker on someone's yellow polo shirt, and look up to find a man staring at me.

"Mamie Katchadourian?" he says, extending his hand. The top of his head is bald, but his eyes are warm and syrup-brown. They wrinkle at the corners. "Hey there. I know your mother. Mothers. You probably don't remember me..."

I study his nametag more carefully, but Viva, behind me, is the first to speak. "Ian Saltonstall. Oh yeah, I know you. Weren't you at—?"

"Julie's wedding," he says, and smiles. "Latest wedding. Yes, hello there Viva. Remember? I danced with you, we did a mean swing, while this one," he points at me, "hid behind some choco-late-strawberry topiary thing."

"I remember those," I nod: chocolate-dipped strawberries in a giant pyramid. I must have eaten ten of them. "Yeah, I remember you. Your wife was there—"

"Emily. She's here, too. Lost her by the auditorium. So, how are you girls? Wow, grown up already. You look like your mother," he says to me.

I flush.

"So, where is she?" he asks.

The confusion is predictable, but feels weird nonetheless, as it's not an ambiguity we're used to navigating. "Which one?" blunt Viva asks.

Ian colors. He's got a nice blush: it makes his skin, which is pale and grainy, suddenly rosy. "Fair question!" he says. "Well, I meant Julie, but either really."

"I don't think she's here yet. Viva saw her reunion packet fifteen minutes ago: she hadn't picked it up. We're looking for Mom. I think she's checking out the Schoolroom." I like the sound of "School-room" on my tongue: it makes me feel old hat, lingo down, as if I'm a student here, or an alumna.

"Yeah, let us know if you see either of them," Viva says.

Ian nods, and something about the way his eyes rove, the way he looks as if he wants to see her first, so he can compose his expression, seems familiar. Viva and I must look that way too, alert: a state of heightened perception. How many people here are searching for a particular someone among all these altered faces? I think of a line from a poem we've been studying in English class: "Time to prepare a face to meet the faces that you meet."

"And you do the same," he tells us.

Viva gives him a thumbs up. "Deal," she says.

He smiles. "You know, it's great to see you girls. That wedding wasn't all that long ago, but I remember you here at the tenth reunion when you were babies. Viva, you were crawling all over the grass, and Mamie, you were the most placid, sweet little thing. You just sat in your mother's lap and stared at everyone with those big, blue eyes. Julie's lap, I mean. Heather was chasing you around." He nods at Viva. "You were on the move! People to see, places to go."

I try to catch Viva's eye—this story seems to bear out her paranoid Brangelina scenario—but she smiles, amused by this image of herself. "I don't remember this place at all," she says.

"Well, of course not," he says. "You girls were barely a year old then. But you mean you've never been back? Really?"

"I have," I say. "Mom took me to a tour fall before last. Heather, I mean."

"You go to prep school?"

"Nope, decided to stay at home."

"Thank God," says Viva. "I would've freaked, if Mamie had left."

"My kids don't have much interest either. Oliver's the oldest, he's twelve, maybe he'll change his mind. Or Sarah, she's more adventur-ous. But they've certainly been here, to see soccer games, and boat races, and these events. Is this really your first reunion since the tenth? Well, of course it is. I would've remembered you at the others. Huh.

My kids are around here somewhere, I'll have to introduce you."

We nod.

"And do let me know, if you see your—mothers—around. Let her know that I'm looking for her." He doesn't seem to notice the pronoun switch.

"He's nice," Viva says, as soon as Ian turns away. It makes me cringe, the way Viva talks about people within their earshot. Mom's the same; it's like they think everyone is deaf. "I do remember him, at that bizarro wedding. He was a good dancer. And one of the only adults who talked to us. Ugh, remember?"

We were thirteen then, and except for one weird Thanksgiving the next year—Grandpa James drinking too much scotch, Julie just pregnant enough to show, smiling and glittery and flitting around, reminding me of a beetle with a hard shell—that's the last time we saw Julie. The whole wedding was strange. She wanted us there, supposedly, but she didn't know what to do with us. You can tell in the pictures that we don't belong. There's a literal gap between us and the rest of the family. Grandma Elizabeth and Uncle Andrew are two feet to our left, as if some invisible person is standing there who doesn't show up on film. To make it easier, Viva said, examining that picture for the first time, to trim us away: snip, snip, no one would even notice the missing girls on the far right. No telltale elbow to give away the deletion. Once at the reception, I caught Julie staring at us, her lips parted as if she were about to ask, "Who the hell are you?" I remember my stockings itched, I remember those strawberries with their shellac of dark chocolate, and I remember drinking champagne with Viva on the beach (the reception was at Grandpa James's and Grandma Elizabeth's house in Newport). "Down the hatch!" we chimed, and clinked glasses. And suddenly my eyes were hot with tears. Viva was crying too, wiping her nose with the back of her hand. "Should we call Mom?" I asked, but Viva shook her head. She didn't look right, because her hair was slicked back and pinned instead of crazy-curly, making her head seem too small. Later we decided that it was some weird reaction to champagne, those random tears.

I'm so lost in this memory that it takes me a second to process the girl planted in front of me. "Hey," she says. She has a shiny forehead, brown hair, and she looks about our age: fifteen or sixteen. "Are you the twins?"

I look down at her nametag. Isabel Benzinger, it reads, and below, Ella (Hoppy) Benzinger, '87.

"We're twins," says Viva, putting her hand on my shoulder. "Don't know about 'the' twins. What twins are you looking for?"

Her eyes, light brown, flick sideways. "The, um, lesbian ones."

Viva's laugh is a bark. "You're kidding, right? No, actually, we're straight, dimwit."

"I'm sorry!" the girl squeaks. "I meant the daughters of—what I meant was—"

"Really, there's no way of salvaging harmless intent here," Viva tells her, then turns to me. "Man, I can't believe you considered going here! Bunch of phobes."

The girl flushes. "I really am sorry, that came out wrong. I'm Isabel. My mother was in the same class as your—" She clearly evaluates whether the next part is safe to say. "Mothers. Ella Hoppy?" She holds out her hand.

Viva folds her arms. "Never heard of her."

I shake Isabel's hand, because really, what's the point? "I'm Mamie," I tell her. "That's Viva."

She looks relieved. "You're the only ones my age here, Mom said. I mean, from the '87 class. All the other kids are younger." She spreads her arms as if we were knee-deep in toddlers.

Neither of us respond to this non-news, so Isabel keeps going. "It's funny because where we live—Atlanta?—everyone has kids real young. My mother is one of the older parents, among my friends, I mean."

"Fascinating," Viva says, but I feel sorry for Isabel. She reminds me of this girl Liddy we go to school with in Hanover, who says all kinds of stupid stuff when she's nervous, not meaning to offend. I try to be nice to Liddy, to compensate for the way Viva's crowd steamrolls her.

"Hey, did you see the class pictures?" Isabel says.

I turn to look where she's pointing. In the corner of the hall are four corkboard folding screens. Photos are tacked all over them. We walk over. Each screen has a heading at the top: '07, '02, '97, '92, '87, '82, '72, '62. It takes me a minute to realize that the screens are double-sided, and '87 is facing the wall. When I walk behind it, it's like being behind a thick curtain. All the people filling the hall are blocked out. It's quieter, as if someone has turned down the volume.

"Wow, check it out," says Viva. The board is covered with black-and-white photos. There are team pictures and candids of kids with their arms around each other. It's funny to see these kids our age in '80s preppie clothes: Khakis and wide-ribbed cords and that ubiquitous L.L. Bean navy sweater with the zigzag white stitches that preppie kids still wear. I saw it on every campus I toured.

"That's my mother," Isabel says, pointing to a girl with a big nose in the front row of the field hockey picture. "Ella Hoppy." I look at the other faces but don't recognize Mom, or Julie.

"Hey, check it out," says Viva, pointing. It's clearly Ian. He's wearing embarrassing nylon running shorts; he must be dressed for a meet. He looks different with his cloud of brown hair.

"And look, there's Beth," I say. She's in a spaghetti-strap dress with two girls I don't recognize.

"Oh wow," Viva says, and this time she touches the picture. Julie and Heather and Beth again. Mom's arm is around Beth, and Julie stands a little apart from them. They're all smiling, Mom in her phony way. She hates posing.

Isabel looks too. "Is that your mother?" she says, touching Julie's face.

It's so weird to hear people call Julie my mother. At home only our closest friends know anything about her, and really Mom, with her outsized personality and paint-smeared clothes, is more than enough mother to go around, even for twins. Viva and I have tried to come up with a better label for Julie, but nothing perfectly applies. "Biological mother" makes it sound like we're adopted, and even though that's technically true, it's misleading. "Bionic mother," was Viva's refinement, and while that accurately characterizes something about Julie—something artificial, not entirely human—it seems too nasty. So we gave up on identifying her more precisely and settled for simply calling her Julie.

Isabel studies her carefully and turns to me. "She looks like you."

I see it too, especially in this picture, with Julie's hair in a ponytail. Of course it's not the first time I've heard that. On the rare occasions I'm around Julie, people always say we look alike. But I never see pictures of Julie at my age. My eyes, my red hair, my strange ears even, with the rims that look like they've been ironed flat: she's a prettier, shinier version of me. Viva and I look at each other, and she makes a face and turns back to the screen.

"Hey, look," Viva points to another picture of Mom, clearly in a play. She's wearing lipstick and a funny '40s style uniform and a cap with a red cross on it. Her hands are clasped, her mouth is open. Her skin, bright in the spotlight, is moon-white. "Whoa, is she singing?"

Suddenly the whole thing feels depressing. There's Mom, our age, in some pinch-waist costume with giant shoulder pads; there's Julie and Mom and Beth, looking happy. Even Mom with her stiff camera smile has sparkling eyes. I feel like I'm watching one of those fast-motion films where a flower grows and shrivels and dies all in one minute. I pull the elastic tie out of my hair and put it in my pocket. Viva looks at me and nods.

"Schoolroom?" she says, and I nod back.

"Nice meeting you," I say to Isabel, and Viva says, "Yeah," in a way that isn't totally bitchy.

Inside the Schoolroom, Viva sees Mom first and points. She's sitting in the far corner by a window, on top of some kid's desk, her boots resting on the chair. I process how dressed down she is, in her black jeans and Led Zeppelin T-shirt and scuffed boots. Just last week she cut off her hair again, and it's standing up in a funny way. At least she isn't wearing the jeans with paint all over them. Sitting on the desk opposite is a guy with curly, blond hair and glasses. It takes a couple of minutes to shove our way over. The Schoolroom is crowded, the aisles bottlenecked with knots of alumni searching the wall panels for their names. Mom is so deep in conversation with the blond guy it takes her a second to notice us.

"Girls!" she says, stretching her arms out. Probably because I have that picture in my head, the one of her in costume, she strikes me as stagey. "Come meet Sam! Sam, these are my girls. Viva, Mamie, this is Sam. He was in my class."

He bows his head. "Samuel Wescott Pitzer, nice to meet you ladies."

The shrill way Viva laughs—*ha ha ha!*, like someone in a 30's screwball comedy—gives away that she thinks Sam is hot. I don't know what it is with Viva and older guys. She barely pays attention to boys our age, but she'll swoon for Mr. Rudopolous, our geometry teacher, who has gray in his beard.

"Genevieve Catarina Howe Katchadourian," she says, extending her hand.

So I follow suit. "Margaret Amelia Howe Katchadourian." I nod instead of shaking his hand, since Viva hasn't let go of it.

"Those are some names," he says, and smiles at Mom, who shrugs.

"Well, as you might expect we had trouble agreeing on names," she says.

"How totally surprising."

"Yeah, I know. Julie wanted to go all *Little Women* on me—she wanted a Margaret Amelia and a Josephine Elizabeth, a Mamie and a Jo Beth, and of course I wouldn't agree to that nonsense. And I like beautiful, dramatic names..."

"Again, I am truly flabbergasted," Sam says, and Mom grins.

"So, anyway, we each got one."

I can't quite squash the spark of resentment I feel every time I hear this origin story, how Viva got the flashy name and I got the frumpy one. Sometimes I think we are the way we are, steady me and hot-tempered, bruised Viva, because our names shaped us somehow.

"I see that." He studies us. "People must tell you this all the time," Sam says to me, "But Lord, do you look like your mother! I mean, like Julie. Though strangely enough—" He appraises Viva. "Genevieve looks a bit like you, Heather."

Mom, whose smile dimmed at the first part of Sam's comment (and I have to believe, if it's weird for me to keep hearing about how

much I look like Julie, it's got to be ten times weirder for Mom),
nods and smiles. "Yeah, I think so too," she says, putting her arm
around Viva. "Not totally coincidental. When we picked a sperm
donor, we didn't get to see a picture of him, of course, but we still
got loads of information. And when we came across this profile a
bunch of things seemed to fit. He was Finnish, he'd been blond as a
child, he majored in film, which Julie thought was a proxy for me—
don't follow her reasoning there. But the thing she insisted on was
'ocean eyes.' 'He has to have ocean eyes,' she kept saying; 'I don't
care if he's a high-school dropout, he has to have ocean eyes like
you.' I said, 'What the hell are ocean eyes?'"

"You do have beautiful eyes," Sam tells her, and they gaze at
each other.

"Gray, his eyes were," Mom says, after a second. "So that's what
sold Julie." She shakes her head. "Girls, Sam was a very good friend
of mine once upon a time. I'm happy you finally get to meet him."

"Well, you should come to more of these things, Recluse," Sam
tells her. "Actually, I met you girls a long time ago, when you were
babies. Here, in fact. I remember you both on the Circle, and Genevieve, you were crawling all over the damn place. Everyone had
to keep chasing you! This was before any of us besides Julie and
Heather had babies, so you both were the hit of the reunion. So cute,
you were."

"Yeah, we were just hearing about that," Viva says. She turns to
Mom. "We ran into Ian Saltonstall."

"Oh, good. Did he bring Emily and the kids?" Sam asks. We
nod, and he says to Mom, "You ever see Ian?"

"Not for years." Her face clouds. There is a way Mom and Viva
look alike, but to me it has less to do with coloring than how you
can see every emotion cross their faces. It's like they're projector
screens. "You?"

"A few times a year. Not as much as I'd like. Nanette and Emily
always got along well..." There's another pause. "Did I tell you
Nanette and I split up? Last summer."

"You didn't, but I heard. I'm sorry, Sammy."

He makes a wry face. "You know, I wonder this about reunions, how many of us losers will show up, the divorcees and unemployed. There's got to be a falsely representative sample of success stories at these things. But fuck it, it is what it is. Sorry for my language, girls."

"Yeah, we've never heard the word 'fuck,'" says Viva. The way she looks at Sam bugs me. She's acting like he's Justin Timberlake. Mom touches his shoulder. "At least you don't have kids."

"That's what everyone says. But what if this means I never do? We tried for years, but Nan couldn't get pregnant, and she didn't want to do any of the fertility stuff, and I was iffy on adoption, and then we started having our problems. And here I am, forty-three, solo."

"It's different for men," Mom says. "Look at Charlie Chaplin, he had kids when he was eighty. You'll find someone. I bet you're hot property."

Sam raps the desk. "We'll see. Dating seems exhausting, I have to say."

"Tell me about it. But what about online dating? That's the thing these days, right? You just scroll through your computer and order someone up."

"Order up some ocean eyes," he says, smiling. "Is that your approach? What's up with your love life, anyway? That was always a rollicking narrative."

"Yeah, right," Mom jerks her head toward us and gives him a stern look. "Well, you can check that box."

"Interesting. Gender?"

"F." She grins. "Her name's Pam."

"Rhymes with Sam!"

"Absolutely, that was the draw."

They laugh, and Viva and I look at each other. Normally Mom is about as flirtatious as a rock wall. Despite the ratty way she dresses, people go after her, and she never seems to notice. It's like she's got some sexual version of Asperger's. And now she's smiling at Sam and her eyes shine. Viva raises her eyebrows. *Who is this person?* we're both thinking.

"Is it serious?" Sam asks.

Mom shrugs. *Shut up already!* her eyes tell him, and Sam finally gets it.

"So who else is here? Who've you seen?" he asks.

"No one. You. Meriwether, who I saw for about three seconds, she was dashing to the bathroom. She's the one who told me about you and Nanette."

"In three seconds. Nice."

Mom laughs. "I know Beth is supposed to come. Joy isn't. You know she's sick?"

"Breast cancer, right?" They both look solemn. "And Ian's here, we should find him. And Lawrence is planning on coming. What about Ginny?"

"She's still in Singapore."

"Oh right." There's a pause. "And Julie?" he asks, casually.

"Supposedly." They exchange another look, and Sam unfolds himself from the desk.

"Well, shall we start scouting?" he says.

"Must we? This corner is so cozy."

"Come on! I'll protect you."

She sighs but stands. Then she looks at us, and for a second her face reminds me of Julie's at her wedding. It's like she's trying to place who we are.

"Girls? You want to join? There's a buffet lunch in the tent by the chapel."

"Is it okay if we just wander?" I say. "We want to see Tommy's race, it's at three."

"Oh, right, Tommy. Well, go past the baseball fields, on the other side of the Circle. You'll see the path down to the river. Mamie, remember, we went to the boathouse after your tour. It's a pretty walk."

"Gorgeous! I used to run it every day," Sam says. "Did you ever run it, H?"

"God no!" Mom grimaces. "Staggered down it, a few times. Remember—?"

They both giggle. Our mother, giggle? But there isn't another word for it.

Mom turns back to us. "It's ten past two now. Should we say we'll meet at four-thirty? On the Circle under the apple trees?" She hugs us goodbye, Sam bows his head, and they cruise off arm in arm.

Of course Sam has barely turned his back when Viva pretends to swoon: she flutters her fingers over her heart. "Oh. My. God!" she says.

"You're sick," I tell her. "What's the opposite of a cougar? A kitten? You're a kitten."

"Just because we don't all have age-appropriate boyfriends," she says. "Come on, you have to admit he's hot!"

"He's a thousand years old." We start picking our way out of the Schoolroom. "Though I think Mom agrees with you."

Viva stops so suddenly we collide. "Mom? What are you talking about? He's a guy."

"So? Remember Charley, before Pam, before Roxie? When we were ten? She sometimes goes for guys."

We shove out of the room. "Let's get refills before we head down to the river," I say. We return to the linen-covered table, pump ourselves jets of coffee. I add milk, and we go outdoors. "This way," I say, heading towards the baseball fields.

"You really think Mom is into Sam?"

"Oh, *qui sait*. But when's the last time you've seen her get all silly like that? Anyway, I think you're right about Pam. I mean about Mom not wanting her here."

Viva frowns. "Yeah, something is going on with them. She's starting to check out. Pam can tell, I bet."

When Viva gets sad the color drains from her face, and she looks as pale as Mom, a ghost girl. I squeeze her hand.

I like Pam, but it's not going to break my heart if they split up. Viva's closer to her. They have the whole sports thing: Pam's a jock: she played soccer in college. Viva and Pam go on early morning runs together. Viva gives me all kinds of crap for my clothes, when I wear knee socks for instance, or anything she deems nerdy, but she doesn't seem to mind Pam's farm girl thing. Or the way she wears her hair in two short braids, like she's six. I was closer to Mom's last girlfriend, Roxie, who met Mom when they were showing at the same SoHo gallery. She had black eyebrows and a long nose, and the way she turned her head to watch me with one eye reminded me of a bird. She taught me how to stretch canvasses.

"What is it with her?" Viva says. "No one's good enough. Pam worships Mom, and Mom acts like she could take or leave her."

"Leave her, more like," I say. "Remember that whole marriage conversation..."

A couple of months ago, we were eating dinner, talking about places to go over the summer. Pam was pushing British Columbia, renting a house somewhere near Vancouver. "We could get married and honeymoon there!" she said. Something about the way she looked at Mom, and the way Mom frowned and bent her head and speared fish with her fork, made us realize that this wasn't a spontaneous, jokey conversation. Later we were in the living room playing Scrabble and we heard them on the front porch. Sometimes I wonder about Mom's hearing. She thinks she's talking quietly, but her voice booms.

"You know how I feel about this, Pam," we heard her say. "I'm all for everyone having the right to marry, so don't turn this into some political cop-out. But marriage is not for me. Frankly I don't believe in the whole damaged, patriarchal institution. The one good reason I can think of to get married is to start a family, and I'm done having babies. If you want those things, you deserve them, and I don't want to keep you from having what you need to be happy. But you'll have to find someone else to share all that with."

We didn't hear Pam's response, but again Mom's stage whisper boomed. "That is not true! I never misled you. Practically from the day we met I've been straight with you." Another indecipherable mumble from Pam, and Mom laughed. "Okay, okay, unfortunate figure of speech. Babe, I would certainly not blame you for not settling for the limited things I have to offer. But I'm just not the marrying type. I don't know how else to put it."

And this time we heard Pam's response, because her voice shrilled in protest. "You would have married Julie!"

When Mom spoke again, it was in what we call her liquid nitrogen voice. "Whatever, Pam." She banged back into the house so suddenly our faces were still pointed towards the open window.

Mom's eyes narrowed, but all she said was, "Hot chocolate, girls?" By the time she finished making it, Pam had come in. Mom poured her a cup too, and put an arm around her shoulder. Pam squeezed Mom's waist, and smiled at us, and everything seemed okay.

We walk past the baseball fields. One kid is kneeling by the team bench, unpacking a cooler of water bottles and a giant Tupperware of orange slices, so I know there will be a game soon. Behind right field I locate the dirt path to the river. I remember walking here with Mom a year and a half ago, after the tour was over. It was October then, and leaves were already beginning to fall, golden ones shaped like spades. Mom kept pointing things out to me: a scruffy bird, bunches of ferns, the crotch of a birch tree where she stooped and laughed and pointed to the H.E.K. scratched into the trunk. "This place does not change," Mom said, and her tone was hard to read: whether she found that reassuring, or otherwise.

The winding path to the river is shady and quiet. I feel protected from all the reunion clatter. Even Viva says, "It's so pretty," her first non-grudging praise.

"Isn't it? Mom took up rowing sophomore year, just because she liked this walk to the Nashua."

Viva snickers. "It's hard to picture Mom engaged in physical activity."

"She sucked, she says. Though she has the right body for it: tall, long legs."

"Does Tommy have the right body?" She gives me a sideways look, as if she's asking something salacious.

"Well, he's strong, even if he's not super tall. Mom says she was just too lazy. Crew is incredibly hard. It uses all your muscles, stomach, back, arms, legs, everything. And it's murder on your hands. Remember Tommy's hands over spring break?"

Viva ruffles my hair. "It's funny, hearing you declaiming about sports."

"Yeah, yeah."

Viva gives me a push. "You know what? I'm going to invent a Mamie doll, and every time you pull its string, it will say 'Yeah, yeah' in that annoying way."

"Oh lay off." We turn a corner and are back in the sunlight, the river suddenly in front of us. I point. "Boathouse."

We watch rowers carry a long, bone-colored scull to the dock, roll it onto the water, and carefully step inside. The scull rocks. The coxswain, a short boy with glasses, takes his seat. With the blades of their oars, the rowers push away from the dock. Viva shades her eyes, but we don't see the St. Mark's boat. They must be in the water already, warming up.

"Come on, it's two-thirty. Let's go to the finish line."

We follow the dirt path by the river. A few people are walking in front of us, alumni in their dressy casuals, one holding a fancy camera, and we pass some students sitting on the bank, but it's nowhere near as packed as the playing fields on the main campus. Maybe because people don't bother with the mile-long walk, or because crew is less glamorous than lacrosse or baseball or tennis. The quiet is a draw for me, though: if I had gone here, I'd want to row, even if I'm nowhere near tall enough. I love the grace of those narrow, pale boats slipping through the water.

We know when we get to the finish line because clusters of people are sitting on the bank, but there's still plenty of room. Viva plops on the dusty ground. I set my backpack on a patch of scrubby grass a few feet away, and sit on top of it. She snorts but scoots over. We face the river, waiting for the race to start, looking for Tommy's boat.

Sometimes I catch myself thinking of him not as Tommy but as tom_malley. He's becoming an abstraction, a handle; I can't easily talk, or worse, "chat" to this tom-underscore-malley with his wink emoticons. In three weeks he'll be back in Hanover for the summer. And then? Do I have anything in common with Tommy Malley in the flesh?

Back at McKinley, we had the smart kid thing in common, and a year and a half ago, that fall, we had the boarding school aspirations. This was before we started dating, really how we got to be friends. We'd compare notes about campuses we'd seen, which ones seemed to have cool kids, which ones seemed full of nerds or snobs or clubbing kids or billionaires (Tommy's dad teaches economics at Dartmouth and his mom works part-time, so it's not like they're loaded, and that worried Tommy. He didn't want to be the poor kid.) Then he applied. And, after I half-filled out three applications (Who is your role model? What is your favorite book and why? If you flew a rocket ship to another planet, what three things would you tell an alien about Earth?) I let them sit on my desk for days. I gazed out the window at the old, soiled trampoline in the backyard, thinking about Viva and Mom on the one hand and Grandpa James and Julie on the other, and in the end, I never applied.

When Tommy got in, I felt something hard to explain: it makes me understand the expression "sinking feeling," because I could literally feel myself scrunching up, almost stooping, when he grabbed my shoulders, so pleased, and said, "Mamie, guess what?" That was March last year. I tried to smile, but I felt envious and crappy and sad.

That weekend a bunch of us celebrated with him at Nick Benevito's house. I got drunk, rare for me, and Tommy and I ended up making out in Nick's redwood hot tub. It was the end of winter; when I leaned far enough back against the shell of the hot tub, I could trail my fingertips into crystals of snow on the ground.

Frankly I thought that night was just a scam, again not like me: usually it's Viva who makes out with guys and then hides the next day. But Tommy never gave me a chance to hide. The next morning at school, he kissed me in the hall in front of all our friends. It was like Insta-boyfriend, add water. Suddenly I was part of a pair, but a different one, with this nice guy everyone liked, who was good at sports but smart too, who was friends with the popular kids and the stoners, who even got along with Viva, and who, for some reason, liked me.

"Crazy," Viva said in our bedroom that night, shaking her head in bemusement at this last piece: he liked me. And, later, she relocated that craziness: "You'd be crazy to dump Tommy."

It strikes me now that Viva and I were both so perplexed by that initial puzzle—he liked me, how bizarre!—that I never considered whether I also liked him. It's as if I was sitting on a shelf and he scooped me up and stuck me in his pocket. I picture Viva's boneless

Mamie doll: pull my string and I say "Yeah, yeah," which is, if you think about it, as much of an assent (Yes, I'll be your girlfriend! Yes, I'll give serious thought to boarding school! Yes, I'll scrap that plan and stay here because Viva can't bear to be left behind!) as it is a dismissal.

The Circle grass is warm from soaking up the sun: through my thin cotton shirt it feels like a blanket. Beside me Viva snores. On the walk back from the boathouse she had to hold my arm, and I was afraid that she'd throw up. How the hell did she get so drunk? In twenty-five minutes? That's all the time we had with Tommy's crew while they waited for the Varsity first boat to race and then row back, while the eyes of his coach were focused elsewhere. Twenty-five minutes for Viva and the other boys in Tommy's boat (Newt, Hank, Carter, and Griffin, the cox) to down a bottle of J & B while Tommy and I sat, thirty feet away, in a grove of birches. Viva is such a lightweight. Always lean, serious running has finessed her into essentials only: bone, muscle, and pale, hairless skin.

"You can handle her?" were Tommy's parting words, over Viva's bobbing 'fro, and I said, "Sure," not at all sure. Somehow that exchange encapsulated the just-over sixteen years of my life.

Lying on the grass I feel not so much drunk as blunted: I decide that I have found, finally, a liquor I like. The rye from Tommy's flask makes everything softer, muted: the sun on my arms, Tommy's mouth on my neck, his hands on my bare back, and the anxiety that has twisted my stomach all day, like a nonsense song I can't get out of my head, a song composed of proper nouns only (Tommy-Mom-Viva-Julie; nonstop, it replays).

Viva snores beside me, and I lie down with my eyes closed, half-asleep myself, rubbed smooth like a river stone by the sips of rye and the late afternoon sun on my face.

"Heather! I've been looking for you everywhere."

"Meriwether! Sit, sit."

"Are those the girls? Whoa, all grown up. Look at them!"

"I know. Quiet, they're sleeping..."

The warm grass under my palms, Viva next to me, the sun on my face: everything that happens feels like a dream. Me waking-sleeping on the grass, Mom ten feet away, under an apple tree, holding court. I tune in, tune out, to snatches of conversation, like a radio in a car driving through some long stretch of nowhere.

"So tell me about Joy," I hear Mom's voice. "How's she doing, really?"

"Better. The tumor was tiny, not even four millimeters, but her lymph nodes were impacted, so... it's unclear. She's in for a hard year. She had a mastectomy in February and after she recovered from surgery they started her on chemo, so she has months of that, and then radiation..."

Tommy's hand on my bra, cupping: the hum of a bee nearby.

"How's she feeling? I mean, mentally?"

"Prepared to fight. She has plenty to fight for. Brendan's in kindergarten, Miles is only eight. And Paul has been wonderful, as you'd expect. You know Paul, right?"

"I met him once, years ago, when they were driving through New England. Miles was a baby then. Paul seemed lovely. Crazy about Joy. He looked at her like she was this magical creature..."

"Jesus, Heather, that was almost eight years ago. I remember, I met up with them in Cape Cod. 2004. Have you really not seen Joy since then? Why not?"

There's a pause. Then Mom says, "Is she losing her hair?"

"Of course."

"Damn, she loved her hair. Poor Joy. Boobs and hair: those were her favorite features."

"I need to show you the photos she sent me of the wigs she was trying on. Hang on, let me find my phone."

After a pause: "Oh my God! She looks like Veronica Lake!" They laugh.

And I'm drifting again, thinking of Tommy's hands on my back, his mouth on my neck, thinking of him whispering "Three weeks" in my ear. Lately it seems like all my conversations with Tommy concern time: We're both sixteen, which he talks about, my birthday especially, as if it signifies something; we've been together for fourteen months; he'll be home in three weeks, for nearly three months. All these numbers add up to a sum he doesn't quite spell out, but I can decode well enough, though I pretend not to get it.

"Or check out this one, Ann-Margaret..."

It's that floating, unsaid expectation that stresses me about the prospect of Tommy this summer, Tommy in the flesh rather than ether-Tommy, tom underscore. Once again I can't tell apart what he expects from what I want. The Mamie doll, with its acquiescent yeah-yeah string. Though I won't deny that the feeling of his mouth on my neck was at least as warm, at least as good, as the rye, or that I love his strong, confident hands, hands that can do things, take apart a circuit board, grip an oar, write an application essay, while my hands just seem to lie on the grass like abandoned paddles.

"She's a clown! God, you have to admire a woman who will buy that wig."

I ask myself the question as baldly as I can, and somehow in my head it's Viva's voice, not mine. Do I want to have sex with Tommy?

"Let's call her."

And my face burns with a memory now: coming home from school a couple of months ago, winter still, there was snow on my boots, though Viva was out running on the sodden trails in her long underwear and nylon hoodie. Mom was sitting in the kitchen, looking just as uncomfortable as me, but saying nonetheless, "Mamie, we need to talk."

"About what?" I said, already wanting to disappear. I spend a lot of time recently affecting a nearly idiotic level of denseness.

"Joyful, it's Heather Katchadourian, I'm sitting with Meriwether on the Circle, and we're wishing so much that you were here! Call us, babe. I'm on Meriwether's cell but you can call mine too, the number is..."

"It's just foolish, in this day and age," I remember Mom saying, "For anyone to get pregnant or get any kind of STD. Birth control is completely effective, especially the pill, though the pill solo makes sense only if you're in a monogamous relationship..."

"Mom, I know all that!" I said, picturing myself composed of acid that could melt smokily through the floor. "Do you think I'm five? And anyway..."

"Honey, I was a teenager too, remember? And a much more foolish one than you, my wise Mamie. I made a lot of stupid choices, and I don't want you..."

"Look, I'm a virgin, okay?" I said at last. Which like some kind of Harry Potter stunning spell—*Stupefy!*—stopped Mom mid-sentence, and before she could switch gears I grabbed my books from the kitchen table and escaped to Viva's and my bedroom. That night after dinner Mom gave me a scrap of paper with a phone number and a name written on it. "That's my gynecologist's number, Dr. Appel, if you want to schedule an appointment. She's great, Mamie, really warm and competent. And don't forget your health insurance card."

Like acid, smoking through the floor.

Though how many of our friends, including Tommy, have said to Viva and me they wished they had Mom for a mother? So young, so beautiful, so hip, so creative, so cool. "So gay," Viva says, making us all laugh.

As if I've invoked her, I hear Mom. "Bethie! Finally!"

"Heather, Meriwether! I have been searching for you guys. It's been too damn long! I've missed you!"

"You too! Is Stephen here?"

"No, he has a big case coming up. And Caroline had a birthday party sleepover, her first slumber party, she didn't want to miss it, and of course that was A-OK by me."

Meriwether says, "I came solo too, I left Leo and Oscar with Bennett. He was willing, meeting new people scares him, and I wasn't going to turn down that offer! Though he sends his love to you both. God, I used to dread flying, and now if I don't have the kids, it's stolen time."

These women can't wait to escape their children, and they have husbands to help them. They haven't had to raise kids by themselves, in a drafty farm house whose wooden steps they taught themselves to caulk.

I must have fallen asleep for a few minutes, because when I

next tune into the Mom station, I don't hear Meriwether's voice any longer, only Beth's, and Beth's is low. "Honestly, Heather, I *need* a break from him. And maybe a 'break' in the real sense of the word. You know, chop chop. Stephen becomes more of a pain in the ass every year. I understand depression, I understand that it's a chemical problem, I truly get all that. But sometimes I feel like I'm living in a cave or a prison, some place with no sunlight. And Caroline is growing up in that environment, no light, no air, like one of those pale, withered plants. I wonder if it's more damaging for her..."

"Well, it's certainly not easy growing up with a parent who's depressed," Mom says.

Beth must remember Mom's father the same second I do, because she says, "Oh shit, Heather, I wasn't thinking."

"My point is I understand. It was hard on my mother too, and of course Dad's drinking made things worse. Though now I think it was his way of self-medicating..."

I drift again, but it's not Mom's father I'm thinking of; I never knew him, he died when she was eleven. Instead it's Julie's dad, Grandpa James, whose image floats before me. With his long, bony face and deep eye sockets, Grandpa James looks like the farmer holding the pitchfork in the "American Gothic" painting. It's a handsome face, but lately the broken capillaries on his nose and cheekbones are making it stranger, as if a child picked up the wrong crayons to color it in: a drinker's face. We have alcoholism on both sides, Julie's and Mom's. Really, it's stupid to decide I like how rye tastes. As if she's tracking my thoughts, Viva rolls to her side and her forehead bumps my shoulder. Gently, I nudge her onto her back.

"...Zoloft?"

"He's tried it. He's tried everything. Paxil, now. But nothing quite works, or, anyway, keeps working. One makes him gain weight, the other lowers his sex drive. Listen to me whine. I just need a break, in the mini-vacation sense. Forget the divorce sense."

"Far be it from me to judge, Bethie. But you know there isn't an easy solution here. Raising Caroline with Stephen is tough, raising her on your own would be hard too. No breaks, speaking of breaks, not unless Stephen is able to parent better than he's been..."

I think of Tommy in the hot tub, both of us holding our beer bottles out of the water into the cold March air, but still the steam warmed the drink: "Beer soup," Tommy said. That made me laugh, and I was still laughing when he kissed me. I remember the collision of all those temperatures and viscosities: the bubbling, hot water, his wet mouth, the hardness of his teeth, the tepid beer, snow brushing my fingertips.

Mom says, "Well, it's not like I had much choice, did I? You know, and this is something I would never tell the girls..." her voice lowers, and my senses sharpen: the rye fuzziness evaporates. "Oh, Beth, you of all people remember. Julie and I were so happy. And remember how much she wanted to have a baby? Like it would legitimize us. Get rid of the whole lesbian stigma. You know how weird she was about being with a woman. And her parents. Remember how they were with me, I mean once we became a couple? Like I'd corrupted Julie."

"Well, they blew how much on that wedding? That, let's face it, you kind of interfered with."

Mom laughs. "Yeah, I guess you could say that."

"Don't get me wrong, Heather, I'm not defending them. I just remember how confusing it was. Here are Julie and Heather, best friends forever, and then there's this whole scandalous fiasco with Julie's very expensive, fancy wedding—"

"Yeah, yeah," says Mom. I picture the Mamie doll Viva conjured.

"Because of which you and Julie have this huge, awful, nuclear falling out, for which everyone blames you. I have to say, I honestly believed you two would never speak to each other again."

"Okay! I get it!"

"And then suddenly, abracadabra, not only are you speaking, but you're in love? Julie Howe and Heather Katchadourian, gay? I mean, it was a bit of a collective shocker, and I was just your oblivious best friend. I wasn't Julie's conservative parents with a golf club membership and a pew at the Episcopal church—"

"Which has come a long way, good old Episcopal Church."

"Very true. Cheers to that." They both laugh. "Look, I'm just saying it's not surprising that her parents have had issues with you."

"Okay, but the point I was trying to make was that Julie wanted to convince them, and, let's face it, convince herself, that she could still have a happy life. And having a baby was a symbol for normality. We were so young, you know: twenty-six when those two were born. No one had babies. And Julie wanted to be the one to carry it, and wanted to nurse, all of that, and of course I didn't put up a fight..."

"Who the hell would? I wish Stephen had been the one to gain forty pounds and get the three-degree tear and have mastitis twice. If I were a lesbian, you bet I'd encourage my partner to be the pregnant one!"

They laugh. "My thinking exactly. So we decided, meaning Julie decided and I said sure, whatever you want, my love, to have a baby, and miraculously, second try with the sperm donor produced twins, of all things. Do you know how rare that is, Beth? Most donor babies, I forget the percentage but it's the majority for sure, are boys. Something about the Y sperms being faster swimmers. But somehow she gets pregnant with not one but two girls. You should have seen our faces in the doctor's office! Beyond shock. And then they came, and it was amazing, of course, but also exhausting as hell, especially for Julie. Who breastfeeds twins for nine months? No one I know. But she insisted, 'breast is best,' and things were good, and then one day..."

"It's like she woke up," Beth fills in, and because I am thinking those exact words, I actually gasp. But Mom corrects her, immediately.

"No, the opposite. It's like she had been awake, and then suddenly she fell asleep. Back to dreaming. You know, in the days, well, years really, when we were secretly fooling around, things would happen and then I could never get her to talk about it. It was like it had happened in a dream. But I always thought, and this is admittedly self-serving, that her life was the dreaming part, I mean, the bulk of it. And these isolated moments of us being physically and emotionally together were the wide awake part. Anyway, I remember her gazing out the window one day and her eyes had this kind of blankness to them. She looked like Sleeping Beauty pricking her finger on the spinning wheel. There was just something glazed and narcotic about her. I remember my heart kind of stopping because it reminded me of how tranced-out she used to get, back in school....

"So I touched her shoulder and said, 'What is it, Sweetheart?' And she said 'Nothing.' Like she was on drugs. The girls were eighteen months old. And it wasn't many days later that she told me she 'just couldn't do it anymore.'"

"1997," Beth says.

"Yeah, right after Thanksgiving. So the girls know all this, more or less, I mean, not the whole prehistory, the canceled wedding with Porter and all that mess, but about her having a sudden change of heart..."

And it's true, I do know this, though it's strange how I've exactly reversed it, just as Beth did: that I imagine Julie waking up, not, as Mom describes her, going to sleep. And I wonder who would have supplied that image if not Mom. I can even picture it like it's on film: Julie's eyes closed and then—Bang!—suddenly open, and the camera close-up to her eyes, terrified, like a victim in a horror film, and big and blue, like mine.

"Here's the part they don't know. Well, I was broken-hearted, and furious...."

"Sure."

"And frankly it seemed unfathomable to have a civil, friendly relationship with Julie. You know, we'd tried that. I'd been her best friend for enough tortured, closeted years. I couldn't imagine going that route again. But we had two kids. We couldn't just go our separate ways and never speak to each other again, not with these two beautiful little girls to co-parent."

"Co-parent? Seriously?"

"Ah, I see you've cut to the end of this story." And Mom's voice is as steely as I've ever heard it. "So we actually contemplated, for about five minutes, each taking one child. You know, like that movie with Hayley Mills that they re-did with what's-her-name. Lindsay Lohan."

"*The Parent Trap.*"

"Each of us takes a baby, *sayonara* family! We go our separate ways with our separate daughters. I imagined returning to Europe, being closer to my mother—well, at least on the same continent. Italy maybe. Julie and I never see each other again. We raise each kid to think of herself as the only child of a single mom, never knowing she has a twin."

"Whoa."

"Well, it was a crazy fantasy, but we were in a crazy state. I was pissed as hell and a basket case, and Julie was in her weird, numb coma. We weren't thinking straight, to put it mildly. So in this psychotic state, we actually got so far as the kids' bedroom, it's still their bedroom today, and looked in on them. They were napping. And they were holding hands. You know, they each had their own crib, but they didn't want to go in them. Or Viva didn't. Mamie would sleep just about anywhere—she was always a great sleeper—but Viva had to be with Mamie. She'd just cry and cry when we put her down by herself. So there they were, holding hands, and Julie said, 'We can't separate them.' And I had to nod because obviously that was true, but I didn't trust myself to talk..." Even now, Mom sounds like she's about to cry.

"Jesus," says Beth.

"So then I said, 'So, you'll take them?' I just assumed... And there was this endless pause, and then Julie said, 'But I can't. Not now, not yet.' Not now, not yet. Like she was sick and had to recover first. And maybe I wanted to prove to her that I could do it. I could be a responsible mother, I would never be the one to leave: not them, or her. And there were logistical issues. She moved in with her brother, for starters. Andrew had this tiny place in the Village, no room for toddler nieces. And then she had to get back on her feet, and then there was grad school, and then this and that, this and that. But it was four or five years before I realized she wasn't ever going to want the girls. It finally dawned on me when she married Will Crockett and moved into that huge house in Fairfield, and *still* didn't ask for them."

"God, Heather. But could you have let them go, anyway?"

"I never would have 'let them go,'" says Mom. "They aren't balloons! I was imagining joint custody. You know, truly 'joint.' Julie having them half the time and weekends alternating. A couple of years down the road I wasn't in that crazed *Parent Trap* state anymore, and being a single parent, this was my earlier point Beth, is no picnic. It's really hard. I would have sucked up some heartache about seeing her at handoffs in exchange for free childcare. Besides, she had wanted them. A baby was her idea, her grand plan. And they should have two parents, not one. They're entitled to that." Mom pauses. "I must say, it still blows my mind, the way Julie totally bailed."

"Frankly, Heather, it confounds everyone. I don't know if you saw her Christmas card—"

Mom snorts. "Beth. Of course I didn't see Julie's Christmas card! But I can imagine. Her, Rob, and the baby. What's-his-name, Benjamin."

"Well, yeah. Exactly. Happy holidays from... and no mention of the girls."

"You know, that makes me angry..."

"I should shut up."

"What I was going to say is, the other scenario would piss me off just as much. You know, if Viva's and Mamie's names were on some fucking card. Because it would be a lie. She doesn't see the girls, she hasn't seen them since Thanksgiving a year and a half ago, she barely calls them. Her parents are better about staying in touch. I'll say that for James and Elizabeth: no love lost between them and me, God knows, but they do make an effort. What I wish is that the conditions were changed so that kind of holiday card, girls' names included, wouldn't be an absurd joke. But whatever."

"Well, I'm sorry, Heather. I mean, most of that isn't news to me, but I've never heard your version. And I'm sorry for whining about my piddly problems. I formally retract all whines."

"So you've heard Julie's version."

Beth snorts. "Is it just being at this place again? Are you also having a flashback? I feel like we're all sixteen, and you two are having one of your bloodbath fights, and I'm, as usual, caught in the middle, trying to calm everyone down."

I have a sudden image of Beth sitting on a yellow couch, plump legs crossed. It was nearly Christmas. Viva and I were in New York with Julie. She was still married to Will then, so we must have been eight or nine. She took us to *The Nutcracker*. She sat between us, and we all laughed when Mother Ginger lifted her giant hoop skirt, yards wide, and all the children spilled out. Afterwards we thought Julie would bring us to La Maison du Chocolat for hot chocolate. I'm not sure why: probably because she had once before, on some long ago trip. So when she said, "Now we're going to a party," we were both disappointed. Julie looked sad. I remember the long neck of the woman who opened the door. Her Christmas tree must have been eight feet tall, with blinking lights. Mom likes colored lights, Julie likes white. I was fingering an ornament when Viva pointed: Beth, sitting on a couch. "Hey there!" she said, reaching for us. Beth rubbed her wrist against ours to share her perfume. Shalimar: we liked the hushing roll of its name. At the ballet that afternoon we had seen Mr. Shonsky from the Hanover grocery, who always gave us free caramels. Manhattan to Viva and me was where you bumped into people you knew in entirely separate contexts. Only when Beth pointed to Julie and said, "Doesn't she look happy?" did it dawn. "You know Julie?" Viva said. Beth looked at us strangely. "Of course!" That was the first time I realized Beth wasn't simply Mom's best friend. I sniffed her perfume on the thin skin of my wrist, and we stared, the three of us, at Julie.

"Sorry, Bethie," Mom says now.

"Does it help to know that she feels incredibly guilty? I mean, about leaving the kids?"

"You mean as opposed to leaving me? Not really, I have to say. Who cares about feeling guilty? Let's see some action!"

"Oh, sweetie."

"I just don't get it. Once upon a time I knew Julie very well, and so did you. Did she strike you back then as being such an epic flake? Seriously: how many people has she bailed on? The girls, but also all the relationships. Count them up: Porter, me, Will Bonehead Crockett. And how long is Rob going to last? I never figured her for such an escape artist."

"Two things," says Beth, after a pause. "First, hardly fair to blame Julie for Porter! I completely understand why you're pissed at her, you have a right to be. Frankly I am too, for the girls' sakes. But

Heather, you of all people aren't allowed to criticize Julie for leaving Porter! Not only is that irrational, it's unjust."

"Okay, okay," Mom laughs. "Point taken. Though Beth, the truth is, I don't feel a damn bit guilty for whatever contribution I had to that relationship ending. Porter was a fucker, and I speak with authority, having fucked him. He would have made Julie miserable. But all right, I grant your point, scratch him from my grievance list. Consider Porter's name officially retracted. You're good at this, Bethie, calming me down."

"Tra la. And as for the more general aspersion of flakiness—well, I'm not going to defend her on that front. Rob seems perfectly pleasant, but in all candor I haven't bothered getting to know him. If he lasts for a full five years I might make an effort, but until then, I don't need another Facebook person to unfriend."

Mom laughs.

After a minute Beth says, "Though Heather, speaking of Facebook: Roxie tried to friend me a couple of weeks ago."

"Shit. This is why I refuse to be on Facebook! I hope you didn't...?"

"I didn't. I 'ignored' her, but my point, Heather, is that you aren't exactly the queen of relationship reliability yourself."

"How can you compare me—"

"You're a wonderful mother, this has nothing to do with the girls. I'm referring to romances here. All I mean is—well, how's Pam?"

"Oh, shut up Beth." But she laughs, dourly.

There's another pause. "So Heather... about that whole *Parent Trap* fantasy?"

"Yeah?"

"Which baby were you going to take?"

It's what I've been wondering too, why I'm listening so hard that I've turned into a pair of ears. Mom says, "That was an insane time. They were babies then. I'm sorry I even considered it. Beth, forget I said that."

But it doesn't matter, because I know; I know with complete certainty, the same way I knew, without having to hear it, that the one who wouldn't sleep in her own crib was Viva; the way I know whose hand was clutching whose.

"Don't you think you're a good mother?" I asked Mom last winter, when she was sitting at the table, looking defeated, and for once, tired and old from some squabble with Viva.

"Within the limits of my personality," she said.

I know how hard she tries, partly to make up for the fact that she's all we've got. That she's it, or more accurately It, in the "Tag, You're It" sense: never planned on being a mother, went with it rather than chose it, never gestated us, never gave birth to us, never breastfed us, but somehow got left with us. I picture Julie tapping Mom's shoulder, *"Tag, you're It!"* and then loping gracefully away, leaving Mom alone, rotating in a slow circle, in a patch of sun that looks like a spotlight. All alone, except for the toddler girls rolling around in the grass.

And it suddenly occurs to me that though Mom and Viva are the ones that everyone says are so much alike, so dramatic, so intense, two of a kind, that Mom and I have this particular quality in common: that she in her own way is a Mamie doll with a yeah-yeah string, not quite realizing what she's agreed to.

The afternoon stretches. First over my legs, eventually over my chest and face, shadows climb. My left arm, pinned under my head, falls asleep, and I roll over to free it. But I continue to lie there with my eyes shut, Viva snoring next to me, and I move as if across the shadows of clouds through different states, awake to asleep to somewhere in between. Nearby I hear Mom's voice weave into other voices, not just Beth's now. It's like one of those complicated minuets in a Jane Austen movie. With my eyes shut and the sun and the shadows slipping over my skin, I only half-follow it. Some voices I recognize, some I don't.

A woman's voice, low and flat, says, "In August we're taking the kids to Lake Como. We've rented a house near George Clooney's. Supposedly you can see his mansion from the patio. The kids are so excited. Sarah has never been to Italy. We took Oliver there before she was born, but of course he doesn't remember..."

"How lovely!" Mom's voice is as phony as her camera smile.

Now and then, a collective, "Oh, hooray!" as a new person or couple takes their place on the grass.

"I come bearing wine and plastic cups. Who wants to imbibe?"

"You still painting, Heather?" someone asks.

"When I can. But designing annual reports pays the bills, and I have college tuition around the corner. Seriously, you all, start saving now. Every so often I get something more interesting, like a logo..."

I wake up to a prolonged discussion about fixing up Sam. A woman named Kirsten is full of candidates: "I know this fabulous person Amanda who would be perfect for you, Sammy. She's thirty-one, but she has her shit together. She has her own wine bar in Tribeca, it's called...."

Beth says, "Oh yeah, I've been there."

Tommy must be back at St. Mark's by now. I wonder if he's thinking of me, maybe writing an email. I picture his fingers on the keyboard, that speedy two-finger way he types. If he's thinking of being in that perfect circle of birches.

Someone named Lawrence says, "And what about you, Heather? Seeing anyone?"

"I've already plumbed those depths. She's seeing a female whose name is Jam. Or is it Damn?"

Mom snorts. "Cute, Sammy."

And every so often, someone mentions us. "Still sleeping?" Or, once, "Look at the Sleeping Beauties!" which makes me think of Mom describing Julie and the spinning wheel.

"Should I put my hat over Mamie's face, Heather? She's right in the sun."

"She'll be fine, Beth. It's past six."

"Well, I don't want my goddaughters getting burnt!"

"You questioning my competence as a mother? Watch your step."

Lawrence says, "You're the godmother? That's an honor Beth! Hey, more wine for the godmother! Pass that bottle, Ian."

Kirsten, who seems to be Lawrence's wife, says, "Sam is

Harrison's godfather. Want to hold your godson, Sam? Jesus Christ, this baby weighs two tons!"

"Hand him over," Sam says, and then: "Oh Lord, I think I just pulled a muscle in my back." They laugh.

Kirsten says, "Hey, isn't anyone else bringing babies to this thing? Aren't Julie and Rob supposed to come? I mean..."

A silence, which Sam breaks, in a way that feels like both changing the subject and spectacularly failing to do so: "Hey, Heather, who is the twins' godfather? We can have a godfather wrestling match."

"Ian," Mom says, in a flat voice.

"Oh, right." Ian laughs weakly. "I haven't been the most attentive godfather, have I? I must owe a real backlog of Christmas presents."

Funny: I always thought we just had a godmother. It followed a kind of symmetry, one parent, one godparent. Beth always sends us great presents: expensive oil paints in April and, when we were five or six, a dollhouse with shaker shingles that we still have in our room. I still play with it sometimes, arranging porcelain petits fours and cream pitchers the size of fingernails on tiny silver tea trays. I remember Beth visiting one summer and helping us paste sheets of origami paper onto the walls. She used one of Mom's palette knives to spread the paste.

"Someone said they're serving cocktails in the tent by the chapel before dinner. Anyone want to mosey? Okay, Emily and I will see you all at dinner. Bye."

A minute later, Mom hisses, "Jesus, he really did forget he was their godfather."

"No, no..."

"He and Julie make quite a pair, don't they?"

Lawrence says, "Don't let Emily hear you call them a 'pair'! She'll bite your head off."

Beth says, "Heather, chill out. It's not like the girls are religious and we offer them spiritual guidance. What's a godparent supposed to do, anyway?"

"What Ian said! Fucking provide presents! Like you have, Beth!" Mom says. "Okay, general announcement to the floor. Ian Saltonstall

is hereby officially fired as godfather. Lawrence, you can take over.
Sam, I'd say you could be one too, but you've already got Baby Jabba
on your hands."

Kirsten protests, "Hey! No one calls my baby Jabba but me."

I think of random things: the way Tommy's skin smells like
biscuits; the sun in yellow pieces on the surface of the Nashua; what
it would be like to be a student here, if I'd actually turned in that
application. Whether I'd feel lonely or simply free.

"I'm going to get one of those cocktails before dinner. You
think they've actually sprung for some decent liquor?"

"They should, the amount of money they're trying to shake us
down for."

"Heather? You coming?"

"No, I'm going to stay with the girls. I don't want them to wake
up and wonder where I am."

"Oh, come on! They're sixteen, they can figure it out."

"No, you all go on ahead."

"Okay, if I don't see you before dinner, I'll save you a seat."

Viva's arm brushes mine, her knee bumps my thigh. We must
have been like this once, in utero, tangled together. As we are still
tangled together. I feel like I'm floating in something warm and
dark, amniotic fluid maybe, or a hot tub, or rye, or liquid sunlight
puddling on the grass. I'm bobbing in this pool, half asleep, when I
hear another voice, a soft one.

"Heather Elena Katchadourian."

"Julia Christine Howe Crockett Azzopardi. Fancy meeting you
here."

I don't hear her steps, but I feel her shadow.

"Wow! Look at them. They look so old! So beautiful..."

"Yeah," Mom says, and it's the most complicated 'Yeah' I've
heard from her all day. "They're sleeping, Jules. Let them sleep."

The shadow retreats. "For how long?"

"Hours. Frankly, I suspect there was some liquor involved."

"Seriously? Where...?"

"They met up with Mamie's boyfriend earlier. He goes to St.
Mark's, he had a race here. Tommy. He's a nice kid. I bet you'd

like him even more than I do. Excellent manners, good with the grown-ups."

"How old?"

"Sixteen. Mamie's age. He's a cool kid, really."

"But alcohol..."

"I'm just guessing. Don't freak. What happens in Vegas stays in Vegas."

Part of me wants to make a big show of yawning, waking up, but I don't. I lie on the grass like I am pinned here. My fingertips feel for Viva's arm.

"I was starting to wonder if you would show up."

"It took us forever to get out the door. Rob had a conference call. And Ben was a pain for most of the drive, so tired and crabby. Of course, fifteen minutes before we get here, he falls asleep. Rob's in the car with him, waiting for him to wake up. If I'd known the Circle had turned into a nap station..."

"Have you been here long?"

"Twenty minutes maybe."

"Seen anyone?"

"I talked to Ian and Emily for a second, they were just coming out of the tent. I swear, Emily hates me."

Mom laughs at that, and Julie laughs too.

"Really, I'm serious. I try to be nice to her, and she's barely polite. It's like she has to keep her eye on me, or I'm going to steal her husband."

"Jeez, how long have they been married? Fourteen years?"

"I know! He's such a sweet guy, too. He deserves someone less menacing."

"Hmm. I'm not sure what Ian deserves."

"Ha. He mentioned you were giving him a hard time."

"Oh, bullshit. Maybe one cross look. He's such a damn tattle-tale." They both laugh. "Beth was saying earlier how we regress, just being here."

"Oh, I want to see Beth! I saw her sitting with you."

"Spy."

"Just for a minute. I saw you all out on the Circle. I was about to come over when everyone else got up and headed over to the tent thing. Thought I'd come say hello to you first."

"Thank you, that's nice." There's a pause. "You're right, Emily is a pain. You should have heard her talking about some Lake Como trip they're taking. Barf. Though she was very nice to me."

"Really? That's surprising."

"Almost too nice. Like she was making a point. Like it was her way of sticking it to you."

"Huh," says Julie.

"I liked Kirsten, though. Lawrence's wife. She seems pretty down-to-earth."

"Girlfriend. They're not married."

"Really? Interesting. I assumed..."

"I think she'd like to get married, but he doesn't want to. Well, that's what I gather. Yeah, I like her too. Speaking of wives—"

"Nanette isn't here. They split up."

"Yes, I know, we had dinner with Sam last time we were in New York. No, I was going to ask if Pam was here."

"Nope. And not a wife, Julie."

"Oh, I just meant—"

"Not a wife," repeats Mom, so decisively that Julie says, sounding confused, "You are still together, right?"

"Yes." Mom doesn't add anything else.

"Okay," says Julie, after a beat. "Well, I should find everyone and say hello. You want to head to the tent? We could wake the girls."

"No, that might freak them out," says Mom. "You go ahead. I'll wake them in a sec."

"Well, it's good seeing you, Heather. You look—" she stops. "I was going to say, great, and of course you look great, you always do. But what is it with you and your hair? It looks like you cut it with an eggbeater."

"Hmm. I was just thinking you looked a little Stepford wife."

"Thanks!" The sharp way Julie laughs reminds me of Mom talking about firing Ian as the godfather, trying to sound jokey, but clearly pissed. Sometimes I think about ways people who are not the

least bit alike overlap. Like Viva and that girl Liddy at our school:
they peel back the foil lids from their yogurt cups with their thumbs
in exactly the same way. Mom and Julie get offended in the same
fake ha ha way.

"You're the one who brought up eggbeaters. Yeah, I don't know
what came over me. I had a freak-out moment. Julie—"

"Yes?"

"Sorry. I just think your hair looked so pretty long."

"Well, ditto. I mean, I like yours longer too."

"Oh. Thanks." After a pause, Mom says, "You know when you
first came over and said my name and then I said yours, you know,
your whole long-ass, law-firm mouthful?"

"Yes, Heather, I caught that."

"Well, just for the record: when I saw you, I wasn't actually
thinking Julia Christine Howe Crockett Azzopardi. What I thought
was just, 'You.'"

"Okay..." Julie sounds baffled. Like she's waiting for something
more, some clarification, but Mom doesn't say anything else. "Kiss
the girls for me, okay?"

"Yeah, we'll see you in a few."

I can't hear her walk away on that soft grass.

"Well, this is beyond peculiar," Viva says.

We're standing at the entrance of another tent, this one in the
backyard of Mr. Stillwell, Dean of Admissions, who, Mom told us,
has been there forever and is practically prehistoric ("You remember
him from your interview, don't you Mamie? He looks like a tortoise?
His daughter Becca was in my class"). We're like rabbits, ready to
make a run for it. Already there are several dozen people here. Some
have commandeered tables for the Class of '87 dinner, and we scan
for anyone familiar: for Beth, and of course, for Julie.

Half an hour ago, Mom woke us in the way she does, brushing
her knuckles on our foreheads. "Wake up sleepyheads," she said. It
wasn't until we were by the car, and Mom had popped the trunk,
pulled out our overnight bag, pitched clothes at us, and reeled off

directions, first for how to get to the Schoolhouse bathroom that has the roomiest stalls for changing "and, if memory serves, the least foul johns," then for how to get to Mr. Stillwell's house ("behind the tennis courts you'll see what looks like a bouquet of maple trees"), that Viva raised one hand like a referee and said, "Wait a minute."

Mom stopped, and I realized ever since she "woke" me up she'd been talking without pause, a burbling stream of chatter ("I can't believe you slept through all that. Quite a party taking place next to you! You must have been so tired. Well we did make a ridiculously early start this morning. Hurry, hurry, we need to don our evening garb. Oh, look, the moon! Crap, does every single person here have a blue Prius?"). Now, she looked sheepish.

"Aren't you coming with us?" I asked.

"Well—" and her eyes drifted off to the left like an answer was hovering in a cartoon bubble she needed to read. She looked abashed, transparently plotting. That's how Viva and I must appear all the time to her.

Then the word avalanche began again, everything prefaced by "actually," making her sound British and prissy. Actually she needs to check us into the inn, remember we didn't have time before coming here. Actually she'd love a quick shower. Actually she feels a bit—she paused and then said, "saturated." She needs a minute to decompress. But we should head over now, they'll be serving dinner in a few minutes, and everyone wants to see us. Beth for one is dying to see us. And, of course, there's Julie. "You have a baby brother to meet, remember?" she said, and despite her best efforts at cheer, she made a sour face.

"Julie's here?" Viva said. "Did you see her?"

"Caught a distant glimpse. So, chop chop, girls, I'll catch up with you in an hour or so, I promise."

"Oh Mom," we both moaned, at the same time. It was one of those twins moments, the accidental harmony, the "Jinx! Can't talk until someone says your name!" syncs, which happen to twins eight times more often than to normal siblings. For some reason this made us all laugh, and Mom seized the opportunity to toss our overnight bag back into the trunk and slam it shut.

"Are you going to call Pam?" Viva asked.

"Exactly, I'll call Pam and just take a breath. Okay?" She was practically hopping in place, and again I couldn't shake the feeling that our roles had reversed, that I was seeing Mom the way she often sees us: bouncing up and down, placating, agreeing to everything—yes Mom, sure Mom—just so she'll let us escape.

It's that vision, that we are she and she is we, that made me release her, though in the same severe way she tends to close such conversations with ominous reminders of curfew. "One hour?"

"Yes, yes, yes," she said.

"All right then," I said, and the severity of my voice—I sounded like a mean governess—made us all crack up again.

"Oh, I almost forgot," Mom said, and she pulled from her handbag, still in their black rectangular boxes, the MAC Viva Glam lip glosses that she'd bought last weekend for all three of us, because the name was funny, and handed one to each of us. "Okay, Viva Glam and Mamie Glam. I'll see you at the Stillwells'. Be good! Make the rounds! Look out for Lawrence Stone, he's the one with the handlebar mustache!" And before we could move, she was in the car, waving, and driving away.

"Bat out of hell," Viva said, eyebrows raised. "Okay, human GPS, lead the way."

While we were walking, Viva asked, "So, did I miss anything? Were you as dead to the world as I was?" Viva and I have a strict policy: no lying to each other, must pool information. We're in a spy club of two, with the same principle marks.

But the avalanche-long answer to that first question stymied me. I tried to organize all the things she missed in my head (the Sleeping Beauty stuff; those baffling allusions to some other wedding; *The Parent Trap* scenario; that bizarro conversation between Julie and Mom), to prioritize them somehow, and froze. Maybe it's *The Parent Trap* piece that I most can't imagine putting into words. So though I knew Viva would take any withholding as a betrayal—because it's exactly how I would feel—for the moment I gave up.

"Equally corpse-like," I said, promising myself that when I had a chance to make sense of it, to put it into some kind of coherent narrative, I'd fill her in.

We sit at a table, waiting for our salads. Viva has baby Benjamin on her lap, her fingers knotted over his tummy like a seatbelt. He's a cute baby, though I can't see much of Julie in him. We don't look related, except that he's inherited those ironed-flat ears. Otherwise he's Rob's baby, and Rob is one of those people you'd have trouble describing to a police sketch artist. Medium height, medium build, brown hair, hazel eyes: his salient feature is indistinction. We met him once before he and Julie got married, when they took us out to dinner at Le Bernardin. They were only dating for about six months before their wedding. Rob is like one of those guys who wins some reality TV attrition show, like *Survivor*, not by standing out or performing spectacularly, but by flying under the radar.

I know Julie's family also sees him as nondescript, from things I've heard them say. At Thanksgiving a year and a half ago, I overheard Uncle Andrew's wife Francine say to Julie's cousin Serena, while they were peeling potatoes, "It's like his plusses are an absence of minuses. He doesn't have a gambling problem, or a girlfriend on the side, or a vagina."

Serena laughed and said, "Really, I think it's about Julie being thirty-nine when they got together. She used to be so damn picky, remember? I've seen this happen with my other girlfriends. Pushing forty, last chance to have a baby..."

"What the fuck? She has us!" Viva shouted when I told her about that conversation later. "Did you say anything to them?"

"I don't think they even noticed I was there," I said, and when Viva contracted her eyebrows, "I know, I should have told them off." I've fantasized about it since: saying, "What do you mean? She has two kids," and watching them blanch. "Oh, of course, of course," my imaginary Aunt Francine responds, waving the vegetable peeler like a baton.

Our table of eight here: Julie, me, Viva, Rob, Lawrence, Kirsten, holding baby Harrison, all rolls of fat, twice the size of baby Benjamin. Next to Kirsten, Sam, then Beth, on Julie's left. One table over, Ian and Emily sit with their kids, talking to a woman with a long neck who must be Meriwether.

Rob, Kirsten, and Lawrence are all discussing preschools. Julie, next to me, has been mostly silent, hiding behind her bob of hair, except for some murmured conversation with Beth about their sick friend Joy. Now she catches me watching her. "So Mamie—"

I wait, but nothing follows. She blinks, realizing that the burden's on her. "So tell me about this boyfriend."

"Oh..." It's not what I've been expecting; I feel like roles have reversed again: she's slipped out of the spot, and now I'm in it. But I tell her about Tommy, and Beth listens too, chin cupped in her hand. Julie listens and nods, but she doesn't say much until I explain how I got to know Tommy.

"I know this is a controversial position, because most people will say it's great to be friends first," Julie says. "But in my own experience, dating good friends can be a bit disastrous. Or at least complicated." She lowers her voice, but nods towards Ian, one table over. "That one was pretty tricky, for instance. And of course, Heather, as I'm sure you know, was my closest friend. Not everyone in this room might agree with me here." She smiles. "She's had her conflicts with poor Ian, for example! But I always found Heather to be an amazing friend, very honest and in general, very loyal."

"I certainly would agree," says Beth, who looks like she's listening carefully, as if she's wondering where this conversation is headed. Next to me I feel Viva stiffen.

"And I'm afraid I screwed it all up by going against my better judgment and getting romantically involved with Heather. I should have known better. It ruined a great friendship, one I still miss."

Beth is biting her lip, but Julie looks intent. She doesn't seem to realize she's said anything sketchy until Viva speaks, and Viva's voice is a pretty good version of Mom's liquid-nitrogen one.

"Julie, for the record, Mom has told us pretty much the same thing."

"Well, of course, Viva, that's my point," Julie says, nodding, but Viva cuts across her.

"Except that she adds this caveat: it was all worth it, because if she hadn't taken that chance with you, she never would have had us."

Julie blanches, making me think of my fantasy takedown of Aunt Francine. "Oh, Viva, I didn't mean—"

I resist the urge, so strong in me, to bail Julie out. In part, it's simply reflexive: here's another Liddy or Isabel Benzinger, Julie's intention to say something meaningful or kind or at least informative being deliberately mangled by Viva. But this is also completely unlike Viva. All our "bionic mother" cracks have always been behind Julie's back. Neither of us ever confronts her about anything— the too-small sweater sets she gives us for Christmas presents, for example, or other age-inappropriate gifts, like the Madame Alexander dolls—because both of us feel our relationship with Julie is already on such thin ice, one hard smack would shatter it. At most, we sulk. Part of me just can't believe Viva is taking her on.

"But girls," Julie says, "It's not like your existence is contingent on us having been a couple. You're my biological children, not Heather's. I could have had you both anyway, regardless."

"Oh come on Julie! That makes no sense," Viva says. "Why would you have had babies at twenty-six if you weren't with Mom?"

Julie's voice is a strange combination of tones, partly beseeching, but also, like Viva's, purely cold. "Actually, I always wanted to be a young mother. Always. I had planned on having children, before Heather and I even—"

"Having us, though? With a sperm donor? Some Finnish guy? Someone with 'ocean eyes'?"

Julie's eyes widen, and she surprises me by laughing. "Oh, right. Hans. That was the name we invented for him, the donor. I'd forgotten about him," she says. "Fair point, Viva. I'm sorry for not—" And there's another pause as her sentence just hangs there, verbless. She stands; Viva, Beth, and I all look up at her. "I'm just going to—" She extends her arms to Viva. At first I think she's reaching to hug her, but then Viva hands her Benjamin. Julie shifts Ben onto her hip and bounces him. She tries to smile at Viva, but she tears up and her smile falters. Then she walks away, toward the bar.

"Shit," Viva says, and Beth reaches over and takes her hand.

"It's okay, Viva."

She looks at me for confirmation, and I nod, though I feel like all my organs have turned to sand. I look at Rob, Kirsten, and Lawrence. They're still talking about preschools, oblivious.

Our salads come, but Julie's chair stays empty. I watch her move around the tent, Ben on her hip. After a few minutes Rob walks over to her. He stretches his arms out in the same silent way she did to Viva, and she hands him the baby. He puts his other arm around her shoulder, and she leans against him. The empty chairs bookending me and Viva remind me of those pictures from their wedding, the visible gap between us and Uncle Andrew and Grandma Elizabeth. Viva stares at her food. The waiters clear the table, including Julie's untouched plate, and as if they're following the same signal, Beth scoots into the seat next to me, and Sam into the seat beside Viva. That finally cheers her up, especially when Lawrence pours each of us a glass of wine.

Beth says, "Lawrence!"

Sam says, "Beth, give it a rest. They can have one glass."

"Pour me some more too," says Kirsten, and soon everyone is laughing again, and ignoring those two empty chairs.

"So Julie dated Ian?" I ask Beth.

But it's Sam who answers. "Oh, lord, yes. Most of junior year. He was completely crushed, remember? Julie the heartbreaker."

"See, what you need to understand about Julie is..." says Lawrence, in such an expansive way that Kirsten socks his arm. "Ouch! Well, we didn't go to the kind of high school that has homecoming queens, but you girls know what they are, right?"

Viva rolls her eyes. "Do we know what homecoming queens are? Dude, we're the ones who go to public school, remember?"

"Oh, right! Well, had we a homecoming queen, it would have been Julie Howe. Prettiest girl in the class, in that treat-her-with-respect girlfriend way. Everyone wanted to date her, and she must have gone out with a third of the guys in our class." Lawrence looks around. "See the guy Rob is talking to? That's Fred Eshelman, he was one of her swains."

Viva squints. "That fat guy, you mean?"

Beth laughs, and Lawrence says, "Well, he wasn't fat in 1987! Fighting trim, right Beth? Right Sammy? Ian was more serious, he lasted a while, but Julie did cut quite a swath through the male population."

"Did either of you date her?" I ask.

Sam shakes his head. "No, no. She was just our very good friend with whom many of our cohorts were madly in love."

"And what about Mom? Did either of you date Mom?" Viva asks.

They look at each other and smile.

"What was the question, Lawrence? The verb was 'date,' correct? You want to field that one?"

"Not especially, Sammy."

There's a pause. "Heather was different," Beth says. "She wasn't interested in relationships—" Then she laughs. "She had fun, in high school. Right boys?"

"Well put, Bethie."

"Good for Heather. All of us should have such fun in high school," Kirsten says, then wags her finger at Viva and me. "Except of course you two. Hard study and strict discipline, right?"

After they bring our main course, a lump of chicken and rice pilaf, I say to Beth, but quietly, so Viva doesn't overhear, "So what's all this about some canceled wedding? Something that happened before Mom and Julie got together?"

"How'd you hear about that?" she says, raising her eyebrows. "Oh, Mamie, that's a long story. Really, you should ask Julie. Or actually, Heather. You should hear your Mom's version, I think, not Julie's."

"Would they be different versions?"

She laughs. "To put it mildly."

I'm still picking at chicken when Rob comes over, holding Benjamin. "This little guy is toast," he says. "I'm going to take him back to the hotel."

"Are you all staying at the Country Inn?" Sam asks, and when Rob nods, Kirsten says, "It's not exactly Paris, is it?"

"No kidding," Lawrence says. "Note the flashlights they've provided every table with so we can find our cars in the dark. This here is rustic living."

"Is Julie leaving with you?" Viva asks Rob, but he shakes his head.

There's a chorus of goodbyes. Viva and I stand up to hug Rob and to kiss the top of Benjamin's fuzzy head. This is my brother: he shares my genes. It feels surreal.

After they leave, Lawrence says, "Does anyone else find Rob challenging to talk to?"

"Like a wooden post," says Kirsten.

"You know who I liked better was Will," Sam says. "Inveterate gambler and all, but he knew just about everything under the sun about baseball. You should have heard him talk about the Negro League. He was interesting, at least."

"Guys," warns Beth.

But Viva says, "It's not like we don't agree! Rob is missing a personality."

Lawrence laughs and pours more wine into her glass.

"Whereas your mother," Kirsten says, "has tons of personality! I love Heather. Why haven't I met her before? Lawrence, we have to have her to the Fourth of July barbecue. And I don't mean just put her on the Evite. Really insist! I want her to come." Lawrence whispers something to her, and she says, "So they can work it out: they're adults. Or they can just not come, I don't care. Haven't we all just agreed that he has no personality?" She turns to us. "You have to come! It's fun. We make this white trash flag cake iced with Cool Whip, strawberries for the stripes, blueberries for the stars—"

"Kirsten, if you can persuade Heather to come, I'll fly out," says Beth.

"Well, help me! She's your friend. Why haven't I met her before? Where is she, anyway?"

Viva and I look at each other. I'm not wearing a watch, so I pull out my cell phone to check the time. It's past nine, well over Mom's allotted hour. There are no messages, except for a text from Tommy: "Miss you mouse xx." Something about the two x's together makes me think not of kisses but of the socked-out eyes of a cartoon figure, someone unconscious or dead.

They clear the plates again and bring us mushy, speckled flan. Emily comes over with her two bored kids to say goodbye. After they leave, Lawrence murmurs, "Three Blond Mice," which makes me think of Tommy's text and how I have no reciprocal pet names for him, like Mouse. Except the secret one in my head, tom underscore, which identifies my distance from him, not any special closeness.

Now Meriwether and Ian take over the two empty seats. "Is that a karaoke machine by the bar? Are we really doing karaoke later? Suddenly I feel old," Ian says.

"Hey girls, you probably don't remember me, I'm Meriwether," she says, and then stares at me. "Oh, wow! It's uncanny..."

"I know," says Ian.

The waiters are pouring coffee when Kirsten stands up. "I should probably follow Rob's responsible parent lead and head to the hotel. Can someone give Lawrence a ride? Thanks Sammy. Bye all! See you in July, I hope! Meriwether, you should come, escape that Arkansas summer. And you two—" Kirsten can't hug us because she has giant Harrison in her arms, but she kisses the tops of our heads, reminding me of the way we said goodbye to baby Ben. Who knows how old he'll be when we next see him? "Really great meeting you girls. Convince your mother to come to our party on the Fourth—we'd love to have you. Bye everyone!"

Viva leans in to me. "I like her." And then immediately she sits up straight. Julie has just taken Kirsten's empty seat, between Lawrence and Ian.

"Julie!" It's a communal welcome; even I say it. It feels involuntary, like crying out when I knock my shin. A beat behind us, like an echo, Viva says, "Julie."

"Hey everyone! Hey girls!" She smiles at us. It's a bright, fierce, impenetrable smile. It reminds me of that red light game we used to play as kids: the kind of smile that stops you in your tracks. Viva and I look at each other.

"Will someone pour me some wine? Speaking of which: is that wine I see in your glasses, Mamie and Viva? Well, special occasion!"

Julie holds up her glass, toasting us. Her smile warms, and we relax.

"Because you never drank alcohol when you were sixteen, hey Julie?" Sam says, and she laughs. Behind her, Ian's arm stretches around the back of her chair.

"So fill me in, you all, I want to hear about your doings. Oh, I do love not breastfeeding anymore, and finally being able to drink! Yeah, Ben's thirteen months, I quit right after his birthday. Is Kirsten still breastfeeding? How old is Harrison again?"

"Couldn't you pump-and-dump? I remember doing that with Leo and Oscar."

"Really? I would feel like such a wino. And pouring breast milk down the sink, I just don't think I could bear it. I really detested pumping..."

The talk winds. I hold my coffee cup in both hands and look at all their faces, picturing that screen in the Schoolhouse with the class pictures. Beth is still recognizably herself, and I'm pretty sure Meriwether was standing by her in that photo where she's wearing the dress with spaghetti straps. I look at Julie, trying to see the prep-school version of the homecoming queen. The homecoming queen last fall at McKinley was Victoria Duggan. I imagine being related to her, the polished kids she'll have some day. I study Julie's face. Just in the year and a half since I last saw her, she looks older, more tired, though her hair, unlike Mom's, has no gray. I wonder if she dyes it. I see her face like it's composed of layers of phyllo dough: just-turned forty-three-year-old Julie, sleep-deprived, tense; Julie in her thirties, flitting in and out of our lives like a bright, elusive moth; Julie in her mid-twenties, in love with Mom; Julie at sixteen, looking like me. Julie sees me staring at her and waves, and her smile seems like a mille-feuille too, the layer on top perhaps good manners, but under-neath, nervousness, and reassurance, and concern, and regret: more layers than I can peel or see.

"Oh, my goodness," says Beth softly, next to me, and I turn to where she's looking. A woman is walking over to the bar. She pours herself a glass of wine, then picks up the mic of the karaoke machine. She's wearing a sleeveless, sparkly, black dress with a low back and strappy sandals with heels, and her short, dark blond hair is slicked behind her ears. Her back is to us; I can see the ridges of her shoulder blades. But it's more the glamour of the clothes, the shiny hair, the high heels, that throw me off, that make me think she's a stranger, until she turns around.

Then I say, "Whoa."

Beth, Viva, and I are on the side of the table facing her, but Viva is talking to Sam, giggling, and doesn't see her right away. Lawrence is mostly turned away from the bar. Julie and Ian have their backs to her. Meriwether, sitting on Beth's left, would see her if she looked up, and now I know she has, because I hear Meriwether echo me: "Whoa."

I put down my coffee cup and grab Viva's hand. "What?" she says, annoyed. I tip my head.

The tent is full of people talking. There's a dull buzz of chatter. But I feel like I have the extrasensory hearing of some nocturnal animal: a bat maybe. Because I swear I hear Mom forty feet away say to the guy cueing the karaoke machine, "Dolly Parton version, okay? Not the Whitney Houston cover." She catches my eye and smiles; even from here I can see the shine of her MAC Viva Glam lip gloss.

"Holy fuck," says Viva. Now Sam looks over.

The music starts. Mom downs her wine in one slug, puts the empty glass on the bar, and takes the mic with both hands. Sam shakes his head, smiling. Then he grabs one of the flashlights from the tabletop and aims the beam at Mom like a spotlight.

She grins at him and begins the song. "'If I should stay / Well, I would only be in your way.'"

"Go Heather!" Sam calls. Ian and Julie, confused, finally turn around, and Meriwether starts to laugh.

"'And so I'll go, and yet I know / That I'll think about you every step of my way,'" Mom sings.

"Woohoo!" shouts Lawrence. Viva looks dumbfounded, as does Ian, and smiling Beth looks like my face feels, like the muscles on her face may just unstring.

"'And I-I-I-I...'" and the "I" goes on forever, and Mom's eyes are shining and almost silver. "'Will always love you.'" Now there are catcalls and whistles. Someone near the flap of the tent shouts, "Katchadourian!" Mom waves but keeps singing. "'I-I-I-I,'" and now she points at the roof of the tent. But then she extends her arm and her leveled finger points straight at Julie, "'Will always love you.'" Her thumb is sticking up, so it looks for a second like she's aiming a gun. But then she tucks her thumb in, looks at Julie, curls her index finger, and beckons.

Julie is shaking her head. Her face is bright pink with that fiery, redhead blush that I also get. She closes her eyes like she might make Mom disappear through a sheer act of will. But she's also smiling; I see every, last, paper-thin layer of her smile. As I watch her, Julie braces both hands on the table and begins to stand up.

JULIE

1994

The door closes, and for a moment I simply stare. My eyesight sharpens. I see the dimple where Andrew karate-kicked the door twelve years ago, just above the knob. Under the light blue paint, I see the elliptical grain of the wood.

"God, she's gone completely around the bend."

"Shut up, Sam."

I could let Heather go, just like that. If I don't follow her, she could be gone forever.

Beth gets up. She grips the metal handle of the sliding glass door to the porch. I see the reflected scallops of her knuckles.

When I stand, I feel them all around me, my friends. They are like waves advancing and receding. I look at Ian's baffled eyes, tilted up. "Julie," he says. In that second I process the relationship between names and identity in a way I've never properly understood. It's like he's reminding me who I am.

There are minutes that protract: here is the dime on which things turn. I see every radial angle of that turn. I could sit down, I could stay. The water friends cling and recede.

I walk out the door.

It takes a second for my eyes to adjust to the dark, and then I see Heather, back toward me, right at the waterline. Her dark gray dress blends with the sky. When I approach, she turns. The word I think when I look at her face is *full*.

"I'm sorry," she says.

Three feet away, I come to a complete standstill. I think, this is a socially appropriate place to stop. In America, that is: not in Japan. And that's such a bizarre thought I smile. Then I take a step closer.

"I thought you weren't going to apologize," I remind her. "I thought apologies were for putting a cigarette burn in my sweater."

Her face puckers. "I didn't mean sorry for him. I meant for coming to Newport. That scene in there." She glances toward the house. Beth stands on the porch, facing us. "I shouldn't have ambushed you."

I wait.

She says, "I heard everyone was coming here this weekend. It seemed like good timing. You'd have reinforcements. People to talk to. You wouldn't be alone."

"Bullshit. *You'd* have reinforcements. You thought I'd be less likely to throw you on your ear, if everyone was here."

"Throw me on my ear! You sound like some Wild West barkeep."

"Speaking of barkeep." I touch her head. Heather's face seems painted on a scrim. Her expression ripples, then stabilizes. "What happened to your hair?"

"Like it?"

"It's extreme."

She raises her left hand to cover my fingers. "I was going for the punished harlot look. Like the French women who slept with the Nazis and were paraded naked down the streets with their heads shaved."

"Appropriate," I say.

"I thought so. Anyway, is this really Wild West coiffure? Wouldn't that be, I don't know, muttonchops?" We both laugh, and Heather shakes her head. "Huh. This isn't how I imagined our conversation going."

"What did you imagine?"

"I pictured every scenario," she says. "Slammed doors. Flung projectiles. You staring right through me. That was the worst. I tried to steel myself in advance. Remember how I used to build my pain tolerance by putting my hand in ice water? I would imagine horrible things you'd say and practice not flinching."

"Yeah, I noticed you exerting control," I say.

Heather looks surprised. "Really? In the house?"

"Just now, when I touched your hair."

Heather smiles. "As I said, this isn't the conversation I rehearsed. I was ready for something more along the lines of your comment inside: thanks for fucking up my life."

"You were ready for that?"

"Well, it seemed predictable." Her fingers are on mine, her eyes look down.

I say, "Does that mean your response was planned?"

Heather laughs. "You mean kissing you? Hardly! That was a crazy impulse. That's the 'scene' I was apologizing for. How did everyone react, by the way?"

"Oh, you know: 'Crazy Heather.' 'What the hell is up with her?'"

We look at the porch. It's not just Beth now. Ginny and Ian flank her.

"Should we wave?" she says. "So they know you're okay?"

I wave. Ian shakes his head.

Heather says, "When I walked out, I thought, what the hell did I just do? Your face kept flashing before me. I came down to the water and felt such *déjà vu*: here I am again, staring at the Atlantic, having burned all my bridges with Julie. Now what?"

"All that advance planning seems pointless if you chuck it out the window when you actually see me."

Heather nods. "Yeah, I know. You rattle me. I practice and practice, then I see you and my best-laid plans fall apart."

"Am I rattling you now?"

"You're confusing me." She ducks her head, but I see the smile she's trying to hide.

"What did you rehearse? So all that prep time doesn't go to waste."

"Seriously?" When I nod, she says, "Partly I wanted to give you the chance to do exactly what you did: some verbal equivalent of slapping my face. You were entitled to that. Then there was stuff in my letter I wanted to reiterate."

"Like what?"

"The part about my love for you is a gift, remember? For you to accept in whatever way you want."

"But that part was bullshit."

Her face ripples again, vying between looking crushed and looking, for the first time tonight, angry. "What do you mean? I was absolutely sincere! I really did come to terms with this in Amsterdam, Julie, it's why I could finally finish that damn letter: I accepted that the only way to love you was to offer love freely, no conditions, no expectations."

She's retracted her hand, but I catch it.

"I'm not calling you insincere. But it was a misguided claim," I say. "Love always has strings, and it always costs. And let's be honest, Heather: your love is expensive! Think about what I must pay to receive it, or to offer mine. It's just not accurate to call it a free gift."

Again I see the fissures in her face. Her eyes shine: they seem to reflect all the moonlight. But her voice, when she speaks, stays composed. "You're not talking about friendship."

"Accepting even your friendship at this point is hardly a piece of cake. You're a controversial figure, Heather. But no." Her hand wriggles away again, so I trap it. "I'm not talking about friendship."

"This is so not how I saw this conversation going," she says, shaking her head. "This is almost my best-case scenario."

"Really? What's keeping it from being that?"

Heather hesitates. "Do you forgive me, Julie?"

"What a question! You're acting as if there's a simple 'yes' or 'no' answer."

"Why not? All big questions are simple."

"Not true. The opposite."

"Oh? Prove it."

I think for a second. "Do you believe in God?"

"Not fair, because you know I'm agnostic." She pauses. "But you believe in God, so... yes, 'I believe in God' is my answer."

"Oh, stop that Socratic thing. Giving a false 'yes' won't corner me into forgiving you, you loon."

"That's not why I said yes," she says. "I want to be where you are. If you're in heaven, I want to be there too. I'm not moldering alone in a grave. If you want to rot in the ground with me, fine: in that case, I retract my belief in God."

"Weirdo," I say.

"Isn't avoidance of death why anyone believes in God? And I thought of another question that proves you wrong, a simple one, with a clear yes or no answer."

I know what she's going to say. She sees the knowledge in my eyes, because she nods. Then she says it anyway. "Do you love me?" When I don't respond, she repeats, "Do you love me?"

"Oh, I thought you were giving an illustration."

"It's an illustration and a question."

"And you think that it elicits a simple yes or no answer?" I ask.

Heather says, "Yes. I think as a general, theoretical question the answer is yes. And I think in your particular case, the answer is still yes."

"Well then," I say. "Yes."

For a second we stare at each other. Then she shakes her head. "I'm confused again."

"Yeah, that's what happens when you try to channel Socrates."

"Clarify," she says. "Are you conceding that particular question has a simple yes or no answer? Or are you actually saying yes?"

"Both, genius."

"Are we talking friendship?"

"I thought that issue had already been resolved," I say.

And because she looks bewildered, and like she's trying to rewind and hear again what I'm referring to, like some panicky court reporter—but mostly because she looks afraid to let herself feel or manifest anything that smacks of happiness—I let her hand go and cup her face. This time I kiss her on the mouth.

After a long minute, Heather pulls back. "Now this is officially my best case scenario."

She's laughing, but there are tears in her eyes. There must be ones in mine too because when I look back at the house everything swims. Now they are all out on the porch: Beth, Ian, Ginny,

Meriwether, Lawrence, Becky, Joy. Sam sits on the rail. Sixty feet away, I can see Ian's open mouth, Sam's grin.

I have to laugh. "They really have no fucking clue, do they?"

Heather puts her arms around me. She says, "I think it's starting to dawn on them."

1997

Before I can unlock the front door, Heather is there, beaming, her arms wide. "Oh my girls! I've missed my girls!"

"Mamie's sleeping in the car," I tell her, and she gives me a strange look, but goes to carry in the car seat.

Later I hear her giving them a bath, singing something silly: "Hey Viva buddy, you are really sudsy, Hey Mamie Mopey, you don't like being soapy." She's left the door open to invite me in. I'm tempted. I want to sit in the heated, steamy room and see Heather be the wet one, kneeling on the slippery tiles, tipping Mamie's head to keep the shampoo out of her eyes.

But I stay in the bedroom.

My ears track Heather and the twins: out of the bath now, it's reading time. Normally I'd help, but I let her do it all herself tonight. She's had two days off. I listen to her read the board book they like best, the one about the nut-brown hare that ends with the father hare whispering to the sleeping kid hare, "I love you to the moon and back." That book always makes me want to cry, especially tonight.

When she enters our room, I'm pretending to read.

Heather says, "What's going on, crabby pants?"

"Did you seduce my brother?" I ask. Her mouth opens. "Because according to my mother—"

"Fucking Elizabeth."

"Well?"

"No, I absolutely did not 'seduce' Andrew," Heather says. "We kissed once. Years ago."

"When he was still a boy?"

"That's absurd," Heather says. But she doesn't stop me when I get up. She just says, "Julie."

"I'm going for a walk." I start down our driveway with some notion of heading to Pirate's for a beer, but walking to town feels too depressing. I'm afraid of crying in public.

So instead I circle to the backyard and climb on the old trampoline. It came with the house when Heather bought it: the sellers had gotten it for their grandchildren. It's stained and has a wonky spring, but when Joe and Buffy asked if we wanted to keep it, Heather said, "You bet!" When I said, our first night here, "I would have preferred them leaving us the washing machine," she said, "Oh Julie, stop being a bore."

Fifteen minutes later that trampoline is where Heather finds me, lying on my back, trying to locate stars. She's carrying the baby monitor and two beers. She hands me one, then climbs up and places the monitor between us. I appreciate her understanding that I need space.

"Okay, listen," she says, after I take a sip. "I'm not sure what that troll told you—"

"Do not call my mother a troll."

"What Lovely Lady Sunshine told you, but I certainly did not seduce Andrew. For one, he made the first move. I was drunk, so I don't recall this with diamond precision, but I absolutely remember that. For two, he was no child. It was that party you had before leaving for your junior year abroad. Andrew was about to start Cornell, so he must have been eighteen."

"Seventeen," I correct. "His birthday is in October."

Even in the dark, Heather looks crestfallen. "Which means I was all of twenty. Look—" She reaches for my hand, but when I retract it, she doesn't push. "It was a stupid thing to do. You were about to go to Italy for an entire year. You were dating Nils, remember, and he was hanging all over you and making me feel like crap. And Andrew always had a crush on me. I know it was dumb. But I sure as hell did not have sex with him."

"Right. You only kissed him."

Heather's voice is weary. "Okay. If kissing were San Francisco and screwing were Washington D.C., what Andrew and I did would be somewhere around Reno on the spectrum. At most, Salt Lake

City. Really, Julie: 'seduce' is a crazy exaggeration. Your mother is blowing it out of proportion. Though why Andrew would tell her... I thought he was on our side."

"Heather," I say, through gritted teeth. "No one is on our side."

"Our friends—"

"No one in my family, I mean."

She says what she usually does: "Give it time." But she says it dully, and I know she's beginning to feel as bleak about them as I do.

I start to cry.

"I wish I could make this easier for you," she says.

"Well, that would be nice, instead of harder. I feel like you keep handing my parents new ammunition."

"Julie, I can't erase my whole stupid life," she says, exasperated. "Look, I'm the first to admit I've made mistake after mistake. You're my one exception: you are anything but a mistake." She reaches for my hand again, and this time I let her take it.

"The fact is," Heather says, "You and I both know that were I as pure as the driven snow, as pure as snow imported from some high-up place in Canada so barren that it doesn't even have arctic wolf tracks on it: your parents would still hate me, because I don't have a dick. And don't suggest that I get an operation. That's really not funny."

"You'd make a beautiful man," I tell her. "Remember when you were Viola in *Twelfth Night*? In those tights? You were hot."

She nods. "I was hot. But if I were some transsexual named Harold—"

"Chip."

"Some transsexual named Chip, your parents would still hate me."

"You could pretend to be someone else. You could do your Yugoslavian accent."

"Julie."

"I know."

"I just wish I could make you not suffer over this. You can't control them. Give it time."

I snort at that tired-out line.

She says, "And if they never come around, well, then they don't. You have me, we have the girls. Can't we be our own family? Why is that not enough?"

"It's different for you, Heather. You don't like your mother, and your father—"

"Is dead. Right. Everything is just easy-peasy for me." Her mouth is a hard line, but I won't be stopped by the Dead Father card this time.

"Whereas I was always close to my parents. Until—"

"Until I mucked it all up for you, yeah yeah," she says, grimly.

For a minute we don't talk. We lie there, looking at the stars.

"It's not your fault," I say. "Well, the Andrew thing doesn't help, but in general it's not your fault. But you need to let me be sad."

"Okay, that's reasonable." After a minute, she says, "Seems like this visit went worse than usual."

I wipe my eyes. "You could say that. My mother said—" I can't finish. Heather waits. "My mother said, she hoped my daughters would never disgust me, because there's nothing more painful."

Heather faces me. Her eyes burn.

"And don't call her a troll, Heather, it doesn't help."

"Okay," she says, after a minute. "Not a troll. Can I call the comment cruel? Will you accept that as a characterization of the remark, not the person?"

I close my eyes. I picture my mother. We're in the kitchen, the babies are upstairs napping, and she won't look at me. She stares at their new backsplash, the apple-green tiles.

"Part of why it's cruel," Heather continues, "is that isn't 'disgust' precisely what parenthood is supposed to remove, exceptionally, for one's kids? All these things that are objectively disgusting, like shit: they become a normal aspect of life. Wiping your child's ass doesn't even make you blink. Or remember Jen?" This is a woman in our moms' group. "Remember when she was holding Olivia up and laughing, and Olivia threw up in her mouth?"

"Gross."

"My point is that your own children should be the one great exception to the condition of grossness. That's what parenting confers. So it's an awful thing to say, because your mother is retracting that essential parental provision." She grips my hand. "The sad thing is it reminds me of something my mother said once. I worry, sometimes, that I have no capacity to be a good mother because my parents were so stupendously defective."

"Well, look at me," I tell her. "My parents were great, so I always knew I wanted kids. And now they've become awful, and I worry I'll say and do terrible things to my children too."

"But we're doing okay, right?"

"So far."

"Sorry about Andrew."

"Okay," I say.

I'm thinking of the night almost three years ago, when Heather and I first got together ("back together" she would say, but the timeline is so confusing it's easier for me to begin it there). Afterwards I made her tell me every last detail about Porter, every time they had sex, every way he had touched her. She cooperated at first and then said, "Julie, please, I honestly can't remember. I was about to tell you something, and then I realized I don't know if I did that with Porter or someone else. Why do you require all the details?"

"Because." Because with details, maybe everything will make sense: like re-assembling the stones to a broken mosaic. I didn't know how to explain it to her.

"You know I had sex with him not because of him, his intrinsic irresistibility, but because of a lot of fucked-up stuff with you. I've explained it before as coherently as I can. Why can't you understand that Porter, in and of himself, simply was not significant to me?"

And I try to understand, but every six months or so we end up rehashing the same conversation. As if the stones will slide in place this time.

That is specific to Porter, but it's also indicative of some deep-down different way of perceiving sex that Heather and I have always collided over. I've slept with nine people in my life: two in high school, three in college, three serious boyfriends afterwards, all who proposed to me, and of course Heather. I can count them on two hands. Heather literally has no idea how many people she's had sex with. I remember asking her once in high school, before we ever touched each other: why all the lovers? After a minute, she said, "Because I'm not dead."

Of those nine people I slept with, I loved six. I used the actual words with all nine, but three I can retrospectively cross off as reaches.

Heather has only loved me.

"We're going to be okay, right?" I say to her. She rolls over and kisses me. Our legs wind.

"Look at your tiny feet," she says. "How do you walk? How come you don't fall over? Tomorrow let me paint your toenails."

"Okay," I say. The baby monitor pokes my side.

2006

There's no proof that if I received Porter's email three years ago, or even three months ago, I would have deleted it. That may be just wishful thinking, that I am so stalwart. But no question it arrived at a time when I was not quite my usual self.

I'm early to get to the cafe, though I don't understand how: I timed everything so carefully. I sat on a bench in Washington Square until exactly 11:45, figuring it would take me twenty-five minutes to cross the Village, yet when I checked my watch on the last block it was not quite noon. I must have been walking quickly—I do that sometimes, when I'm preoccupied, like when I'm planning an exhibition. So I slow down, hunch my shoulders, and walk like I'm eighty-five years old. Is this what it'll be like to be an old, old woman?

Samz is the name of the cafe. I wonder if it's a cutesy spelling or someone's last name. I poke my head in the door to check if Porter is inside. One man who looks about forty sits in the back, and I stare at him, but twelve years wouldn't change Porter that much.

Then I spring back, like there's a force field around the cafe. I refuse to be the first one here.

Two storefronts down a street vendor has set up his folding table. It's covered with a cloth. Dark green velvet, opulent: it makes me think of church. Out of place in SoHo in May, where it's already so hot that looking at velvet makes me sweat.

Did I remember to put on deodorant? Yes.

All morning, no surprise, my head has buzzed. I barely read three pages of my novel in the hour I sat in Washington Square. Partly that was the novel's fault. I picked it up on my way out, not because I was interested in it but because it fit into my green purse while the book I was actually reading didn't. At the park I cursed myself for switching books instead of purses, because there was no way a story about some Armenian fisherman was going to hold me, not today. Though to be fair, it's hard to imagine the book that could.

Instead Porter's email keeps unrolling in my brain. Short, I know it by heart.

Julie (if this is really you),

Forgive the out-of-the-blue message. I've been wanting to contact you for a while—quite some time, actually—and I've at long last "screwed my courage to the sticking place." Are you ever in New York these days? I'll be there for work the last week of May, and would very much like to see you. Alternatively, I could meet you—well, just about anywhere. But I'd rather not do this over email. There are things I need to tell you, and it's a conversation best conducted face to face.

Love, Porter (and if this isn't Julie, I'm really not a lunatic)

Two weeks ago I saw his name in my inbox and caught my breath. My ears hurt, which is about the strangest physiological effect I can think of: not inside my ears, but the rims.

There was a time, I like to think, that I would have deleted the email without opening it. I have it in me to be very surgical. But now is not that time. And who knows, maybe I'm kidding myself about that prior resolve. Maybe there was never a moment when curiosity wouldn't have compelled me to hear what he had to say. I had barricades up, granted, but they weren't very obstructive ones, and the truth is Porter never did try too hard to get through.

The vendor has earrings spread all over the green cloth, organized by color in rainbow stripes. For some reason, the yellow ones grab my eyes. I never wear yellow, but I can't look away to the colors I do wear, blue, green, black, and sometimes, when I feel like breaking rules, jarring the eye, red and pink. ("Redheads shouldn't wear shades of red": my mother drilled that into me when I first started choosing my clothes, and though I remember red being my favorite color, I listened to her, as I usually do).

"Try some on?" the vendor says. I can't place his accent: West African, maybe. He holds out a hand mirror.

Even as I shake my head, my fingers close on a pair. They are clear butterscotch and square. They remind me of cough drops.

Here are the things I thought when I opened Porter's email.

He has AIDS and wants to warn me in person. That thought almost stopped my heart, before I remembered all the blood tests I did when I was pregnant. I don't have HIV. So my mind flitted: okay, he hasn't infected me, but he still has AIDS. He doesn't know whether I've been tested; informing me is the responsible thing to do.

Or, forget AIDS, he has whatever: cancer, a brain tumor. Something terminal, and he wants to say goodbye. That seemed less plausible.

Or, he's in some recovery program and he's ninth-stepping me. I'm on his list of people to make amends to.

But isn't the rule that you only make contact if it will do people more good than harm to hear from you? Though I don't know if my reaction to his email, while I couldn't characterize it as pleasant (prickling ears, near heart attack) qualifies as harm-inducing. Wouldn't Porter nevertheless assume I was intractably, for life, situated in the "harm" category? I've certainly given him no reason to believe otherwise.

Then I thought: since when did Porter give a shit about how his actions make me feel?

Or, he wants to get back together. His latest relationship has exploded (big surprise) and in the consequent self-scrutiny he thinks about me, The One Who Got Away. I put that epithet in caps because the only way to even consider this possibility is to make fun of it immediately, by using my most withering and ironic Dorothy Parker internal voice.

Still, that possibility is unsettling enough that I feel a current again around the rim of my ears, and I must forestall further consideration. So I pick apart the actual text of his email.

The first earring goes in, though I have to push the wire hard, but the second sticks. Has the hole actually closed? I calculate when I last wore earrings. I used to love them, I used to wear them every day. I picture a pair of teardrop turquoise ones. "They make your eyes so blue." Who said that? In my head it's Heather's voice. I press again, tentatively. I'm less afraid of pain than of bleeding all over this guy's jewelry.

The text of that email made my internal Dorothy Parker lick her lips: lots to satirize here. To begin with: what the fuck is up with the *Macbeth* quote? Does that even contextually make sense? If I remembered right, that's Lady Macbeth talking, and she's exhorting Macbeth to kill Duncan. I looked it up to confirm (I have a bunch of Penguin editions from some college Shakespeare class) and I was right. I smirked a bit over this, Porter's inappropriate allusions. Well, I was always the stronger student.

I push the earring in, hard. It hurts, more sharply than before, but finally fits. It doesn't slide so much as force through the flesh in a sticky way that makes me think of cutting meat. I touch my ear lobe, trying to be subtle about it, then look at my fingertip. No blood.

There are other, less bitchy, notations I made. The email was short, but carefully written. He has his commas in the right place, and Porter didn't always pay attention to those, even when it mattered. I remember proofreading briefs for him that were full of comma splices. He's picked his verbs carefully but oddly. "Conducted": there's something formal about that word. It's the kind of diction you'd use in a job application.

"There are things I need to tell you face-to-face" was the first bit to snag my attention, the line that set off that reptile brain chain reaction: AIDS/Cancer/Ninth Step/Regrets Letting Me Go. The phrase that I found myself chewing over that night was a different one: the offer to meet me "just about anywhere." Seriously? What if I said Hong Kong or Nairobi? He's full of shit.

But "just about anywhere" looped in my mind when I emailed

him back twenty-four hours after opening his message. I kept it short. I was too self-conscious, after my snotty critical scrutiny, to give him much to work with.

I'll be in New York Saturday May 28. I can meet then. Say noon? Name a place. J

Before sending it, I replaced J with Julie, because J sounded too intimate, and then I cut Julie altogether. He knows who it's from.

What I left out: it so happens I will also be in New York May 27, and 26, and 29, and 30, and, heck, pretty much all of May. Officially I'm apartment-sitting for Andrew, taking care of their dog while he and his wife Francine honeymoon in Portugal. Really, I'm hiding, wound-licking, and trying to figure out what the hell to do about Will. No one has used the word "separation" yet, except my lawyer Joe Lymon, whom I've known since I was eight, and who told me yesterday that I should file for divorce. That is, Joe used the word "separation" only to discount and trump it. ("By no means do I want to interfere, Julie, and I promise to say nothing about this situation to your father. But I must advise you to formalize your separation and file for divorce. It's foolish to subject yourself to further risk.")

I look at myself in the mirror the vendor handed me. The earrings are swinging pieces of candy. For a second I'm pleased. Noticing, he says, "Just forty-five dollars, ma'am." But the movement of my smile catches my eye, and I'm immediately sorry. It's like seeing your reflection when you're tripping on acid: horrible, but impossible to tear away from.

I process my face, how pale, how drawn; the wrinkles around my eyes and, suddenly, also my mouth. How old I look. Well, at least not fat: after three weeks of fretting and eating the strange dry goods in Andrew's and Francine's pantry (crackers that look like bark, bags of seeds) I must have lost eight pounds. Still, my face is too disturbing, and I hand back the mirror.

"Anything wrong, ma'am?" His accent rounds the ma'am to mom. I pull the earrings out.

The one that was hard to stick in clings, and I think of meat again, of a hook in a fish. Fishing with my father and watching some giant silver thing—a flounder?—thrashing, desperate to breathe; my father ripping the hook from its lip as I cowered behind an ice chest. How old was I? Eleven? The smear of blood on the floor of Uncle Henry's boat.

A hand on my shoulder.

I think, irrationally, that I would recognize the feel of that hand, its precise weight, if I were in a stadium and a thousand people came up behind me and touched me there.

I turn to see Porter. There's an awkward second of looking at each other, and then I quickly look down, and we hug.

I have a vague sense that the hug wasn't what I scripted. I would have had some other game plan, surely. But none of the possibilities—a handshake? A step backward while crossing my arms in a way that radiates chilly distance?—none of them seem right, and besides it's over, it's done. *God grant me the serenity to accept what I cannot change.*

Before I can think, he's leading me to the cafe, his hand still on my shoulder. We're standing in line, taking sidelong glances at each other, and we haven't yet said a word. How strange. He must be thinking the same thing, because he laughs suddenly and says, "Well, hi."

"Hi," I repeat.

It's hard to look at him but hard to look away, like my face in the hand mirror. I could have predicted that Porter would age well. The trick is the bones. I used to tell him he had a beautiful skull. His hair is receding on either side of the center point, giving him a sharp widow's peak. In a few years he'll have Jack Nicholson's capital M hairline, but it suits him somehow. He looks, and the thought makes me want to laugh, like Count Dracula.

"You look gorgeous," he says, and I turn away, because I know it's a lie. The mirror image is too present for me. The last twelve years haven't treated me as kindly as Porter, which is no fucking fair.

"What am I supposed to order?" I study the baffling menu. It's written in chalk on a giant blackboard, and the decorations are chalked too, tall cups of coffee emitting, like smokestacks, blue ripples of steam.

"They make the coffee to order, one cup at a time. It's good. The thing I've had before is Canopy of Heaven." He laughs.

"Weird name. Sounds like an erotic massage parlor, doesn't it?" His face changes. He regrets saying that, I can tell. Why? Because it will remind me of what a dissolute pervert he is? Unlikely that I'm going to forget that fact. For some reason, seeing Porter uneasy makes me feel more composed, undoes the problem of him looking sexy.

I say, "Okay, I'll have that too," and when we get to the counter, Porter orders "Two Canopies, large, cream, not too sweet."

I remember all the times he ordered for me. Menus conflicted him; he wanted to sample everything. Rabbit or lamb? It would send him into a tailspin. I didn't much care what I ate, except that I drew the line at organs. So we got in the habit of Porter ordering for us both, and we'd trade plates. Thinking about that now makes me smile: how symptomatic of Porter, to be incapable of committing to an appetizer. And I thought I was being so accommodating, so flexible. Ha.

"What are you smiling about?"

"Nothing."

We sit, and I look around. The cafe is shabby-precious. There are wooden tables of all sizes, some as big as dining room tables, some like desks. Ours is the kind of round side table you'd see draped with a doily in a grandmother's living room. There are lamps so pretty I'd want them in my house, those fake Tiffany stained glass ones that Will never let me buy. But there are also lamps with torn shades, and wobbly floor lamps taller than me. The chairs we're sitting on are mustard velvet.

Velvet: fuck.

I look down at my right hand, closed in a fist, and feel the earrings in them, the cold stone warming in my balled fist, the filament of wire. Well, they will have to wait. Under the table, I open my purse.

It's the loudest zipper in the world. I hate this green purse that holds boring books and contraband and unzips so loudly that Porter stares. It goes straight into the garbage when I get back to Andrew's. I can feel myself blushing. I say, "So."

"So," he repeats. And then something I'm not expecting: "Hey, did you hear about Geri Rosenblatt?"

"Sure." She was my friend Kevin's older sister. Dead at forty-one, she had a horrible, fast decline from ALS. The last time I saw her, she was so small and contorted in her wheelchair that she reminded me of a chicken wing.

"I still can't believe it," Porter says. "I remember her flying across the monkey bars like Tarzan."

"I didn't know you knew her."

"We went to grade school together."

Which makes sense; Porter is Geri's age. Was her age.

"Did you go to her funeral?" he asks.

"Yes. It was awful."

"I hear poor Mrs. Rosenblatt was completely destroyed." He looks at his hands, turning a salt shaker around and around.

"Well, can you imagine, losing a child?"

Porter stares. His eyes narrow. "No, I can't, actually." And the way he says it, measured, pointed, I'm not sure what he means: if it's just another convention, more of the "how awful! how dreadful!" opining, or if he's saying he himself doesn't have children, so can't imagine the loss, or if he's in fact saying the opposite. That he does have children, therefore the loss is inconceivable in a different way. The way that starts the minute you have a child, when your mind plays horrible tricks: I love you so dearly, you small thing, how will I ever protect you from dying? Immediately producing fantasies you repress just as quickly, stomping on awful mental fires.

I look at him, wanting to ask, but resist because I don't want to answer. We regard each other for a few seconds, it feels longer, and I realize it's the longest I've looked into his eyes. Dark brown, the feature hardest to extinguish. Sometimes I dream about them, and that's all that happens: his eyes stare at me. Nothing scary, but I wake up miserable.

"I almost went myself," he says, at last. "And then I thought you might be there and it felt... complicated. Like I would be going partly to see you. Or alternatively, I wouldn't go because I was afraid of seeing you. Anyway, it was confusing, so I didn't go. And the more I've thought about it the more I've realized it's time to stop being so chickenshit."

I consider his email again. I wonder when Porter started throwing around the word *alternatively*. I'm thinking "Complex feelings about a mutual friend's death" wasn't on my speculative list of reasons why Porter, after twelve years, would contact me.

"So I decided it was time." He rotates the salt shaker again. "Do you know what the ninth step is?"

I have to laugh. He looks surprised, then smiles.

"I'll take that as a 'yes.' What's so funny?"

"Oh, nothing. Just, that one was on my list. For why you wanted to get in touch."

"Really? What else was on the list?"

I shake my head. "You were saying?"

His smile has deepened. It's a smile I recognize, the flirtatious, putting-on-the-charm one. Now he sobers. "So you know about the ninth step. It's when the person in recovery makes amends to people he harmed through his addiction. Has anyone ever ninth-stepped you?"

"My cousin Serena. You remember her?"

"Sure."

"Well, it was pretty silly. She got sober three years ago. Even though we've always been close, her drinking never had a negative impact on me. Frankly, I'm not sure I'd call her an alcoholic. It seemed more like she was going through a stage in her life where she needed to evaluate everything and purify herself. Anyway, when she made amends to me it was for all these things that happened when we were kids, way before either of us began drinking. Like I had this pillow I called 'Softy.' One time when I was maybe five and Serena was six, she was mad at me about something. I caught her with Softy in her lap, stroking him. I asked her what she was doing, and she looked at me with really mean, *The Bad Seed* eyes, and said, 'I'm smoothing out Softy and making him hard.' That's the kind of thing she brought up: hardening Softy."

Porter is laughing, as I knew he would, and I feel a rush of pleasure that immediately makes me ashamed and suspicious of myself. It reminds me of being on an early date, when you trot out all those scripted stories guaranteed to charm.

"'Making Softy hard'! That also sounds like a naughty massage parlor." He smiles at me. "Man, I would have loved to know you when you were five."

"You did know me when I was five," I remind him, and that erases his smile.

"True. So..." His eyes find mine again; I feel pinned by them. "Well, you know the drill. I make amends to you, for hurting you in ways influenced by my addiction."

I shake my head. "First of all, I don't see how you accomplish that, Porter. I mean, we're not talking pillows. You cheated on me with my best friend. What's supposed to happen here? You say you're sorry and I say, Oh, no worries? I have to say, the thing that pisses me off about the whole ninth step ritual is that it functions like a Catholic confessional. Just by copping to something you receive absolution. That strikes me as way too fucking easy."

Porter studies me. "You've gotten tougher, haven't you?" he says at last.

"It just seems conceptually ridiculous," I say. "Heather understood. She once said to me, explicitly, 'This is not an apology.' She knew making one was absurd."

I stop, because Porter's face has changed from looking contrite to almost angry. "Heather," he repeats, and his mouth twists. "Now that you bring her up—"

I'm already shaking my head. "I won't talk about Heather."

"That sounds familiar," he says. I look at him, baffled. He's turning the salt shaker again. "Okay," he says, finally. "You said, 'First of all.' What's the 'Second of all'?"

It takes me a beat to reorient. "Second of all, isn't there a rule about the ninth step? You're only supposed to make contact if it will do more good than harm, something like that?"

"Right." Porter actually looks ashamed. "Well, that's true. Like I said in my email, I've been mulling this for a while, whether I should contact you. Phillip—he's my sponsor—we've had conversation after conversation about it. On the one hand, you're pretty high up there—frankly you top the list—of people I owe an apology. You were the primary victim of my addiction. On the other hand—"

I'm bristling, again. "Victim?" I repeat. And then, considering, "Addiction?" It strikes me suddenly that Porter keeps using that word. I haven't heard him say "sober" once. "Wait a minute. What are you supposed to be addicted to?"

He frowns. I guess "supposed to be" wasn't particularly diplomatic.

"Oh, don't tell me you're a sex addict!"

I see in his face that I'm pissing him off, but he controls himself, and after a minute even laughs. "Why is that so hard to believe? I expected it to make perfect sense to you."

"Oh my God." Again, anger is a transfusion jolting through me. I know it's a bit unfair to Porter, because this rage over phony addictions is not exclusively about him. "Talk about bullshit concepts! Sex addiction is so indicative of our society, the way we exonerate all kinds of bad behavior and turn deviants into 'victims.' Don't get me started. In fifty years people will laugh about our generation. Really, this Oprah woe-is-me culture will seem ludicrous and baffling to our descendants."

Porter's eyebrows rise. "Listen to you, Nancy Reagan," he says. "'Just say no,' huh? When did you turn into such a fireball?"

"Okay, let me ask you this," I say. "Do you want to fuck Queen Elizabeth?"

"The First or The Second?"

"The Second. The seventy-whatever-year-old one. Because if you want to fuck her, then I'm open to accepting the designation 'sex addict.' Otherwise, I think you're kidding yourself, and trying to excuse bad behavior."

Porter smiles his twisty smile and shakes his head. "Well. I don't want to fuck Queen Elizabeth in the puffy suit. Now the First, especially if she looked like Cate Blanchett in that movie: different story."

For some reason, we're smiling at each other.

"Look, it's not like I wasn't expecting skepticism, nor is it the first time I've heard it," Porter says. "But Julie, it's simply true that sex addiction shares many of the same attributes as chemical addictions, like narcotics or alcohol, or behavioral addictions, like gambling."

Gambling: my face clenches. If Porter notices, he ignores it. He's ticking things off on his fingers. "You feel out of control. You behave self-destructively and irrationally, acting against your better judgment and own best interests. You do anything for a 'fix.' You hit bottom. Want me to tell you about hitting bottom?"

Part of me wants the whole seamy story. I want to know why my perfect boyfriend chopped up my heart in so many bits that, twelve years later, I still feel like some Frankenstein creature, hanging together with sutures and glue. But part of me doesn't want Porter humanized. I don't want to feel sorry for him.

There are different roads that could lead to, and one, I feel, looking into his magnet eyes, is a hotel room. I'm entirely aware that when I got dressed this morning, I put on my most flattering dress, morning glory blue, the one that people say makes my eyes so bright.

"Not really," I say.

Porter looks disappointed, but concedes. "Well, you'll have to take my word for it, Julie. I hear the skepticism—"

He reminds me of our couples therapist, Dr. Sheffold, the drill he makes Will and me do: "What I hear Julie saying is that my gambling makes her feel anxious and insecure." "No, Will: you handing our life savings to bookies in Vegas and getting us into debt for who knows how many years makes me want to kill you!" Sheffold, cutting in: "Julie, please articulate your frustration in a less hostile way." When did Porter start the therapy talk? It's as strange on him as the commas and the fancy adverbs and the nonsense *Macbeth* quoting. It's as if he's in drag.

"I hear the skepticism, I truly do. But don't any of those behaviors sound familiar to you? Don't you know any other addicts? I mean, aside from the pillow-smoother?"

"Of course," I say. "There's my father, remember?"

Porter nods. "Right, the Dewar's. Did he ever get sober?"

"No, he refuses to think he has a problem."

And the truth is, I've never suggested he does, though it

becomes clearer and clearer over the years that Dad's drinking is not just contextual, being part of the highball generation. Andrew tried to talk to him about it once, and Dad blew up. To James Howe, alcoholics sprawl on sidewalks holding brown paper bags. He bristles at the concept of "highly functioning alcoholic" at least as intensely as I bristle at "sex addict." "I happen to like the taste of wine!" he snapped at Andrew, who, telling me the story later, said, "Less coherent an argument when applied to vodka shots, no?"

"And there's Will," I add, then stop.

Porter stares at me. I'd forgotten how intense his gaze is. Or, rather, remembered but muted it. It's like being caught in a laser beam.

"Hold that thought, Julie. I'm going to the bathroom."

When he leaves, I try to compose myself. Porter has no clue, of course, how steeped I've been recently in twelve-step jargon. Since I've been staying at Andrew's, I've gone to half a dozen Al-Anon meetings. There's one in Park Slope that centers on gambling, but that's far away and a pretty esoteric specialty. For all the shit I've been giving Porter, I recognize the universality of the recovery rubric. Yet it rubs me the wrong way. Or rather, my response is conflicted. Sitting in my metal folding chair in a church basement that smells like a basketball court, I feel the serenity prayer course through me like wine: "God grant me the courage to change...." Yet removed from it, my empathy falls away. I'm walking rage again.

Yesterday that rage walked me right over to Joe Lymon's office. And I admire Joe's straight shooting. "Look, Julie," he said to me. "Those marriage vows mean what they say. Have you ever really listened to them? 'For better, for worse. For richer, for poorer.' Your condition is inextricably tied to Will's."

I remember when Will and I first opened a joint account, the banker, a round-faced Latino who thought he was hilarious, encapsulated its pros and cons. "On the plus side, if Will suddenly has a heart attack you have money, Julie. On the minus side, you can clean him out and run off to Atlantic City." At the time, we laughed about the prospect of a heart attack representing a "plus side."

Joe Lymon, again: "Of course, divorce is an efficient solution to that inextricable tie."

It pisses me off how clueless I was about Will's gambling. Oh, I knew about his weekly poker game because we'd host sometimes. I want to smack myself when I remember buying triple-creme cheeses and Spanish olives for it. But I had no idea about the horses, the basketball, or the $34,000 he lost over the weekend of Spencer Carbondale's bachelor party (and fuck Spence for having a bachelor party in Vegas, I bet I'm not the only wife cursing him).

I was brain-dead clueless until I tried to figure out if we could afford in vitro ($15,000 a shot, 25% chance that the embryo will take: a form of gambling in itself), and started combing through our financial statements, three months ago.

Sometimes I think all the pressure to get pregnant over the past two years is responsible, in a way I intuit more than forgive, for Will's compulsion. All that unsexy timed sex and the ovulation kits and sperm counting and peeing on sticks and since I turned thirty-six a year ago, the up-the-ante talk about fertility treatments.

And there's the confusing way it makes us play double roles. In the doctor's office, my being a mother is an optimistic finding: I've gotten pregnant "successfully" in the past, I should be able to do so again. Of course, I was twenty-six then, and it strikes me that I first started feeling old when obliged to regard my ovaries that way. "As an older woman," Dr. Preminger characterized me, and I was startled: *Who, me?*

Socially, however, I'm childless. Not really; of course all my good friends know about the twins. But I learned a long time ago not to out myself at cocktail parties as a mother, because the follow up questions stung too much. "Oh, you have daughters? Oh, they don't live with you?" Judgmental face. "Do they live with their father?" And, after I said, "No, they're with my ex-girlfriend," the inevitable "I see...," the raised eyebrows, the awkward "Excuse me, I need to get another drink." I made Will understand, finally, that there's no point in having such conversations with people until they actually knew me and had their minds made up about the kind of person I was.

I didn't tell Will, after all, until our fourth date, which he talks about ruefully: "By then, you'd hooked me." But I remember the way even his face changed, and the way I had to explain my whole life. And how he was relieved, how his face re-composed, when I said I wanted another child. Maybe because he wanted children himself someday, but also maybe because he could regard me as not, after all, *unnatural*: this woman who left her children, who sees them only a couple of times a year. If I were a less shitty mother, would I have gotten pregnant by now? I wonder if Will asks himself my question.

Porter returns. "So," he says, sitting back in his chair. "Who's Will?"

"My husband."

"I figured." He's rotating the salt shaker again. I look at his hands. I could swear he was wearing a wedding ring before, but now he's not. I look more carefully and see a paler stripe of skin around that finger. Could he have removed his ring, just now in the bathroom? And why would he? I picture again some hotel room, Porter behind me, unzipping my blue dress.

"Are you married?"

He looks up, his mouth twisting. "What's the Facebook characterization? 'It's complicated'?"

"I don't know, I'm not on Facebook. Isn't Facebook for kids?"

"Luddite," he says, quite tenderly. "Actually, I knew you weren't on Facebook, I looked a while ago. But you'll succumb. Everyone will. And when you do, promise you'll friend me?"

"Hmm," I say.

The flirtatious smile again. "Really, you should join. Then you can see pictures of my kids."

That jolts me. "You have kids?"

"Two. Callum is five, Maggie is three."

"Maggie? For Margaret?"

"Short for Magnolia, actually." He laughs at my expression. "It was her mother's choice, I was iffy. Yeah, I remember how opinionated you always were about names."

"I like Callum," I tell him, and he laughs again.

"Thanks for the thumbs up, Baby Name Police."

This conversation seems so strange: I never imagined being this civil. Back when Heather and I were living in Hanover, after the girls were born, I occasionally used to see this guy we called the Porter Clone who looked like Porter, especially from the back. Something about the set of his shoulders. I saw him at the butcher, on the Dartmouth campus, once at a park where we were picnicking with our moms group. And my reptile reflex was always flight. Of course it made no sense for Porter to be in Hanover. But I liked to rehearse what I'd do if I ever ran into him, and these fantasies constellated around my eyes. I'd give him some freezing look. Or I'd just look through him, like he was smoke. I never imagined speaking to him, or even nodding: just silently delivering the message that he was invisible.

"The reason I asked is because I have a Margaret," I say, finally.

His face changes. It becomes chillier. "But you don't call her Maggie, do you?"

How strange: my ears are prickling again. "What?"

"She's Mamie, right?"

I stare. Porter fans his fingers on the table top, regards them, then looks back up at me. "And she has a twin, correct? Her sister is Viva?"

"Correct": He sounds like he's deposing me.

"How—?"

"I met them once."

I'm racing, trying to understand. When the girls were with my parents in Newport? That would make sense. But surely they would tell me, if they ran into Porter. Unless, for some misguided reason, they were trying to protect me?

"How?" I repeat.

"When they were babies," he says. "1996. I bumped into Heather, just before Thanksgiving. Didn't she tell you?" I stare, bewildered. His mouth is a sharp line. "Interesting. What are they? Ten now?"

I can't make my mouth work. I nod.

"I gather they don't live with you."

It's a statement, not a question. How does he know? Well, of course there are any number of ways he could know.

I feel flooded, not with anger this time but shame. I'm horrified, for reasons that don't fully make sense. I'm scattered pieces that need reassembly. Porter's the one who Done Me Wrong. He's the one with the hat extended. So why do I feel like the deviant, the one being judged? A word shapes in my mind, like a bubble, and pops: unnatural.

"Julie," he says, and his voice is softer. What I want, and the irony of it strikes hard, is some kind of absolution. Hail Mary Mother of God. Grant me the serenity to accept what I cannot change.

He says, "There's one thing I need to know," and I look up, but his face doesn't match his voice. It's grim. "So when we were together, when we were a couple," he begins, and even though I know what he's going to ask just before he says it, I still can't absorb the question. "Were you sleeping with Heather?"

I have felt plenty angry over this last half hour, but it's the first time my anger is purely focused on Porter, rather than a spillover of other things, like my resentment of Will. For all these years I've thought of myself as so firmly against Porter, so furious with him, but also so baffled by him. Suddenly he feels as recognizable, and as ugly, as my face in the hand mirror.

My voice, when I respond, is acid. "No, Porter. Remember? That was you."

It's like I've stuck a pin in a balloon. He recoils, he deflates, and I see on his face the same kind of horror and shame I must have been projecting seconds ago. It's like someone hit a rewind button, except now it's a film of Porter, not me.

"Julie, I'm sorry," he says, but I'm already disentangling my purse from the chair back and standing up.

"Forget it, Porter." It sounds much less like forgiveness than a final judgment. Before he can stand I'm out the door.

I move fast, fast, because I don't want him following me. My legs race to match my mind. I half-run back to Andrew's apartment. My sandals click, click, click on the sidewalk. I can feel the blister forming on my left heel. Stupid shoes, stupid purse, but I won't slow down. The whole conversation replays in my head as I move, and it's only during this mental review that I process he did after all, and at the eleventh hour, sneak in an apology.

Strange to know that I'm not angry at Porter, any more than I was angry at him when he was telling me that sex addict bullshit. Strange, though hardly surprising, to know who the real target is, at this moment, of my loathing.

It's only when I'm at the door and scrabbling in my purse that my fingers close, in place of keys, on the butterscotch earrings. I stare at them like they're tea leaves, like they might tell me something I could use.

2012

Standing on the Circle with Heather, I had the oddest feeling that we'd slipped through a wormhole in time. The metallic bark of the apple tree still looked like dragon hide; the moonlight silvered the grass. It could have been 1986 again; we could have been breaking curfew. We talked in those same harsh whispers.

"I'll figure this out," I said.

"I'm not holding my breath."

My sigh shuddered. She softened. "Because if I did, I'd suffocate. But here's hoping." And she rapped the apple tree, knocking wood, her smile thin.

The whole next day I walk through my house in a daze. Rob dropped me and Ben off, then took the train straight into the city to catch up on work. I barely slept in the hotel the night before, and I'm so tired I feel drugged. But my skin is electric. I can picture the bundles of nerves: blue and red wires like those inside the Invisible Woman my parents got me at the Natural History Museum when I was eight. I remember holding her, her cool plastic skin. Looking at the pink coil of her intestines, the chunk of liver, the fronds of lungs.

Tired, wired.

I shuffle through the house, half-listening for Ben to wake from his nap. I touch everything. The edge of the Baccarat ashtray hurts when I press my thumb, hard, on the corner.

Upstairs, I open the drawers of our walk-in closet. I heft the Marc Jacobs purse Rob gave me last month on my birthday. Meaty red, it reminds me of a tongue; I rub my finger over the thick zippers. Too many zippers, and the wrong color, but he tries so hard. Watching me as I pulled it out of the tissue.

In the mirror, I'm a ghost of myself.

For two hours, the whole stretch of Ben's nap, I walk around the house, touching. In one hand I hold a balled Kleenex to staunch the snot, the tears. Everything is leaking out of me. I will shrivel like some dried fruit.

I remember doing something like this in the days before I left Heather: walking through our house in Hanover, fingering objects. Staring out the window to locate more things to touch: the rusting spring on the trampoline; the glass candies we bought in Venice, just before I got pregnant. I pressed my thumb then, as I do now, on the sharp edges of the candy, wanting to draw beads of blood.

Same, but different. Because then, I was touching and looking at and holding our things, to ask myself one question: can I let this go?

I remember putting on a green sweater of Heather's: cashmere, a hole in the elbow, as soft as the twins' blankie. She had it back in high school. I used to borrow it. I remember it folded on the shelf of our double room sophomore year. Always on the top of the pile, because it was worn, in constant rotation, by one or the other of us. I put it on and looked in the mirror. It smelled of Heather, nuts and lemons.

Can I bear to leave this? I asked myself, and eventually, I thought yes, I can.

But now, I touch objects with opposite intent: will they help me stay? Anchor me, keep me from floating all the way up? Can I bear to be here, with these zippers and electrical cords, these curling metal pipes? (Somehow that's what I keep touching: the sutures, the bundles of nerves).

Can I make myself stay?

By the time Rob comes home for dinner, I know I can't. I jangle like keys. I drink a glass of wine, arrange cheese on a platter. The whole time I'm rearranging wet wedges of cheese (I can feel the sticky coat of them on my fingers, no matter how many times I wash my hands), I rehearse what to say.

But when we sit and I start, as soon as I say "Heather," it goes to hell.

"Heather," he repeats. My parents do exactly the same thing, pucker and spit her name. Like she's indigestible.

But am I so fucking digestible? I remember the blaze of Viva's eyes back in the tent, the way she said "Julie, for the record." Like my name, I, was disgusting.

"I'm so sorry," I tell Rob, and again his mouth twists over how inadequate these words are. How inadequate I am.

Rob is kind.

Once one is forty-three, once one has been breaking up with people for, oh, thirty years, three quarters of a life, a spectrum forms. Patterns emerge. There are the breakups where you run on anger and lack of options. Crystalline ones. Porter was like that: I never even told him goodbye. I just looked at a spectacle that flipped everything and made words beside the point. With Will, though our therapist might have disagreed, there was really, as my lawyer told me, no choice. And I remember the relief of that. I was extricating myself from a weight that would drown me if I held on. No choice, no option, consequently no blame.

Even if I did feel, at least in my mother's eyes, that much more cracked and dirt-caked.

But Rob has done nothing wrong, except choose badly. He's tried, he's kept trying. His double-exposure face, watching me lift the Marc Jacobs purse out of the tissue paper: hopeful but already settling into disappointment at my disappointment.

To be recognized; that's the thing about Heather, she recognizes me.

Rob's recognition is partial and tragic: he sees that he's let me down, but he doesn't see what I want. Of course it's the same for me. I understand, again and again, an awful cognitive loop, that I'm making him sad. But I don't have the power to change things, to make him smile instead. It's like all we clearly perceive about each other are the ways we discourage. We don't brighten or elevate or cheer each other up.

It's hard to leave someone so kind. It's only possible because it's harder to stay.

And I can't shake the feeling that this is a relief to him: Veruca

Salt going down the bad nut chute. I have finally hit the bottom of his steadily lowering expectations. Almost since we first got married, Rob has maintained—or mildly insinuated—that the shiny, confident, "normal" woman he fell in love with was a mask, that I lured him in with some performance of self-aware stability. I can't deny it.

"I wish you'd figured all this out sooner and saved us a lot of time and trouble": that's as harsh as Rob gets, and I wince, then cry.

I'm as transparent as the Invisible Woman, all the ghastly parts of me exposed: here are my barnacle kidneys, my blue-red, defective heart.

My high school boyfriend cried more when I ended it. It seems suddenly obvious to me, it's the light that shines on our mutually blasted expectations: Rob never really loved me. I was more of a legitimate loss to a sixteen-year-old boy than to my husband. I picture Ian Saltonstall wiping his nose on the ribbed cuff of his sweater.

Why does it matter if one loses something as insubstantial as an Invisible Woman?

He can find a replacement, real flesh. Like that day trader with the cap of hair, short as Astroturf: Alice Copeland. I know he likes her. When she's come to parties I've envied her cool, brazen, burgundy hair. Once or twice I've sidled behind Rob and seen her name on his inbox. He's lowered his laptop, been a little too quick to make her disappear. I've been jealous of her.

Or, rather, I've identified her as someone I ought to feel jealous of, if I had functioning feelings, if I weren't so numb.

"Alice," I start to say.

But before I can get out anything else, he looks up. His eyes are both molten and icy. He says, "Fuck you, Julie."

2012

I've had plenty of crappy conversations in the past two weeks. My mother's voice kept rising in a kind of operatic shriek: "You're getting divorced again! Who are you, Elizabeth Taylor?" Yet of all these conversations that make my life of late feel like some off-the-rails rollercoaster, this one is the scariest.

I feel sick, but when I tried to go to the bathroom earlier, Heather shook her head. "No recreational vomiting in this house," she said, sotto voce.

So I sit at the scratched kitchen table, clutching my mug of tea with both hands. I make myself look the girls in the eye. Mamie is easier: she's clearly skeptical, but I can see in the guarded smile she throws my way a willingness to hear me out. Viva, though, is Earth's toughest audience. She scowls, bracing her knees against the table.

Heather, leaning in the doorway, is no help at all. Every time I look at her, her eyes and mouth seem out of sync. She's either smiling but hard-eyed, or her mouth is a straight line, while her eyes sparkle. She knows she's letting me down. When I glare at her she throws her head back, her crazy haircut making her look like a scrub brush, and laughs.

"Sorry, Jules," she says, not remorseful at all. "They won't buy this coming from me. You have to make your own case." She folds her arms, and it strikes me, belatedly, that Viva and Mamie aren't the only ones needing to be convinced.

"Thanks for all your moral support, Heather."

Her response is more cackle than laugh. But then she sobers. "Now listen up, girls," she said. "Family meeting time."

At that, Viva almost spits. "Family!"

"Viva, why don't you shut up and listen to what Julie has to say?" Heather says calmly. I register this—at the twins' age it's acceptable to say *shut up* to one's kids.

Not very patiently, Heather says, "Julie? Floor is yours."

"Well," I say, but immediately I'm tongue-tied. Viva's freezing glare keeps turning me into stone. I look back at Heather helplessly.

"Come on, Jules," she says, impatient, but trying to sound encouraging. It reminds me of the way I talk sometimes to the baby: the phony trill.

"I'm not sure where to start. How about I'll answer any questions you have?"

Heather rolls her eyes, but Mamie speaks up. "Okay. Tell us what's happening with the baby. Are you going to leave Benjamin with Rob?"

"No!" I say, shocked, and right away all three of them react. The girls look relieved, on the one hand, but also pissed. Even though their expressions, Viva's especially, are transparent, I can't seem to stop what I say next: "Why would I leave Ben?"

"Because," Viva says with a snap—God, have I thrown her a juicy bone—"You abandoned us. Remember, Julie?"

I look at Heather. Her face is grim, but she nods. "Viva, don't be so mean. Check your tone, please. Julie, Viva made a legitimate point, if poorly phrased. So…" She looks at me somberly. "Your ball."

"I'm sorry," I say, and when Heather doesn't respond, I look back at the girls. "I'm sorry. You're right. I know that I've damaged your trust, and you have no good reason to have faith in me." I give Heather a long look, hoping she sees I'm addressing her too. "I've been the world's crappiest mother. It's okay that you don't see me as your mom, that's perfectly understandable. All I can say is that I was immature and stupid, and I got freaked out about how my parents and brother were reacting to my relationship with Heather. How they were all willing it to fail. That's not an excuse, I know." I grip my mug. "Listen…" I catch Viva's eye, and even though it's not malevolent now, I freeze again.

"We're listening," says Mamie, gently.

"Go on," says Heather.

I take another breath. "So about Ben. I'm not leaving him, but his dad wants him too. So for the short term we'll do lots of commuting. I'll take him to Connecticut to be with Rob, and I'll pick him up. I'll do loads of driving." I laugh, weakly. "Rob works of course, so he'll mostly want Ben on the weekends."

"So on weekdays he's living with us?" Viva asks. "A baby in the house? How do you feel about that, Mom?"

Heather shifts her weight. "Well, I did think that the diapers-and-bottles phase of my life was long over," she says. She smiles at me. "Only for you, babe."

Babe: it keeps me going, it's like a fortifying shot.

"We haven't worked out details, of course," I say. "Rob needs to be near the city for work. Maybe eventually we'll move closer to Greenwich—"

Now both girls are sitting upright like I've jammed sticks down
their spines.

Heather raises a placating hand. "Not until you're done with
high school, kids. Nothing changes in the next two years, so don't
freak out. And wherever I may eventually live…" Her eyes are back
on me, stern again. "It's not going to be in fucking Greenwich."

So it's also okay to say *fucking* in front of one's kids. Noted.

"Now does that cover logistics?" Heather asks, pleasantly.

Viva harrumphs. "Where's it going to sleep?"

"He," Heather says, and her stern look is now aimed at Viva.
I've been familiar with that look for a good thirty years, "has options.
One thing this freezing old house has is space. Okay, onto the next
topic."

"How's Rob doing?" Mamie asks.

I feel my face sag.

"Who cares about Rob?" Heather snaps. "Sorry, Julie, that
wasn't very diplomatic. Let me rephrase that: Rob really isn't your
business."

"I want to know," says Mamie.

"He's okay," I say. Actually I appreciate Mamie's concern;
Heather's hostility towards Rob rankles more. "He's angry at me,
naturally, and he feels pretty shell-shocked. Though in a funny way,
I think he wasn't that surprised. I will do everything I can to be kind
to him, and to make this as easy as possible for him, and we don't
have conflicts about money." I try a joke. "This isn't the first time
I've gotten divorced."

"Yeah, about that," says Viva.

Another bone.

"So, lovely that Rob's not about to hang himself," she goes on.
"But what about Pam? Pam's completely brokenhearted. And we
loved Pam."

Mamie shifts in her seat. "You loved Pam," she says to Viva.

"What?" Her eyes blaze, but Mamie looks back coolly: the
gorgon-freeze thing doesn't seem to work on her.

"Just saying. I liked Pam fine, I didn't 'love' her. More to the
point, Mom didn't love her."

"Her heart is broken!" Viva shouts, looking at Mamie, then looking at Heather. "Why doesn't anyone give a shit about Pam?"

Heather unfolds her arms. "Listen, Viva, Pam's on me. That isn't Julie's fault, any more than Rob is my fault."

"Rob," Viva says, glaring, "is your fault, Mom."

"What I meant," says Heather, assuming the not-so-patient trill again, "is that it's one's own responsibility not to hurt or betray one's partner. I was the one who had an emotional contract with Pam; Julie's the one who had a contract with Rob. The third party is not to blame for the breakup."

"Hmm. What about…" I can't stop myself from saying, "if the third party also has an emotional contract of sorts? That is, is it still okay to sleep with someone who's attached if one is also friends with the person being betrayed?"

"This is a hypothetical question?"

"Say, for instance, best friends with that person?"

Heather's eyebrows contract. "You really want to be having this conversation now, Julia Christine? Has that topic not been canvassed to death in years gone by? Do we not have enough else on the plate?"

"Okay, okay. I was just wondering."

Heather rolls her eyes and turns back to Viva. "In sum: you should blame me for hurting Pam, not Julie. My fault, not hers."

"Believe me, I do blame you," Viva says.

"Glad that's sorted, then," Heather says, and gives me a twisted smile.

"So what are you going to do?" Viva asks.

"About Pam? Nothing. It's over. I'm sorry I hurt her, I truly am, but that's the risk you run when you fall in love, Viva, and if you haven't figured that out yet, believe me you will. And one thing I will say in my defense." Heather lifts her chin. "I never deceived Pam. She always knew exactly how ambivalent I was. I assure you that this recent state of affairs is not a shocker to her."

"Oh, so she knew you would leave her for Julie?" Viva's voice is waxy with skepticism.

"What she knew was that, given an opportunity, given, in other words, Julie whistling," Heather gives me a wry smile; I feel a hot flutter in my chest, "I would come running. Pathetic but true!" she says, as Viva's eyebrows continue to lift.

"Well, that just fucking proves my point: it is Julie's fault for, whatever, whistling. You wouldn't have left Pam if Julie hadn't motivated you."

"Oh, come on Viva, you're being deliberately obtuse! *I* left Pam. My choice. Pam has always been jealous of Julie, and rightly so. But that isn't Julie's fault, it's mine. Pam banked on the fact that Julie was never going to want me back, but she was, nonetheless, always freaked out by her. Why do you think I never joined Facebook? Pam thought I'd start chasing Julie—"

"You hate Facebook," Mamie says.

"True. Facebook is for chumps. Anyway, the point is Julie barely knows Pam, Julie did not betray Pam, Julie is not accountable for Pam's suffering. Which will, at any rate, be short. She's young and resilient and adorable. She'll do just fine. Believe me, I was holding Pam back. As moderator, I declare this line of inquiry complete. Let's move on."

"You can't be a moderator and an interested party at the same time," Viva objects.

Heather reflects and then sticks out her tongue.

My eyes are suddenly wet. I don't know whether it's happiness or grief: for the past two weeks, I've felt bipolar.

"Julie?" Heather says right away. "You okay, babe?"

Babe, again. "Yeah, I'm just—" I choke it off. "You're a good mom."

"I try," she says, doing jazz hands.

Viva and Mamie say, "She's okay," at the exact same time, and then, "Jinx! Can't talk" at the exact same time. We all laugh, and it feels, for the first time this afternoon, almost tolerable.

"Oh, screw you both," Heather says, smiling. "So, more input from the peanut gallery? Somehow Julie has managed to skate through the last five minutes of this inquisition making one smartass, totally irrelevant comment, drinking her tea, and weeping. You are a beautiful weeper, Jules."

"Okay, I have one," says Mamie. I've been feeling like Mamie's on my side, so the hardball takes me aback. "How do we know you aren't going to leave us all again?"

There's a long pause. I look at Heather, but her eyes have gone flat again.

"Yeah, that's where I thought that multiple divorces angle was going in the first place," Heather says.

"All I can say is I won't," I tell Heather and the girls. I am careful to look into each of their eyes. "I have loved your mom," I say to Viva and Mamie, and it feels strange to say "your mom" but that's the bed we've all made. "I have loved her since we were kids. Younger than you two. Since she was prancing around our freshman dorm wearing some crazy, silk bathrobe. I kept running from it..."

"Exactly," says Viva, and Mamie nods. "You kept running. So what makes this time any different?"

Though Viva's eyes aren't freezing, now, I still clutch for words. I don't look at her for help this time, but after a pause, Heather speaks.

"The fact is, Julie can't promise that she'll never leave me. Though I do expect her to promise," and her eyes hook me now, "to never leave you two again. Whatever happens with us, she's going to be a more stable presence in your lives. That's only fair. Agreed, Julie?"

Tears again. I nod.

"However, she can't promise to always love me, though I appreciate the optimism. No one can authentically make that promise. In a nutshell, this is why I've never had much patience with weddings: all that swearing to love until death do us part is magical thinking. The most you can do is hope you will always feel the way you currently do, and promise that you will do what you can to stoke and nurture that commitment... Yeah, that pretty much encapsulates my beef with weddings. Though that said...."

When I look up, Heather is staring at me. "Julie, if we're going to sail this ship again, and you see the extra cargo." She inclines her head toward Mamie and Viva. "Never mind that I'm going to theoretically have an at-home child in my life from age twenty-six to, let's see..."

"Sixty," Mamie says.

"Sixty?" Heather is aghast.

"Well, yeah. You're about to turn forty-three, Ben just turned one, that's seventeen years until he goes to college..."

"Sixty!" Heather repeats. "Fuck."

Mamie and Viva both laugh. "Mom, you suck at math," Viva says.

I keep my eyes on Heather. "You were saying."

"Right. So, if I'm going to hazard these waters again, until incipient geezerhood, I think the least you could do, Julia, is...."

Pause. It reminds me, suddenly, of high school: how we used to kick butt at charades.

"Marry you?" I say, when she doesn't complete the sentence.

"You know, it would be a lot more romantic if you proposed. Since you're the one whose commitment has been a little shaky, historically speaking. Under a cloud of suspicion and all."

Her eyes, on mine, glitter.

"Does it count as a proposal when one is being strong-armed into making it?"

"Strong-armed? That seems unfair. Gently cued."

"Or when one is still technically married?" I say. "And is one's credibility undercut by the fact that one has been married twice before?"

"Almost three times," Heather smiles.

"Yeah, if you hadn't screwed that first one up..."

"Ha. You ought to thank me for saving you from both a real creep and a truly farcical divorce rate. Three! That would have been fucking embarrassing."

I snort. "Thanks so much. You have my undying gratitude."

"Any time, babe."

I can't pull myself away from her eyes.

"Waiting," she says, after a minute

"This will convince you? For real?"

"I'm starting to feel high and dry here."

I close my eyes. I take a breath. I am Zen. I am a leaf floating on water.

"Heather Elena Katchadourian, will you marry me?"

She stares at me for another minute, then bobs her head.

It's only now that I notice the twins' pop-eyes.

"Seriously? But you always said—" starts Viva, and Mamie, over her, harmonizing, "I thought you didn't believe?"

"Yeah, yeah," says Heather. "One adapts. I've been holding out for that one." She aims her finger at me.

I stand up, I close the distance between us, I kiss her, kiss the girls. Viva's probably three inches taller than me now, Mamie is just my height.

"All good?" Heather asks, smiling at them: smiling at me.

"You really love each other," says Mamie, wonderingly.

"Always have," I say. The tears track down my cheeks. "Since she sashayed around in that crazy red bathrobe like some Euro starlet."

"Yes, I was terribly glamorous," says Heather. She kisses the top of my head. She whispers, but loud enough for the twins to hear, "See? That could have been worse."

2012

I'm not aware of making a sound, but Heather's arms are around me.

"Bad dream?" she asks, in my ear.

"Can't sleep."

I'm facing the wall. She holds me, quietly. "You always get sad when you're away from Ben."

"I just feel—" I catch my breath. "I feel like I've wasted my life. I barely know the girls, and they're almost grown up. They'll be leaving in a year..."

"Two years," says Heather. "Twenty-two months. Wait a bit: you'll be desperate to have them go."

I laugh, reluctantly.

"Anyway, do you think that's the end of parenting? Do you think your mother has stopped worrying about you just because you supposedly grew up? Hardly. You have them for life."

I consider. "Sometimes Viva looks at me like she hates me."

"Sometimes Viva looks at *me* like she hates me. Babe, I have news for you: sweet little Ben is going to hate you, too. Kids grow in body mass and brain development and disdain for their parents. It's the natural order of things."

"I've wasted your life too, you know. I've blown more than fourteen years."

Her hands reach for mine. "Listen," she says. "I won't deny that I missed you terribly. But I'm not going to second-guess anything that has gotten us here. Because right now, tonight, I'm very, very happy."

"Really?"

"Truly. Aren't you happy?"

"Yes," I say. It comes out as a sob, and Heather laughs.

"Good, because you sound it."

Which makes me laugh, too.

"And listen, Julie: There's one very good reason why you shouldn't see those years as wasted."

She pauses, and I say, "Ben."

"Ben," she repeats.

"Why are you so sweet to me?"

"Because I want unlimited access to your boobs."

"Ha."

"So stop beating yourself up already."

"Okay."

"Really? You're actually going to listen to me?"

"Yes."

"Then go to sleep."

So I go to sleep.

2013

I have dragged my feet every step of the way over this, wedding three-and-a-half, but it's the one thing Heather has been adamant about. "Your parents need to see this," she said. "The girls need to see this. And what the fuck? Am I not as good as Will or Rob?

State of New Hampshire says I am, so there." So, though the whole production seems beyond absurd, here we are.

My first wedding: horror show fiasco. That was the one I actually enjoyed planning. I cared about the flower arrangements, the *amuse bouche*, and the processional music (not Mendelssohn's "Wedding March" but classier Bach's "Jesu Joy of Man's Desiring"). Of course I never did walk down the aisle, at least not in the intended sense. The second one, I didn't want to waste my parents' money again, so Will and I got married in Bali. It was tiny, just ten people: my brother, Will's sisters, Ian and Emily Saltonstall, who were in the vicinity in New Zealand, our parents, and, randomly, a stoner college friend of Will's who lived in Jakarta. My third wedding was at my parents' house, less ornate than that original Porter disaster but a real wedding nonetheless, catered and polished. My mother planned that one, though Rob took care of the music.

In short: Wedding 1, I was a basket case surviving the single worst day of my life on adrenaline and spite; Wedding 2, I felt queasy from what I hoped was morning sickness but what turned out to be some weird reaction to fish curry; Wedding 3, I just remember feeling oddly dissociated: oh, that's a pretty cake, oh, that's a nice table arrangement.

Over the years, my boyfriends have seemed less like derivations from a common mold than like reactions to the last romance (frat boy followed by sensitive poet followed by investment banker), and the same principle of overcorrection seems true of my weddings.

Yet here we are.

Mamie hands me my shoes, which are beautiful but impossible. They are gunboat silver and as pointy as skis: they both look and feel like knives. I never would have picked them, but Viva was so excited ("Julie! These are perfect!") I bought them to please her. I put them on and look up, shocked.

Mamie smiles. "Yeah, I broke them in for you. I've been wearing them in the attic. Didn't you hear me up there? Clomp, clomp, clomp."

I want to cry. "They don't kill!"

She laughs. "They don't kill."

Now Viva pokes her head in the door. We let the girls pick their own clothes, and while I think the color of Viva's dress is too mature for her (it's blood red), there's no question she looks stunning, like some goth flapper.

"Oh Viva," I say. "You're gorgeous."

She says, "I was about to say the same thing to you. Love the shoes!"

The three of us face the antique standing mirror, which wobbles and has a crack across the top, but which we nonetheless like because it makes us look tall and thin. "It makes normal humans look like Mom" is how Mamie puts it. I have an arm around each of them.

We admire ourselves until Viva says, "No more preening. People are starting to show up. Mamie, Tommy's downstairs, and Julie, Grandma Elizabeth just got here, that's what I was coming in to say. Grandpa James is parking."

"Oh crap," I say. "Will one of you deal with Grandma Elizabeth? I'm not up for her yet."

"On it," says Mamie, and we head downstairs.

Tommy is talking to my mother at the bottom of the stairs, and I greet them both. He hugs me.

"Wow," he says. "You look great, Julie."

"And you look very handsome, sweetheart."

Mamie slides her arm through his, and I hear her say, "Wait until you see Mom."

My mother raises her eyebrows, but that's as close as she comes to some Elizabeth Taylor/Jennifer Lopez crack. She says, "You do look very pretty, darling. Mamie, I love that color. And Viva, you look terribly sophisticated." Viva grins at me, and I know she can decode the implied critique. "Now will someone point me to my grandson?"

We've had to borrow vases, pitchers, even mason jars from all the neighbors. Mamie and Viva came home from the farmers' market this morning with an entire car full of flowers. I see calla lilies, never my favorite—they look too sculptural and waxy. But I love the sunflowers, the poppies, the fiery dahlias, the gold parrot tulips. I think, randomly, of a pair of yellow earrings on a green cloth.

The doorbell rings, and I open it to the Saltonstalls. Ian looks handsome and overdressed in his navy suit, Emily is wearing something shiny and emerald green. When she sees me, she says, "Oops! I didn't mean to match the bride."

"Hardly the traditional bride," I tell her, and she laughs.

Ian hugs me. He smells like peppermint. "So," he says.

"So."

He whispers in my ear, "Am I the only one who has been to all four of these?"

I whisper back, "You and my parents and Andrew."

"Can this one please, please be the last?"

"Deal."

I turn back to Emily, worried that all the whispering will have her in a snit. Emily has always hated me. But she clasps me in a hug.

"Congratulations, Julie."

"Thanks."

She's still, astonishingly, hugging me. "I really, really like Heather."

And for some reason, I'm about to cry. "Me too."

"You okay, J?" Ian says to me.

I smile and say, "Very."

The room starts to fill. I keep opening the door. Why not? Every wedding of mine, I've hidden away, waiting for my music to begin, waiting to perform. Even at the Porter fiasco, I timed my entrance perfectly. Now, I don't need to.

People are surprised to see it's me opening the door. "Well! Julie!"

But I feel as light and golden as wine. I open and open. My father, whom I later see with Ben in his lap. Beth and Stephen. Grace Katchadourian, who has let her hair go white. My cousin Serena and her partner Teddy. Lawrence and Kirsten. Meriwether. Sam, with some woman with wavy brown hair; I wonder if this is the wine bar owner I've heard about. Andrew and Francine. Ginny, all the way from Singapore. Joy and Paul. Joy gets a special hug: I haven't seen her since she finished chemo. She looks thin but happy. Growing back, her hair is light brown fuzz. "You feel like a duckling," I say, touching it. "I want to stuff you in pillows."

I kiss cheeks and open the door. I look out the kitchen window to the garden and see the trellis, where we'll get married. Also drenched in flowers, it appears to be on fire.

Sam says to Beth, "Do you know what Heather has planned? Some crazy serenade?"

Next to him, Lawrence laughs. "All I know is I brought my video cam."

And then behind me I hear bubbles of noise, oohs and ahs and catcalls. I turn to see Heather coming down the stairs. She refused to let me near her dress, though she modeled it for the twins. All week it's been hidden in the attic. "Bad luck baby." So this is the first time I see it: saffron yellow, clingy, with a long, swishing skirt. She looks like a mobile flame. When she catches my eye, she beams. "Hey you," she says, in her carrying voice.

I feel my life around me like disturbed water, settling.

ACKNOWLEDGMENTS

Grateful thanks are due to Leland Cheuk, for plucking this book from the slush pile, and for everything 7.13 Books stands for. Leland is the kind of publisher and editor writers dream about: ethical, judicious, respectful, and honest.

Thank you to Charli Barnes, for designing yet another dazzling cover. Thank you to Robin Black, Sylvia Brownrigg, Kathy Fish, Alice Hatcher, and Michelle Ross, for saying kind things about this book, and for writing fiction that bends my brain.

Thank you to the editors who published parts of this novel, particularly Mark Drew and Andrea Gregory.

Thank you to my colleagues at Mills College, who read drafts of this book: Diane Cady, Sarah Pollock, Kirsten Saxton, Thomas Strychacz, and Kara Wittman.

A wide-armed thank you to the friends who have done the same, and who have been tireless and patient supporters of my writing: Chris Belden, Susie Britton, Garrett Croker, Daniel Duane, Sarah Stearns Fey, Judy Garvey, Jennifer Granick, Dorothy Hale, Sarah Hoenicke, Alexandra Kamerling, Randy Kline, Robert Landon, Yasmina Din Madden, George Malko, Amanda Marbais, Jeffrey McCarthy, Diana Newby, Brian Normanly, Alexandra Quinn, Jennifer Reese, David Robinson, Karie Rubin, "well-greaved" Traci Shafroth, Chessie Shaw, Cassidy Smith, Sallie Bland Smith, Mark Smoyer, Emily Kaiser Thelin, and Rebecca Vicino.

Thank you to my family, who helped me make this book in all kinds of big and small ways: my mother Jill Oriane Tarlau, who trimmed the fat with her big blue pen; my sister Margot Magowan, who read and edited very messy first drafts; my sister Hilary Magowan, who bugs all her friends to buy my books; my mother-in-law Charlotte Connor, who used up printer cartridges on my behalf; my father Peter Magowan, who thought this novel would make a good movie, and whom I miss every day; my daughters Nora Wagner and Camille Wagner, who can tell you which characters have which favorite flowers.

A very particular thank you to my husband, Bryan Wagner. When I was banging out the first draft of this novel in New Orleans in 2012, Bryan carted our girls to summer camps and stood on very hot lines with them for snowballs so I would have time to write. I couldn't have done this without his support and love.

Finally, this novel is partly about the peculiar and intense kinds of friendships one develops as a teenager, so a warm shout-out is due to my form mates, class of 1985. Love to you all!

ABOUT THE AUTHOR

Kim Magowan is the author of *Undoing* (2018), which won the 2017 Moon City Press Fiction Award. Her fiction has been published in *Atticus Review, Cleaver, The Gettysburg Review, Hobart, New World Writing, SmokeLong Quarterly,* and many other journals. She is the Fiction Editor of *Pithead Chapel.* She lives in San Francisco and teaches in the Department of Literatures and Languages at Mills College. You can find her on Twitter (@kimmagowan) or read more of her work at www.kimmagowan.com.

7.13BOOKS

55636569R00136

Made in the USA
San Bernardino,
CA